WITHOUT BORDERS

STACY REYNOLDS

WITHOUT BORDERS

STACY REYNOLDS

Affinity
Rainbow Publications

2025

Without Borders
© 2025 by Stacy Reynolds

Affinity E-Book Press NZ LTD.
Canterbury, New Zealand

First Edition

ISBN: 978-1-991357-24-3 (paperback)

Editor: Angela Koenig
Proof Editor: Lisa M
Cover Design: Irish Dragon Designs
Production Design: Affinity Publication Services

ACKNOWLEDGMENTS

Many thanks to my book club, Sapphic Reading Group, for all their support and encouragement. Our meetings are often the highlight of my month. Saying thank you to my sister, Diane, will never be enough for the love and strength you've given me over the years. Even when you had little strength of your own, you always found enough to pour into me. Another big thank you to my Aunt Peggy, who not only saved my life when I was five years old but always treated me like a writer even when I wasn't sure I believed it myself. Peggy and Diane, you are my heroes. It goes without saying that everyone from Affinity Rainbow Publications is wonderful. From the minute I met anyone associated with Affinity, I've been treated as a friend and respected as an author. Thank you all.

DEDICATION

For my daughter, Misty Sunshine.
Your love of reading encourages me to keep writing.

TABLE OF CONTENTS

CHAPTER ONE

When I heard that my colleague, Kevin Paskey, was shot while reporting live from Ukraine, I dropped everything and sprinted for the boss's office. Desire to be the first and only candidate to take Kevin's place fueled my urgency. Becoming a war correspondent wasn't a passing fancy. It was the culmination of my work, my education, and my talents. It was a want that was so persistent, it had become a need.

My high-top Vans squeaked on the tile in the hallway before the editor's office as I skidded to a halt. All the executive offices in the building had glass walls, so it wasn't like she hadn't seen me coming. Nor would my request be a surprise because it was no secret that I wanted to go to Ukraine. Now that opportunity was at my door, I would make sure it knocked.

I burst into the glass cube and made my request.

"Send me," I said, out of breath. My heart was beating so

fast that if she said no, I probably would have died on the spot from a massive heart attack.

Pamela Kemp, editor and chief of Titan Global News, looked up from the proofs scattered across her desk and raised her left eyebrow. I knew what that look meant. It meant she wouldn't hand me the assignment without a major discussion. I would have to convince her that not only was I worthy, I was also hands-down the best candidate for the job.

Five years ago, when I'd interviewed for the job with Titan Global News, I was terrified Pamela wouldn't hire me as a general assignment reporter. When she did, I was even more terrified that I would let her down. Working my way up the ranks, I currently held the lofty title of political correspondent covering the state legislature in Austin, Texas. Pamela's tutelage had made me earn every bit of my experience. However grateful I was for the opportunities that had come my way, the time had arrived for me to move forward. In my mind, being a war correspondent was the next logical step.

"Jesus, Sheppard, ever since you saw that fucking movie, you've been insufferable," Pamela said.

It wasn't only since the movie *Civil War* came out, a story about a pair of journalists covering a future war in the United States that I'd longed to become a war correspondent. It was something I'd dreamed of my entire adult life. We both knew what I was asking for, but if she was going to agree to let me go, it would be because I made my case clearly and concisely, leaving no room for doubt that I was the best candidate. Since the first moment I'd opened a blank notebook with my pen ready to bear witness to the events there, or the first time I held a camera up to my face and twisted the focus, I had wanted to be a war correspondent.

"Send me to Ukraine," I said.

This time both eyebrows rose, giving her an expression not simply surprised but also interested. "That's amazing," she said, looking at the expensive gold watch on her left wrist. "It took approximately four minutes for the news of Kevin's injury to run from corporate to the newsroom."

A burst of fear leapt from my heart when I thought she was putting me off. My desire to cover the war in Ukraine far outweighed any objections she might have. She knew me, and she knew I could do this. I was willing to stand there all day, hopping back and forth from one foot to another until it annoyed her enough to respond. She had to send me; she just had to.

Leaning back far enough to make her leather desk chair creak in protest, Pamela continued to observe me. Although I'd been with Titan for five years, her *Vogue* good looks and overwhelming confidence could still make me feel like a rookie reporter trying to impress upper management with my art of making obituaries sound exciting.

"Why should I send you?" she finally asked.

I had my response ready. In fact, I had practiced it over and over since being assigned to the college newspaper my freshman year. I'd rehearsed it enough to not even need notes. My time would come, and now, with the war in Ukraine, I finally had the experience, the knowledge, and the opportunity.

I held up my hand to count off the reasons. "I'm a writer and photographer. You get two for the price of one. I've been studying photography since I was old enough to hold a camera." My dad bought me my first point-and-shoot when I was eight, and I'd never looked back. "I have a good eye for composition and form. Up to this point, Titan has been buying photos of the war in Ukraine from a freelance photographer. Taking the pictures myself will save the company thousands of dollars."

This brought me to my second point. Although my ego wasn't as big as some, I still had enough of one to take pride in my accomplishments. I waved to the awards hanging on the wall behind Pamela that showcased my talents as a writer and journalist. "Several of those have my name on them, confirmation of my ability to tell a story.

"Three. I don't have kids, a spouse, or any binding relationships to get in the way." I had friends, sure, but no one I couldn't leave behind for a few months. My parents had long since passed away. I had no siblings. I dated some, but romantic entanglements, and I seemed to have a way of avoiding one another like a germaphobe avoided cold and flu season. "My passport and visa are all up to date. Plus, I've been a card-carrying member of Reporters Without Borders for years. Being ready to leave on a moment's notice is a priority.

"Four. I'm in good physical condition." What I didn't say was I was in peak shape compared to Kevin, who was known to hoist more than a few drinks after hours and couldn't make it through a two-hour meeting without sneaking outside for a smoke. "I work out at least twice a week. I can run a fair distance without getting winded. These are all things a war correspondent needs to be able to do."

That brought me to my fifth and final point.

"Many people are more comfortable opening up to women." Playing the female card was a long shot, but it still supported my point. "You know that being a woman these days can be more of an asset, especially since you're such a badass yourself.

"And finally, there isn't anyone who wants to go who can do the job better than me." I held up my hand to prove I had hit all my main points. When the news of Kevin's injury reached me, I had instantly made a do-or-die decision. Either Titan sent me, or I would quit and go freelance. I hoped I wouldn't have to offer that ultimatum because going would be much easier with the backing of a corporate giant. Freelancers ran a higher risk of dying or being wounded due to a lack of equipment and money. Just the thought of trying to say those words paralyzed me with fear but my determination to go was stronger.

Pamela kept staring at me as if seriously considering what to do with me. I stood there like an idiot with my hand in the air, looking like I expected her to give me a high five and whip out a company credit card. I shoved both hands in my pockets and tried not to fidget, but I couldn't stop. Usually, I wasn't so forward. I'd grown up with enough insecurities and therapy to know that I had imposter syndrome which led me to believe my achievements were false. On some level, I knew that I was more than qualified, and I was the best candidate for the job. None of that eased my anxiety as the seconds ticked by. Pamela continued to stare at me like I'd just asked her to let me have her job.

After another endless moment, Pamela reached into a desk drawer and pulled out a book that she tossed onto the desk before me. It looked like one of those manuals put out by the military or even the Boy Scouts back in the 1960s. Instead of having a glossy cover like similar publications, it was an eye-catching orange with a bold print title, *Safety Guide for Journalists,* and the subtitle, *A handbook for reporters in high-risk environments.*

"We've already sent the request to add your name to our embedded contract to replace Kevin," Pamela said, trying unsuccessfully to hide a mischievous grin. Signing an embedded contract meant she'd promised I'd be good while I was in Ukraine and follow the rules. "I've had you on my shortlist since the beginning, but the upper brass wanted to give Kevin a chance."

Holding the book was as good as holding a signed contract, as far as I was concerned. She wouldn't have given it to me if she wasn't going to send me. It took my brain a minute to process this.

"I know you have a very different style from Kevin," she continued. "I expect you to send in a different kind of story. Even if doing so means you have to think outside the box."

I picked up the handbook. The words *high-risk* and *safety* jumped at me. I was going where people were shooting at one another and tossing bombs around like a high school gym class throwing big red balls on dodgeball day. I nervously rolled the book into a tube, then forced myself to unroll it. I was going to Ukraine. I needed this information.

It was happening. I would laugh in the face of danger. A lifetime of hoping, dreaming, and preparing was within my reach. I would be fearless. All this danger was exaggerated anyway. They always highlighted the people who got hurt, kidnapped, or killed. Hundreds of journalists or scribes had covered wars since wars began and had come away unscathed. Being a war correspondent would be getting back to real journalism. For me, that was what counted.

Covering the political scene in America, where politicians passed out insanity like Halloween candy, had worn me down. I was convinced politics in America had become a one-way ticket on the crazy train. With this country's growing hatred, violence, and bigotry, covering something as cut-and-dried as war would be a relief. War was black-and-white. Politics was an endless sea of gray.

Pamela was talking again. She told me that she had requisitioned some essentials for me. I was to report to Marge, our office manager, and pick up supplies. She tossed a large envelope across her desk. I picked it up and opened it. Inside was money, a lot of money. There were stacks of tens, twenties, and even a couple of hundreds. There was also a stack of hryvnia, the Ukrainian currency, and another pile of Russian rubles.

"I would recommend splitting up the money in three or four different places. If you get kidnapped or robbed, you won't lose it all," Pamela said. "Also, the first thing you'll need to do when you get there is hire a fixer. Kevin's fixer died in the same incident that wounded him."

I tried to rein in my reeling mind and pay attention. I didn't know the first thing about hiring a fixer, except I wanted someone who could speak English and knew the country, the politics, and the players. A good fixer could mean the difference between a Pulitzer Prize and getting crap stories. Hiring one was a decision I decided to worry about when I got to Ukraine. I liked to look someone in the eyes when I heard their pitch.

Which reminded me, I needed more critical information. "When am I leaving?"

"Next Tuesday," Pamela said.

Today was Wednesday, so I had approximately a week to get ready. I had a million things to do, and the clock was ticking. Impatience and anticipation fought for dominance in my brain. I needed to get moving. It was a struggle to bring my focus back to the present moment. I was going to Ukraine to cover the war! My heart was pounding, and I wanted to stand on top of the building and shout it to the world.

Pamela gave me some more instructions. I shouldn't wear bright clothing that might attract attention. Make sure that someone always knew my approximate location. Don't wave my money around. Under any other circumstances, this information would have been cause for alarm. It was practical stuff anyone in a dangerous situation needed to know. Brushing aside her cautions, I vaguely assured her I would be careful.

"We've made you a reservation at the Raddison Blu in Kyiv," she said. "It's a base hotel where most of the press is staying. There aren't any vacancies, but I paid a bundle to have them hold Kevin's room for you. The last I heard, the lights were on, but they still have blackouts and brownouts."

I could only imagine the cost of having a room at such a place. It also meant that keeping a story under wraps or trying to get a scoop would be difficult. There were no secrets when journalists lived in small spaces. Most of us couldn't help bragging about whatever story we were working on or what awesome interview we had scored. I'd never met a journalist who didn't have an inflated ego, myself included. Visions of camaraderie and exchanging exciting stories, danced in my head.

"One more thing, Nicole, and this is probably the most

important," Pamela said. She waited until I gave her my full attention. "You can't be openly gay there. I'm not telling you to go back into the closet, but I am telling you to be very careful. You're going to a place that killed women like us not long ago. That's another reason the big brass was reluctant to send you. I fought for your right to go. Don't repay me by getting killed."

I assured her that I understood, even though I was kind of offended that she'd brought it up. I wasn't going over there to pick up a mail-order bride. I was going to cover the war. I had always been kind of open about my sexuality. It was part of what made me who I was but not my entire existence. However, outing myself to everyone I met in a country where gays and lesbians were still persecuted wasn't part of my itinerary. Other people weren't that comfortable about open sexuality, especially in many foreign countries. I watched the documentaries. I'd read the stories. But hell, these days, being out was even becoming risky here in the United States. I would never deny it if someone asked outright, but this assignment was too important to let a little thing like homophobia stop me.

"I'll see you again before you go, but as of now, transfer everything you're working on to me for reassignment," Pamela said. "Report to Marge in supply. She'll provide everything you need. Take the rest of the week and get everything in order." She stood, and for a brief, awkward moment, I thought she would hug me. Instead, she stuck out her hand. I shook it firmly and tried not to gush. She hated mushiness.

I left her office and took the elevator three floors down to where our office manager lurked in the basement of the Titan

Global News headquarters. Once the elevator doors opened, there was a long hallway. The squeak from my sneakers echoed irreverently. At the end of the hallway on the right were two large double doors that opened to the press room. Before almost everything had become digital, the giant machine had turned out thousands of papers daily. The noise level had resembled standing directly under a jet, and the smell of ink had permeated the whole building. Even now, the scent of past issues lingered.

The double doors on the opposite side of the hallway opened to Marge's domain. Instead of a desk, she sat behind a long counter. Behind her were towers of shelves, all neatly arranged and labeled. It brought to mind the layout of an auto parts store where I could tell the counter person, I needed a carburetor for a '92 Dodge. Although she had to have been expecting me, Marge didn't acknowledge me at first or indicate that she knew what I was there for.

"Nicole Sheppard," I said. "I'm here to get supplies for going to Ukraine."

"Wait here," she said without looking up.

She pushed off the high stool behind the counter and disappeared into the stacks behind her. While I waited, I pulled the *Safety Guide for Journalists* from my bag and flipped through it. The first thing it said was to always keep the guide with you. That seemed a bit obvious, but okay. Then, there were the usual pages about how the guide had come into being and how important the work on it was. Yadda. Yadda. Yadda. It wasn't until chapter three that I got some helpful information. I skipped through the parts about what to do in case I was kidnapped. I had no intention of being kidnapped I scoffed to myself.

For some reason, I assumed that anyone in a foreign country who went and got themselves kidnapped had to be asking for it on some level. My arrogance caught me a bit off guard as I went back to the beginning of the chapter. I was not the kind of person who usually blamed the victim. If I was kidnapped, I would be smart about it because I would memorize this book.

While I was skimming the information about what to pack, Marge returned, pushing a small cart piled high with luggage and equipment. I had thought the list in the book was long, but she had brought a small mountain of gear.

Marge dumped the pile on the counter between us. The first thing she held up was a tan tactical vest with the word PRESS written across the front and back in big red letters. She came around the counter and dropped it over my head. It was heavy but not too heavy. She fussed around, circling me twice and showing me how to tighten the clasps, buckles, and strings.

I'd read somewhere that getting tactical vests to fit women was a problem for modern soldiers. Fortunately for me, Marge had foreseen the possibility of at least one female journalist going. I was five-four and weighed around a hundred and forty pounds. The vest was not uncomfortable, but it was bulky. It also had tons of pockets, Velcro, and carabiner hooks. That made me happy. I loved the thought of keeping an extra supply of pens in one of the ammo pockets.

"Tactical vest." Marge thumped the breastplate directly under the word PRESS. It made a soft, hollow sound. "It won't stop a bullet completely, but it could mean the difference between being wounded or being dead."

She thumped the breastplate again, this time directly on

11

the word PRESS. "This is supposed to keep you from being identified as an enemy soldier and keep someone from deliberately shooting at you. That doesn't mean you won't get shot. Plus, most of today's warfare involves drones. I want you to remember this crucial fact. Drones. Can't. Read." She thumped her crooked knuckles against the PRESS to emphasize each word.

Of course, just printing the word PRESS in big red letters across my chest wouldn't stop someone from shooting me. If that were the case, everyone in the country would print PRESS across their chests. It was cynical of me to think that way, but not everyone lived by a moral code like, don't kill women and children, don't shoot innocent bystanders, and don't frag someone just trying to report the news. Still, I was glad to have the vest, and I would proclaim my nonparticipation to the heavens if it kept me from getting shot.

Next, Marge plopped a matching tan helmet on my head. It also had the word PRESS written in big red letters across both sides. I felt like a kid playing soldier with the neighborhood boys. "Roger that," I said, slipping into character.

She scoffed at me and ignored my attempts to crack jokes. It was something I always did when I was nervous. I assumed she probably thought I was just another dumb kid asking for trouble because I wouldn't pay attention to my elders. "What's your blood type?" she asked.

"O negative."

"Good. That makes you a universal donor." She dug around in the pile on her desk and pulled out a Velcro patch with O NEGATIVE written across it in red letters smaller than the word PRESS but still visible. She affixed the patch to the back of the tactical vest. She took another one and attached it to my messenger bag. A third patch was stuck to a giant knapsack she pulled from the pile of stuff. It gave me the creeps to think of enemy soldiers strapping me to a gurney and draining my precious O negative to keep their war machine running. I swore they'd have to mop it up off the floor first. Another joke about back-alley blood transfusion died on my lips. If it ever came to the point where I was the one needing the transfusion, I would be glad my blood type was plastered all over my stuff.

When all the supplies had been tallied, they filled three big bags, and I hadn't even started thinking about my clothes. Marge had stuffed one bag full of items like toothpaste and shampoo, soaps, candy bars, and other things that might be hard to buy.

"What's all of that for?" I asked.

"War cuts off supply chains," she said. She ought to have known since she's practically been around since World War I, I thought sardonically. "You can also use some of it for currency. Believe me, if you've got five bucks but there isn't any toilet paper anywhere to be found, that five bucks becomes useless and a roll of Charmin is pure gold."

My new stash of electronic equipment included two phones. One of them was a satellite phone. A laptop, an iPad in a special drop-resistant case, and a cool solar charger for everything were also included. I did love my gadgets, but it was a lot. I was a bit overwhelmed by the sheer mass, and I was generally considered a pack rat.

"How the hell am I supposed to cart all this stuff around?" I asked.

She shrugged. "My job is to ensure you get what you need, not what you do with it after you get there." She helped me out of the tactical vest and stowed it and the helmet in the duffel bag on the cart. "Always, and I mean always, wear the vest and the helmet when you leave the hotel. I don't care how uncomfortable they are. You'll get used to them."

I nodded solemnly. Every bit of information I received impressed upon me that where I was going would be dangerous. I still wasn't afraid, but it was no time to pretend that I was bulletproof.

Having adequately supplied me, Marge removed a document from her desk drawer. It was an itemized list of everything she'd just provided. I put my signature at the bottom. Marge peered at it for a long minute as if she suspected I'd forged my name. Finally, she signed and dated it, made two copies, and handed me one.

We left the basement through the press room and started up a ramp leading to the employee parking lot. While I pushed the cart to my car, Marge walked alongside me. She waited while I loaded everything into my trunk.

My previous interactions with her had been brief conversations over pens and notebooks. In the past, she'd guarded them diligently. She'd told me more than once that reporters tended to be wasteful. That was why this influx of supplies had left me a little off guard. Once everything was secured, I turned to say goodbye. After a long silence, she cleared her throat. I was amazed to realize that she was having trouble speaking. The thought of all the people who seemed to care about me now that I was going, caused me to fight back some tears of my own.

"Don't get killed," she said gruffly. She turned around

and wheeled her empty cart back inside the building.

"I'm not planning on it," I said to her retreating back.

CHAPTER TWO

The rest of the week went by in an instant. Preparations for my trip consumed every waking minute. The office threw me a small going-away party the Friday before I left. Even Kevin appeared on Zoom. He'd already sent me a list of his contacts and other helpful information he thought I might need. He seemed different from the arrogant son of a bitch that had gone to Ukraine. He was more subdued. That was understandable since he'd almost had his leg blown off. The doctors said, physically, he would make a full recovery. A full mental recovery, if that was even possible, would take a lot longer. A good five minutes of our conversations consisted of him telling me to keep my head down. He seemed relieved to be home. For his sake, I tried not to look too ecstatic about taking his place.

I listened to him drone on about how important it was to stay with the troops I would be embedded with and to make sure I paid attention to the curfews and warnings. Sure, he was only trying to help, but this was my going-away party, and other people wanted to give me their best advice for staying alive in a war zone. He didn't need to monopolize my time. Besides, I had the ten-page memo he'd sent me the day before.

The following Tuesday, my best friend Hannah drove me to the airport. We'd been friends since we'd worked on the university newspaper during our college days. Her talents had taken her in a different direction from mine. She now worked as a marketing rep for a large pharmaceutical company. "Marketing is where the money is," she'd told me on more than one occasion. Maybe, but the excitement for me was in journalism.

During the drive, she didn't say much. At the terminal, she hugged me long and hard. She had been my wing woman since college, and now I was flying solo. She'd never understood my desire to test my mettle in a war zone. All the time I'd talked about becoming a war correspondent, she had thought it was a fantasy of mine. Not anything I would ever actually do, like she would never become a high-powered lawyer or eventually become president. We both pretended she wasn't crying and my watery eyes were the result of allergies. She begged me to keep in touch and to please be careful. I promised.

"Don't get killed," she said, hugging me one last time before I entered the terminal.

Even under ordinary circumstances, flying stressed me out. During takeoffs and landings, I would cling to the armrests until my knuckles turned white. There was no way something this big and heavy was just going to hop into the air. Visions of airplane parts scattered over miles of terrain flashed through my head at every takeoff and landing.

Instead of flying directly into Kyiv, I had to take a commercial flight to Lebanon. From there, I hopped a military transport to Kyiv. It was a courtesy flight for journalists and humanitarians. Fortunately for me, there was space available, and I squeezed in between a pallet of stuff marked Red Cross and an overweight businessman yelling into his cell phone in Russian.

Flying into Kyiv airport was harrowing. The tension on the plane was at a level I'd never experienced before. The pilot made announcements in English, Russian, and Ukrainian, that so far, the airport was available and not under any recent attacks. That didn't rule out the existence of missiles, drones, or attacks on the ground. This announcement didn't do much for my peace of mind.

It was early evening local time when we finally touched down. Before this conflict started, Kyiv International Airport had been a gleaming modern facility with all the latest in transportation opportunities. Now, it resembled an old clunker held together with plywood and duct tape. Shadows of its former glory occasionally peeked through the many cracked windows and caved-in walls.

The next test of my jangled nerves came once I made my way to the baggage claim. Dozens of hawkers greeted me. Each sought to get a bit of cold, hard, American cash. I had my camera bag and a carry-on with me. The waiting mob knew I was a journalist even without seeing the word PRESS across my chest in two-inch red letters.

"Press? Need a ride?" one tall, mustachioed man asked in broken English. "I'll take you to the hotel. Very safe."

Another promised to get me there faster than any of the others. Still another asked if I had any items I wanted to sell. I shook my head and bravely waved them all off. I felt bombarded with them coming at me from all sides, but I needed a fixer. Before I chose anyone, I wanted to be able to consider my options.

Then a young woman leaning against a post near the baggage carousel caught my attention. She looked to be in her twenties. She was short, but it was hard to tell how tall she was as she leaned against the post. Her blond hair was short and neatly trimmed. She wore a pair of green cargo pants and a Hard Rock Café T-shirt that boasted a location in Los Angeles. Her expression was curious and thoughtful as she watched me wade through the crowd. It was possible she wasn't a fixer. It wasn't a profession many women aspired to. It was more likely she was someone's daughter or girlfriend. Our eyes met, and she gave me a slight smile and nod. She straightened and sauntered toward me.

"You need a fixer?" She had the bluest eyes I'd ever seen. Her English was good enough for me to assume she was fluent.

"Tell me why I should hire you rather than any of these others." I waved around, taking in all the nearby hopefuls. She was a curiosity.

She followed the trail my hand made and pulled some papers from a plastic case hanging from a lanyard around her neck. "I'm embedded and registered with the press office," she said. "I know Kyiv. I live here my whole life. The city map is inside my head. Besides my native Ukrainian, I speak English, Russian, Spanish, and Italian. Well, very little Italian. I have a large family, many contacts. Some even work in government. I'm a good driver. I never crashed. I'm strong. I'm healthy. I work cheaper than them." She ticked off each point on her hands. She gave off an air of confidence that only the young had. I liked her.

"Why has no one hired you yet?" I asked. "Why should you charge less than them?"

"I'm a woman," she said. Looking around, I realized there weren't many women here. Other than me and this girl, the few women present either clung fearfully to their male counterparts or rushed to get out of the way of the mob.

That brought the point home to me more than anything else; I was in a different place with a different culture. Women here hadn't made the strides we'd achieved in America. Even if she had the blessing of the Ukrainian government, she no doubt thought she deserved less than her male counterparts.

"How much do they charge?" I asked.

She thought about it for a minute. Then, she pointed out one tall dark man negotiating with the overweight man who'd disembarked from our shared flight. "He says he is the best but does not know the area like me. He doesn't have the contacts I have. He charges one-hundred-and-fifty US dollars a day."

"What's your name?" I asked.

"Tatiana Eristova," she said.

"Okay, Tatiana, my name is Nicole Sheppard. I want to hire you as my fixer, and since you're the best, I will pay you one-hundred-and-fifty US dollars daily." I held out my hand to shake on it.

She looked surprised for a second, then shook my hand and grinned. "You won't regret it, boss," she said.

While we negotiated, my two huge bags were on their second or third trip around the carousel. I grabbed one, heaved it off the conveyor belt, and jerked my head toward the other. While she struggled with the large suitcase, I wondered if I shouldn't have hired someone stronger. The bag was almost as big as she was. But she latched on to it and wrestled it upright. Strength didn't seem to be an issue.

"Follow me, boss," she said.

As we weaved through the crowd, we were besieged by beggars, peddlers, and others asking for cigarettes, chocolate, or coffee. Tatiana yelled at them in three different languages. The majority backed off. A few lingered, looking for an opportunity to approach me again. Tatiana bullied a path through to the doors leading to the parking lot.

Most of the glass at the front of the airport was either missing, cracked, or taped over because of the bombing. Sheets of plywood had replaced the glass in the doors with the word *shtovkati* written across the wood in red paint. When Tatiana stopped and pried the doors open, I assumed the word meant *push*.

Once we were outside, I stopped and looked around. Piles of rubble lay everywhere, hastily swept up in heaps to clear the roads. I pulled out my camera to get a few shots. I was sure the destruction was nothing Titan's readers hadn't seen before. I'd seen plenty myself. But seeing it in person was new to me. I knew one reason I was here was to have a fresh pair of eyes. Everywhere I looked, there seemed to be something I thought needed documenting.

Tatiana waited for me to finish. "Before Russia invaded, this was a beautiful area. Very modern. Like a park in New York City."

Her voice sounded so sad. The area around the airport had probably been cleaner before the war started, but beautiful might have been a stretch. I tossed my camera strap around my neck and grabbed the suitcase handle again. Circumventing the airport parking area reminded me of playing a video game. Every obstacle we conquered placed two or three more in our way. There were police barriers to cross, giant craters to avoid, and some spills with ominous signs posted in one or two places.

"Toxic," Tatiana said. "*Otpyta*. Poison."

I nodded and snapped a few more shots. What kind of poison would be in an airport parking lot? I made a mental note to myself to find out. Again, it brought home the notion that I was in a different place, and OSHA was nowhere to be found.

Tatiana led me to a beat-up old Land Rover with the word PRESS painted on the side in red letters about a foot tall. Either she had been certain someone would hire her as a fixer, or she was a great optimist. The car had seen some distance. It was the color of desert sand. It sported numerous dents, scrapes, and a crumpled front fender. The damage made me wonder if Tatiana had been completely honest about her driving skills.

She must have guessed what I was thinking. She gave the car an affectionate pat. "Don't worry, boss. It was beat up when I bought it. Not pretty but practical. My cousin is a mechanic. He keeps it running." She opened the back and tossed my suitcases in.

I kept my camera bag with me but allowed her to relieve me of my carry-on. She pulled a tactical vest from underneath the seat. It also had the word PRESS written in big red letters across the front and back. A sense of pride crossed her face as she slipped it on. "I have an extra," she said. "If you need one."

It came as no surprise that she had a tactical vest or two with the word PRESS on both sides. In the United States, you could pick them up at any Army-Navy surplus store. If there wasn't a surplus store handy, they were available online through a multitude of websites such as law enforcement sites. You could even order them where you ordered paintball supplies. All you had to do was get some stick-on letters, and you could pretend you were a card-carrying member of the press corps.

I assured her I had my own. While digging through my oversized bag to find it, I was conscious of a prickling sensation on the back of my neck. I had to will myself to calm down, telling myself it was unlikely a sniper was crouching on the other side of the parking lot just waiting to blow me away. Still, I'd just landed here and violated the number one rule of always keeping my vest and helmet on. It wasn't like me to be so careless. It was a relief when I found the vest and helmet crammed into the bottom of the duffel bag Marge had packed for me. I slipped the vest over my jacket and securely fastened the helmet under my chin.

Once we cleared the airport parking lot, Tatiana took off like one of the jets on the runway. While we drove, I asked her about her life in Kyiv. She was twenty-three. Until recently, she had been a student at the University of Kyiv where she'd studied engineering. Before the war started and the university shut down, she had wanted to help build a better infrastructure for her country. Engineering was even more critical now because it would be vital to rebuilding their city and country after they chased the Russians out.

Her decision to become a fixer was purely economic. Fixers earned the best money, and they were in high demand. She had plenty of time to return to engineering later. After graduating, she intended to take a year off and travel. She calculated that she'd have enough money saved to do that by the time the war ended.

I admired her determination. Lots of kids her age wanted to take a year off and see the world. If this kid could save up enough money to do that when this conflict was over, more power to her.

Earning her way meant she didn't have to ask her parents for money. They were unhappy about her working as a fixer. They believed it was not a proper occupation for a young lady. Still, she said they'd raised their children to be independent and self-sufficient, so they limited their protests.

She didn't seem that much different from any other twenty-three-year-old woman I knew. It amused me to listen to her prattle on about how she was a grown-ass adult and could look after herself. Had I ever been that self-confident, I wondered? Was I even that sure of myself now that I was in my thirties?

In addition to her parents, she had two older brothers and an older sister. Both her parents came from large families, so there were tons of aunts, uncles, cousins, nieces, nephews, and various hangers-on who made up her circle of care. Both her brothers were off fighting in the eastern part of the country. All her siblings were married and starting families, but she saw no reason to settle down. She wasn't seeing anyone seriously.

Her mother taught law at the university, and her father

was a city planner. I mentally filed that away, thinking once we got to know each other better, perhaps her father would agree to an interview about the damage the war had caused. I pulled out the notebook and pen I'd connected to my belt loop and made myself a note under the heading of story ideas.

Our trip to downtown Kyiv allowed me to observe some of the damage inflicted on the city. Some city blocks were virtually untouched, while others were nothing but piles of rubble. What surprised me was that some buildings had entire rooms intact while other parts lay heaped on the ground. Some had tarps flapping in the wind to keep out the elements. I couldn't imagine people still living there, but on the second floor of one building, I noticed a woman cooking something on a barbecue grill while a man sitting at a nearby table fiddled with some gadget. The rest of their apartment was completely gone.

While I marveled at the resilience of humanity and made more notes to track down these people to interview, Tatiana kept talking. She said her life had been good before the war. She had gone to school, socialized with friends, and bicycled down the idyllic streets near her home. The Russians had destroyed all of that. A certain degree of hatred crept into her voice when she spoke of the invaders. I was getting a picture of life before the Russian invasion, and I had to be careful and not idealize the picture too much. I was sure many things about Kyiv had not been as picturesque as she made them seem.

A mix of vehicles stood parked in front of the Radisson Blu Hotel, a long black stretch limo, a military Jeep, and an ambulance, among others. A sandbag barricade blocked the hotel's front entrance, with just enough room for a luggage cart to slide through.

Two teenage boys ran toward the car and began speaking to Tatiana as she dragged my bags out of the back. She gave one to each boy. They nodded happily and headed back inside with my giant bags in tow. I gave her my reservation information so she could translate and check me in.

The inside of the Radisson Blu was like nothing I'd ever seen before. Instead of a quaint, picturesque hotel lobby, I was standing in the middle of a bad episode of some network TV hospital drama. One of Kevin's articles had been about how local hotels had opened their lobbies for makeshift hospitals. Although I knew about the temporary triages, the actual sight was something completely different. It was chaos. People wearing scrubs rushed around, dodging hotel guests and staff. Gurneys and stretchers lay end to end across the lobby and down the hall. Almost every surface that, in normal times, would be covered with vases filled with artificial flowers or plants, now held supplies or cast-off clothing. A few of the longer tables were even being used as makeshift beds. Wounded men, women, and children moaned or cried out for help from whatever space they could occupy. As horrifying as it was, very few of the wounded were soldiers.

An older couple stood over a blanket-covered, person-shaped mound in a far corner. The woman cried quietly while the man held her close. My heart ached for them, but I snapped a shot anyway. Could I have been any more of a ghoul? It was morbid and intrusive to record their grief, but how else would I get their message out? It was my job.

There were not enough places to sit, so people in various

stages of distress sat on the floor and leaned against the wall. One teenage boy sat cross-legged on the front desk holding a bloody towel against his head. Other wounded lined up at the door. The smell of urine, blood, and something rotten, overpowered the smell of antiseptic and bleach. Hotel staff deftly navigated the mess, avoiding both patients and medical personnel.

News crews carrying cameras and other gear rushed past us and out the door. Another group of journalists stood before the front desk, arguing in what sounded like German. Dirt and what looked like motor oil, or possibly even blood, covered their tactical vests. A couple wore their helmets while the others tucked theirs under their arms or clipped them to their vests. The excitement of it washed over me like a tidal wave. I was here in the middle of it all.

Tatiana waved me to the front desk, which doubled as a nurse's station. A harried desk clerk who looked like he hadn't slept in days, said he'd be with us in a minute. He ran his hand through thick, dark hair that looked like he always used his fingers instead of a comb. He shoved a small pyramid of bandages out of his way and used both his index fingers to type something into the computer. Tatiana took charge and made sure everything was in order. It was already obvious she was an asset. It took several minutes for her to say I was Nicole Sheppard from Titan Global News, and I was moving into Kevin Paskey's room. The desk clerk responded with a lengthy explanation before he handed me a key card.

"He says they have been using the room for wounded. It was empty, and they did not know exactly when you would arrive," Tatiana told me. "He asks if you don't mind waiting in the dining area while they clear out the room and get it cleaned. He says he will have staff fix you a meal."

As tired and jet-lagged as I was, a pang of guilt shot through me. I didn't want to toss out someone who was hurt so I could take a shower and a nap. I relayed this to Tatiana, who, in turn, told the clerk. When he finished speaking, she turned back to me.

"He says not to worry. The patients waiting there are not critical. Only minor wounds. He will find another room where they can wait until the doctor can see them." I glanced around the lobby, where about a dozen medical personnel rushed back and forth creating a sense of urgency in the spacious foyer. From the looks of it, the doctor wouldn't be ready anytime soon.

"I would be happy to wait for them to clear out the room," I said.

Once we settled that business, Tatiana took a card from her pocket and handed it to me. The information was in English and Ukrainian. It looked like an ordinary business card with her name, phone number, and other identifying information. Her bank's name and a long string of numbers were on the back of the card. I looked up quizzically.

"You give that information to your payroll. They will deposit my pay in that account," she said.

Good to know. I slid the card into my back pocket. I took out one of my money envelopes and handed her a wad of twenties. "For your first day."

She looked at the wad. I thought for a minute she was going to protest it was too much for a ride from the airport. Much to my relief, she grinned and stashed the bills away in the pocket of her cargo pants.

"Tomorrow we will meet the press secretary. She will tell us where we can go during the morning briefing." She smirked. "Then, I will take you to the real story." She gave me a jaunty wave and danced around an incoming gurney on her way out the door. It would be a race for her to get home in time for curfew.

Instead of going to the dining area, I raised my camera for more pictures of the wounded, the nurses, and the doctors. It was unlike anything I'd ever witnessed. This scene was something Kevin had never covered. His angle had been more on the logistics of war, on troop movements and military strategies. I wanted to get to the heart of this story. Why and how had one of Kyiv's ritziest hotels become a makeshift hospital?

I photographed a young woman I assumed to be a mother trying to soothe a crying child of about four or five years old. The child had an ugly gash on the side of her head. There seemed to be copious amounts of blood, but I knew from experience that head wounds tended to bleed profusely. The child's clothes didn't look old but were torn in several places, and she had a few other scrapes and bruises as well. The mother wasn't unscathed. A portion of her forearm was covered in a rapidly purpling bruise. Maybe they'd been injured during some of the shelling I could hear in the distance.

"Out of the way, Press," a French-accented voice spoke from behind me. I whirled and almost took the speaker out with my swinging camera. It hit the tray she carried, and her brown eyes glared death rays at me for a few seconds before she bent to pick up her supplies. I started to help, but she impatiently waved me away, saying I'd already contaminated her sterile instruments.

She wore a white lab coat over some ordinary green medical scrubs. A red-and-white stick figure logo over her right breast sported the words *Medecins San Frontieres* and *Doctors Without Borders,* in French and in English. Embroidered over her left breast was the name *DuBois*. An alligator clip held a great ball of her brown hair off her neck. A stray tress fell over her forehead as if longing to escape the confines of the clip. A stethoscope was draped around her neck like a scarf. Despite the lines of weariness, her eyes, although shooting daggers at me, had an inner sparkle that I swear held the echoes of her laugh. I very much wanted to hear her speak again.

When several French curses broke from her full, wet lips, I got my wish. Although I'd taken four years of French in college, I was not fluent, but these words I understood perfectly. "Shit!" might not have been pronounced the same, and it might be spelled differently in every language, but the tone was unmistakable. I volleyed between begging her for forgiveness and trying to introduce myself. She scorched me with those beautiful brown eyes again.

"I said, out of my way, Press, or I'll sew that camera to your forehead," she threatened.

I backed away, trying to blend in with the wall. A young man dressed in similar medical scrubs rushed up to the beautiful woman and handed her a tray of fresh supplies while taking away the ones I'd contaminated.

The doctor carried the tray with the sterile instruments over to the woman and child. Her expression changed to one of compassion and kindness as she knelt before the child and said a few words to the mother in Ukrainian. The doctor's speech was slow, and her forehead creased in concentration. I suspected learning Ukrainian was a recent talent for her and probably half the people here. Both mother and child visibly relaxed under her care. The conversation went back and forth for several minutes.

While this happened, the doctor rubbed the child's wound with some rust-colored solution. She removed a small packet from the pocket of her smock. When she pulled out a needle, the child's eyes widened, and she began to cry. The doctor waited until the mother pulled the little girl into her lap. The mother started singing in a low calm pitch to the frightened child. I inched closer to see if I knew the tune or recognized any lyrics and kept pressing the shutter button, capturing the whole thing. Once the crying stopped, the doctor went to work stitching the cut.

The doctor finished quickly. She talked to the child and the mother the whole time, keeping them both calm. When she finished, the little girl rewarded the doctor with a semi-toothless grin. The doctor pretended to look for something in her pockets, and when she pulled out a chocolate bar, the girl laughed and snatched it out of her hand.

After giving the mom some final instructions and a tube of medication, the doctor sent them on their way. Even though she gave them a reassuring smile as they left, she wilted a little when they were out of sight. Then, the doctor disappeared through a door to an office off to the side of the lobby. I wanted to follow her and ask dozens of questions, but I didn't want to intrude. I didn't want to make her mad again.

The lobby was beginning to clear. Somehow, while I'd been preoccupied with taking pictures, a small bit of order had been restored. The desk clerk waved me over and told me in passable English that someone would serve me dinner now if I went to the dining room. He pointed in the general direction of the double doors off to his left. There were about a dozen large round tables in the empty area. Each had seats for between six and eight people, depending on how intimate we wanted to get. White tablecloths covered each, with place settings for six. I sat at the table closest to the lobby, making sure the door the doctor had disappeared through was in my line of sight.

The desk clerk carried in a tray with food and drink. The aroma coming from the tray was intoxicating. I hadn't realized how hungry I was. The odor almost caused me to snatch the tray from the poor guy's hands and devour the contents. I politely thanked him and let him fuss over me for a few minutes. It seemed to give him some satisfaction to pretend everything was normal.

The meal was stew, a couple of rolls, and water. There was a cup of something smelling a bit like coffee. I hoped it was and not some tranquilizing tea or something. I could have used the caffeine buzz. The desk clerk apologized several times, saying they offered a much wider variety of dishes during regular times. He said they had the best dessert selection in all of Kyiv. I assured him the stew was fine, excellent even. Satisfied he'd done all he could, he told me my room would be ready soon and excused himself to return to his duties.

After I'd eaten everything in front of me, I sat back and surveyed the scene. As dusk settled in, the dining room began to fill up. The medical personnel began to shut down operations. Some of the other journalists started to arrive.

They wore flak jackets and carried their protective helmets, the word Press prominently displayed. They piled their cameras, bags, and other gear near the dining room door. One of them carried a case of what appeared to be beer. They were a boisterous bunch, and several joined me at the table when they spotted me still in my flak jacket.

A tall, balding man in his fifties turned to me and introduced himself as Shawn Glass. I knew who he was—the biggest name in war correspondents. He was a large man, not fat, just larger than life. He had covered almost every conflict in the world during his thirty-year career in the news business. He'd won all the awards, including a couple of Pulitzers. I'd also heard through the grapevine that he was an arrogant ass.

"You must be Kev's replacement," he said. He popped the cap off a beer bottle and set it on the table before me. "We liberated this from a group of Russian soldiers."

"Nicole Sheppard," I said, picking up the beer and taking a drink. It was lukewarm and extremely bitter. But accepting a beer was part of establishing myself among my colleagues. Creating a camaraderie with these men and women was essential to my survival. While we competed, we were also comrades. In situations like these, traveling in a group was safest.

"It's a pleasure to meet you, Nicole." Glass lifted his beer bottle in a toast. "Here's hoping you don't get shot like ol' Kevin did."

A two-person CNN crew of reporter Elizabeth Sexton and cameraman William Alvarado took seats on the other side of our table. Another television crew from the BBC consisted of three people: Alexandra Fischer, Ben Meade, and Elwood Carey. They all offered friendly greetings.

After the introductions, the talk turned to the day's events. They'd spent the morning in Kherson, where the Russian troops had begun pulling out. There had been widespread looting. Incredible piles of rubble had replaced the buildings. Citizens were living in makeshift shelters fashioned from the remains of their homes. While these newspeople talked about bodies in the street, they laughed and drank and tried to see who could come up with the most horrendous thing they'd covered today. It was scary and exciting.

Their morbid sense of humor didn't put me off. It was that same objectivity we were supposed to have that made us good reporters. Developing a little bit of gallows humor was the way most of us coped with too much death and destruction. I looked forward to grinding the edge off my horror at how easily they talked about death.

The desk clerk beckoned to me from the doorway. My room was ready, and he'd already sent my larger bags up. I stood and offered the usual good-byes. The desk clerk asked if I wanted to take the elevator but quickly warned against it because the electricity was erratic, especially at night. I assured him the stairs would be acceptable. I picked up my camera, iPad, and messenger bag and gratefully climbed the stairs to my fourth-floor room.

The room still smelled of antiseptic and another, more ominous odor. Everything on the surface appeared clean, but my nose told me the disinfectant had missed something. I decided it didn't matter if the sheets were clean. Thankfully, they were. I changed into shorts and a T-shirt, crawled into bed, and was asleep in seconds.

Without Borders

CHAPTER THREE

It was probably a combination of my alarm going off, the distant explosions, or Tatiana pounding on my door that woke me. When I stumbled to the door and opened it, my fixer stood there with a paper bag, a thermos, and two cups. She thrust one of the cups in my direction.

"Coffee, boss," she said.

I was grateful for her offerings since I'd been told coffee was hit or miss at the hotel most mornings. A tempting aroma emanated from the paper bag. Tatiana handed it over. "Syrniki, cottage cheese pancakes," she said. "My mother makes it fresh when she can find all the ingredients."

Gratefully, I took the coffee and the syrniki. The pastry was still warm and delicious. I finished it in three bites. We needed to get moving. The press secretary was on her way, and if I wasn't there on time, my troop liaison would leave without us. Tatiana seemed almost as nervous as I was. We could meet the press secretary and get an assignment, then we could go our own way.

"Some of the other fixers told me the press secretary is not sending them to the front lines," Tatiana said. "Many of the journalists are upset by it."

I could imagine. Typically, journalists had their own ideas about the stories they covered, and if the local government wasn't assigning them to the troops who were doing the actual fighting, they could get ugly.

Tatiana outlined our day. She thought we would start in the city by interviewing some local businesses. Many of them were anxious to speak to the Western press. They wanted to talk about how they'd coped with running a business during the uncertainty of war.

"Are you sure you're not a journalism student?" I asked her.

She gave me a big grin. "When I decided to become a fixer, I did much research," she said. "I found out what the people wanted to know. Then, I researched how to get that information. Finally, I made a list. All I needed to complete the task was you, boss."

I packed a few toiletries and some candy bars in my messenger bag to use for bribes. Dressed comfortably in jeans and a nondescript T-shirt, I pulled the flak jacket over my head and fastened all the loops and buckles. I adjusted my helmet to where it sat securely on my head, and I was ready to go.

"You look good, boss," Tatiana said. "Very professional." I felt like a kid playing dress-up on Halloween. The fashionable journalists wore a tactical vest and helmet in Kyiv, so I should fit in.

Downstairs, the lobby filled up quickly. The journalists, camera crews, fixers, and soldiers were all waiting for the press secretary. Their presence pushed the medical personnel back into a corner of the lobby, near what used to be the hotel business center. The beautiful doctor stood over in a corner talking to a couple of other medical types while they waited for the first wave of wounded to come flooding through. A different desk clerk went back and forth between the two groups, trying to direct them while other hotel staff ran the gauntlet to get to their assigned duties.

A woman in her mid-forties with short brown hair and a stern expression entered the room. She wore a red dress that fell to a tasteful length below her knees, with matching high heels, but not too high. Her jewelry was a simple gold necklace and small diamond studs. She portrayed the perfect picture of a confident but conservative government servant. Two harried-looking aides followed in her wake. She ignored everyone vying for her attention and went for the stairs. She stopped on the third riser and turned to address the crowd. All talking ceased, and everyone turned their attention to her.

"For those of you who don't know me, I am Inga Tupoleva, press secretary to the Ukrainian government." She made a brief statement about what newsworthy events had happened overnight. She paused for effect. "If you will get with one of my aides, they will give you assignments for today."

I expected the group to rush the two young men standing next to her, but everyone proceeded in an orderly fashion. One of the aides leaned over and whispered something in Tupoleva's ear. She looked out over the crowd until she spotted me standing next to Tatiana. She waved us over.

"You are Nicole Sheppard with Titan Global News?" she asked. I nodded and turned to introduce Tatiana. Tupoleva took a long look at my fixer, long enough to cause me some concern.

"Your father is Dimitri Eristova?" Tupoleva asked Tatiana. "I know your father well. Does he approve of this line of work for you?"

"He has given me his approval," Tatiana said respectfully. Tupoleva nodded and told us one of her aides would give us our instructions, as well as the rules and regulations she expected us to follow. For our first day, we could shadow a particular unit here in Kyiv. They would patrol the city, looking for unexploded missiles or bombs. An aide stepped forward and instructed us where to find our assigned official. He also handed me a sheaf of papers that rivaled the *Safety Guide for Journalists* in size and sheer volume.

"These are the rules of behavior we expect you to follow while you are in our country," he said in heavily accented English. I thanked him and tucked the tome away in my messenger bag.

Once we were in the Land Rover, Tatiana told me she had a different idea in mind, but if I wanted to follow the press secretary's instructions, we could do that instead. I thought about it and asked her where she believed we'd get a better story. She grinned and took off in a direction opposite to what the aide told us.

Our first stop was a coffee shop. The name of the place was Good Brew when translated into English. Boards covered the broken windows, but a handmade sign said they were open. An additional disclaimer said some items on the menu might not be available due to supply issues.

The barista greeted Tatiana as a good friend. She came around the corner and hugged her. Tatiana introduced her as Mila Kiryanova, owner and proprietor. Mila was tall, with her dark brown hair tied back in a ponytail. Fine lines of exhaustion stuck out from her dark eyes. She invited us to sit and brought us coffee and pastries. At first, I protested, not wanting to take goods she could sell to paying customers. I always felt a little bit guilty taking free food and drinks from people I interviewed. I already knew she wouldn't take my money. She waved away my protests, so I repaid her the only way I could. She sat across from me, and I encouraged her to tell me her story.

She and her husband had opened the shop five years earlier. Business was good. They had many loyal customers, and word spread throughout the city about the quality of their goods and services. Things had gone along in that vein until Mila's husband unexpectedly had a heart attack and died three years ago. Mila had been devastated but knew he would want her to go on.

She didn't shut down when the war broke out, but supplies had dwindled to almost nothing. Mila's ten employees had scattered to the wind. Two had died trying to travel to their home cities along the eastern border. Two others had returned after a few days when they'd realized Mila was back in business. Mila didn't know what became of the others. Sadness fell across her face, and she said she feared her other employees were dead.

Since their part of the city often lost power and they had no place to go, Mila and the two remaining employees lived in a storage room in the back of the shop. It was cramped, and sometimes, they wore on one another's nerves, but they made it work.

She took us to the back of the shop to show us where the three women lived. Three cots were neatly lined up against the wall. Above each cot was a shelf with clothes, toiletries, and a few personal items. Mila said it was okay to take pictures. I focused my camera on the beds and the shelves above them. One had a small snow globe of Kyiv, and a picture of Mila and someone I assumed was her husband in a small gold picture frame. It amazed me to see how the three women had pulled their lives together and met the war with resilience and determination.

There were cartons and boxes stacked everywhere else. Whenever an item she needed became available, Mila bought as much as she could. Who knew when sugar or flour would become available again?

She assured me she gave what she could if anyone came to her in need, and she knew hoarding was against Ukrainian law, but surely it was okay if she gave to anyone who came asking to her door. I had Tatiana tell her that I didn't think her scoring three or four bags of flour would cause someone else to starve. I said that because in the short time we'd been there, Mila had given out three separate orders to people who came asking for help.

"It's not about the money anymore," Mila said. "It's about Ukraine helping Ukrainians."

This woman's kindness and generosity made me want to give her the best possible story. I had to wonder that, if the United States was in a similar situation, would the majority of Americans help their fellow citizens? It distressed me to think that, given the current climate in my home country, most would adopt an every-man-for-himself approach. We spent several hours with Mila and her two remaining employees. People came in and out. Some of them paid, and some didn't. One or two expressed frustration and anger that not everything on the menu was available.

"Blame it on the Russians," Mila told them.

Our next stop was a watermelon farm outside the city limits. I had no idea Ukraine produced many of the world's watermelons. They were something you picked up for your Fourth of July barbecue. I'd never thought much about where they came from. My grandfather had grown some in his garden when I was a kid. My cousin and I had to pull weeds for a week after we stole his first ripe one. This field consisted of several acres. It would have been an impressive sight if the bombs had missed. As it was, we were faced with several acres of mounds of dirt, vines, and massive amounts of watermelon pieces drying in the sun and being picked apart by flocks of birds.

The thought of spending a summer without watermelons didn't bother me too much, but I had to wonder how devastating the impact would be on the economy as a whole. Watermelons were cheap. Even people below the poverty line could buy them. If Ukraine was a primary supplier, then the prices would skyrocket, and people everywhere who once enjoyed this large refreshing fruit would have to do without. I felt the loss on behalf of everyone who ever salted a slice and spit out the seeds after.

We met the farmer at the edge of his field. He was an older man in his sixties. His skin was weatherbeaten and dried out like aged beef jerky. His back was permanently stooped from years of bending to tend to his crops.

The drones had destroyed his fields, he said. Some days, the bombing seemed endless. He couldn't do anything except watch as missiles tore through row after row of fruit. Now he had nothing to send to the market. He would not be able to meet his mortgage and feared he and his wife would lose their home. I took dozens of pictures of the destruction. It was almost like the Russians had taken a giant shit in the middle of his fields and then laughed about it.

As we prepared to leave, the farmer insisted on giving us one of his few remaining melons. At first, I tried to say no, but he insisted. He refused to let me pay him for it. All he wanted was to know that someone gained pleasure from eating what could be his last harvest. I put the melon in the back seat next to my bag. These simple acts of kindness were what I wanted to share with my readers.

It was getting dark, so we headed back to the hotel. Tatiana said if I didn't mind, she would like to give the melon to her mother to make a fruit drink they called quass. How she described the drink made me uncertain, but Tatiana assured me it was delicious and refreshing. Since her mom had practically fed me breakfast, I gladly handed over the melon.

When she dropped me off at the hotel, I was ready for a nice, delicious, refreshing drink, even if it wasn't quass. If I was lucky, I could scrounge up a soda somewhere. I also craved a nice juicy cheeseburger and a basket of hot fries to go with it. I hiked my bag up higher on my shoulder and strolled through the doors, not expecting much in the way of dinner.

The hospital triage in the hotel lobby was still in full swing. Patients again lined the walls leading to the door of one of the conference rooms. Nurses and staff rushed around, bobbing and weaving past hotel staff. I looked around for Doctor Dubois. She was back up against a wall, wrist-deep in a young soldier. She said something to the nurse standing across from her. The nurse shook her head. The doctor turned away, her shoulders slumped. She wrote something on a piece of paper and dropped it on the blanket. The nurse pulled it up over the soldier's head. He hadn't made it. Even though I didn't know him or anything about him, I felt his death as an acute loss.

I watched Doctor Dubois as she wiped away a tear. She pulled a tissue from her smock pocket and gently blew her nose. I wanted to stride over, sweep her in my arms, and hold her until she was all cried out. She looked up and saw me watching her. I got a sad smile.

"How was your day, Press?" she asked.

"Better than yours, it seems," I said.

She nodded, turned away from me, and went through the office door off the side of the lobby. I thought about following her, but the rest of the journalists swung through the lobby doors and swept me along with them into the dining room. The BBC news team had won the Man Booker Prize, the British equivalent of the Pulitzer. I was happy for them but a little bit jealous as well. To not celebrate with them would have been rude, and I allowed them to bring me into the dining room to ply me with cold beer and vodka. The celebration went on well into the night.

It seemed like something was not quite right about the loud and boisterous partying going on when a few feet away, young soldiers were dying. I could only imagine what the doctor would think of us laughing and raising our glasses to my British colleagues. Although it would seem rude not to offer my congratulations, I couldn't get over the image of Doctor Dubois pulling the sheet over the dead soldier. My attempts at joining the camaraderie were halfhearted at best.

I wasn't much of a drinker. Not like I had been back in college. Foreign beers were more robust than the American beer I was used to drinking. I was tipsy before too long between the beer and joining every toast with the vodka provided by the Ukrainian press office. It was their way of making amends to the press corps after they'd denied access to the front.

Since I'd been keeping one eye focused on the door, I was the first to notice Doctor Dubois when she reentered the lobby.

"Does anyone know her?" I asked the table in general. All eyes turned toward the lobby. It was the CNN reporter, Elizabeth, who answered.

"She's Marie Dubois from Doctors Without Borders," Elizabeth said.

"I call her the stone-cold bitch," Shawn said nastily.

"Don't mind him," Elizabeth's cameraman, Bill, said. "He's just put out that the beautiful doctor won't give him the time of day."

"It's no secret she has no great love for journalists," Elizabeth agreed. "Probably because Shawn keeps hitting on her."

"She's a heartless dyke," Shawn said. I immediately took offense. His words slurred a little, and he was probably drunk, but I still expected more from someone who was supposed to be enlightened. It was cowardly of me, and I was ashamed, but I let the slur slide. The last thing I wanted to do was pick a fight with Shawn Glass.

Instead, I mumbled something about an early day the next day. I intended to go to my room and pass out, with the possibility of throwing up beforehand. I was almost at the entrance to the dining room when I noticed Marie standing there watching me. The other journalists cheered me on as I headed for the stairs. A couple of them made bets on whether I would make it as far as the staircase before I toppled over. Marie stepped over and grasped my elbow.

"Come on, Press, I'll take you to your room," she said.

The catcalls from the journalists increased at her offer. We journalists were an obnoxious bunch. When I mentioned that to Marie, she laughed and agreed. I allowed her to guide me up the stairs to my room. Once inside, she steered me toward the bed and unceremoniously dropped me on it. She almost came down with me since I hadn't let go of her yet. She extracted herself, stood, and straightened her clothes. I tried to mutter some kind of apology.

"Look, Press, I have a feeling you are not quite as jaded as the rest of our press corps, but as a whole, I've found most journalists are nothing but a bunch of drunken gossipmongers who will sleep with anyone willing, and do anything to get the story they want, whether it's ethical or not."

Each word was like a dagger straight to my heart and soul. Sure, some journalists behaved that way, but most of the ones I'd known were good, decent people just trying to tell the truth. I wanted to defend my fellow journalists, but she didn't give me a chance.

"Maybe you better hold off on the vodka while you're here, Press," she said. "Now get some sleep and come see me in the morning if you need aspirin." She patted me on the head and left. I briefly wondered if she was a lesbian. Then, I fell asleep.

During the next few weeks, I caught brief glimpses of Marie while coming and going. Sometimes she came in when I was going out, or I'd see a flash of her smile as she boarded the bus to take her team home for the night. If I hadn't been so wrapped up in keeping ahead of the multitude of stories that came at me, I would have thought Marie was avoiding me. Every time I saw her, I was determined to prove that not all journalists were unethical drunks. Maybe I could do a story about Doctors Without Borders, and she would have to talk to me then. Even my ethics didn't put me above doing a story about someone I had a crush on. Every morning, I found myself lingering about, hoping to catch a glimpse of her.

More often than I should have, I wondered about her story. What had brought her here? What motivated her? Who was she? Would I ever get the opportunity to find out?

Chapter Four

When Tatiana knocked on my door one morning a few weeks later, I practically assaulted her for the thermos of steaming coffee and pastries she held out to me. It had been a grueling few days with the two of us shadowing a small Ukrainian unit assigned to keep Russian troops out of the city.

It was my element. I walked with the troops, jotting down notes while we weaved in and out of the debris from bombs. During a couple of firefights, I stuck my camera right in the middle of the action. At times, I was close enough to feel the bullets as they brushed by me, close enough to cause my clothes to flap. The young soldiers began to tease me about believing I was invincible. But one of the most famous war photographers of all time, Robert Capa, had said, "If your pictures aren't good enough, you're not close enough."

The days began to run into one another. Tatiana typically

knocked on my door every morning with food and coffee. We'd head down to the lobby and check in with the press secretary or one of her minions. Then, we'd spend the day with the unit we were embedded with, dodging bombs and bullets. Sometimes we would go in a different direction to chase other stories, but for the most part, we followed the press office instructions.

Every evening when I returned to the hotel, sometimes right under curfew, I'd check to see if Dr. Marie Dubois was around. She often stayed later than the other medical personnel. If she missed curfew, the hotel manager tried to find her a room, but I'd found her sleeping on a gurney a couple of times. If she was awake, we always talked a bit. I'd come to realize how much I looked forward to seeing her and talking to her on those days. Sometimes, I would rush downstairs in the morning and pretend like I was impatiently waiting for Tatiana while simultaneously trying to flirt with the doctor.

"You're a lifesaver, you know," I said to Tatiana on another morning as I devoured the food she brought. Doctor DuBois and her crew had not yet arrived. "How does your mom manage to get the ingredients she needs to make enough food to feed her family and still have enough left over for me?" I asked.

"Mamma has never gotten used to not cooking for her whole family," Tatiana said. "Remember, I have two brothers. They ate tons of food. Mamma still cooks like they are coming home for dinner. I don't ask where she gets the food. I'm not sure I want to know. I grab the leftovers and bring them to you."

"Well, I am grateful to her for making it and to you for

bringing it to me," I said honestly.

We gathered up my gear and toted it to where the Rover was parked outside. I walked around the car to get in. That was when Marie and her crew pulled up. It had been a couple of weeks since she and I had done more than mutter a brief greeting to one another, ships passing in the night.

"Good morning, Press," she said, smiling at me.

"What's up, Doc?" I retorted and climbed into the Land Rover. Tatiana got behind the wheel. Before she started the Rover, she turned to me.

"What the hell was that?" she asked. "You call that flirting?"

"I call it saying hello," I said. "Do you think she was flirting? No, she wasn't flirting. She was just being nice. Do you think she was flirting? I don't even know if she's into girls."

"She's into girls," Tatiana said. She started the car. "She's just not into reporters."

"How do you know that?" I asked.

"I've seen her around."

She'd piqued my interest. "Around where?"

"I have seen her in Podil. I'll take you there."

"What's Podil?" I asked.

According to Tatiana, Podil was the bohemian area of Kyiv. That was where the biggest gay bar in the country was located. It surprised me that Kyiv still had an active nightlife while the city was under siege. When I asked about it, Tatiana shrugged and said there had to be a place for people to have fun and release some of the tension. As long as they stayed off the streets, the local police left them alone. One good thing that had sprung up from the city being under siege was that the police had more important things to do than to harass the local gay community.

"Wait! You're gay?" I asked. I'd assumed she knew I was, even though we'd never discussed it. In my case, I felt it was apparent. It never occurred to me that my young friend might also be attracted to the fairer sex. Most kids these days seem to identify as bisexual or trans. My gaydar must have been off. I felt kind of stupid that I didn't notice.

"Yes, boss," she said, laughing. "That's why I knew you needed me as your fixer. I gotta keep you safe, and I need to keep an eye out for pretty girls for you."

I laughed at that. My fixer was five feet, two inches, and maybe tipped the scale at a hundred twenty pounds. The image of her protecting anyone was funny. She had proven herself as a reliable and knowledgeable fixer, though. "I am fortunate to have you," I said.

"You bet you are," Tatiana said, roaring out of the parking lot.

We drove through the city. I had an appointment with her dad to discuss the city's emergency plan and possible long-term solutions.

It was a great interview. Tatiana's father, Dimitri, was knowledgeable and pleasant and answered my questions thoughtfully. Tatiana waited outside while he showed me to his office. Once we completed the interview, he escorted me out and invited me to dinner.

"Great idea, boss," Tatiana said as we walked across the parking lot to the Rover. "We can have dinner, then go out."

"What do we do about curfew?" I asked.

Tatiana pointed to a yellow sticker in the corner of her windshield. I had not noticed it before. "Diplomatic sticker.

Unless we do something stupid or are in imminent danger, the police won't bother us."

She took me back to the hotel so I could shower and change. I dressed carefully. I picked out a clean pair of jeans and a blue button-down shirt that wasn't too wrinkled. I wanted to look my best in case we ran into Marie.

I was nervous about going to a bar in a war zone. But Tatiana said she had overheard one of Marie's assistants say they were going out tonight. What if she had a girlfriend? Tatiana assured me that Marie didn't seem to be with anyone but admitted she could have someone back home. Although my fixer assured me there didn't seem to be a significant other in Marie's life, I still fretted though I don't know why. It wasn't like we were dating or anything. But the heart is a nondiscerning organ when it comes to romance. It refuses to listen to the brain.

The house Tatiana lived in looked like something Frank Lloyd Wright designed for people who lived in Wonderland. On the one hand, it was all glass and angles. On the other, it had what almost resembled turrets and different designs that reminded me of mushrooms. It was larger than the average home in the city, but it seemed to fit into the neighborhood. This part of Kyiv appeared untouched by the war, except most windows were either boarded over or taped up. The shutters were closed. Tatiana told me it was a protective measure in case of bombing. They had been lucky so far, and no missile or drone had come close enough to blow out the windows.

Tatiana's mother was another surprise. I was expecting a dowdy older woman dressed in a colorless, shapeless dress with stockings falling around her ankles and a kerchief tied around her hair. Instead, Tatiana's mother was in her late forties, maybe early fifties. She was slim but not skinny. She had the same shade of blond hair as her daughter and a twinkle in her blue eyes. She wore a pair of designer jeans and a peasant blouse. She graciously welcomed me with a kiss on both cheeks.

"Welcome, welcome, Nicole," she said in almost flawless English with just a touch of an accent. "I am Pasha. Tatiana has told me so much about you. "

She smiled and placed a hand on my upper arm. She told me how much she and Dimitri appreciated that I had hired Tatiana. She ordered me to sit at the dining table and put a glass before me. It was the quass Tatiana had told me about. Quass vaguely resembled a smoothie but combined different fruits to enhance the flavor. The ingredients were rye bread, fruit, and berries. According to Tatiana, there were many ways to make quass, depending on the fruits and berries used. This particular batch was one of Pasha's recipes. I took a cautious sip, not knowing what to expect. When that first chilled drop touched my taste buds, they cheered. It was delicious, and I had to restrain myself from chugging the glass.

"It's wonderful," I told Pasha.

"Thank you," she said humbly. "It's getting harder and harder to make, though. I fear the damage done by the Russians to our fruit crops has made some of them scarce."

That was a shame because this stuff was great. It wasn't quite the consistency of a milkshake but it was thick and creamy. Pasha then thanked me for the watermelon, saying it provided the bulk of the fruit in this quass. Dinner was *holubtsi*, stuffed cabbage, and potato pancakes. My previous experience with Pasha's cooking had set high expectations, but this was beyond good food. I had to restrain myself from overeating.

Pasha and Dimitri were the perfect hosts. They kept the conversation away from talk of the war. They asked a lot of questions about Texas. Neither of them had ever been to Texas, but some years ago they had visited New York City. I extended a blanket invitation if they ever decided to make the trip. I found myself liking them immensely. I only hoped they were as safe here in their home as they seemed to believe.

When we prepared to leave, Pasha expressed some concern about us being out at night. It wasn't so much the curfew that concerned her but rather the people who went out after curfew. The change brought on by war had also brought out some of the worst of humankind. The crime rate in Kyiv had dramatically increased with the war. Dimitri assured his wife that we would be fine. Before coming home, he'd caught up with his staff on troop movements. The fighting in the city had died down, he said. He did throw in a warning for us to be careful and wished us a good night.

No one stopped us as we made our way to the club. The name of it was *Tenats Klub*, Dance Club in English. I liked the name. It was simple and easy to understand the function of the business. Many gay and lesbian bars in the United States tried to elevate themselves with names like Ropers or Casbah. Being straightforward was a good tactic in a country with a long way to go with human rights.

Tatiana parked the Land Rover in the parking lot of a partially bombed-out bank across the street from the club. The lot was full. It made me wonder how many people thought about how safe it was to be out dancing at night in Kyiv. If the citizens didn't see it as dangerous, I would put my worry on hold. As soon as we stepped out of the car, I could hear the beat of the dance music thumping against the club walls like it wanted out.

I expected a line of anxious patrons at the door, and I wasn't disappointed. Most clubs in America had bouncers screening people and only allowed in those they deemed worthy. The same appeared to be true here. I couldn't help but wonder if we would exceed the occupancy rate. I guess the fire codes were suspended if they even had city fire codes. Any fire department personnel probably had their hands full with fires created by explosions. Why worry about a bunch of idiots trying to party like the end of the world wasn't imminent? When the bouncer saw Tatiana, he recognized her and waved us right in. There seemed to be many things I had left to learn about this remarkable young woman.

It was no wonder the beat tried to escape the confines of the building. There was nowhere to go inside. Half of Kyiv's young adult population seemed present. The line at the bar was three or four deep. The dance floor had so many people, that the dancers had no room to move, so they jumped up and down. The volume was so loud, I couldn't hear what Tatiana was saying. I knew she was talking because her lips moved. Even if she shouted, I wouldn't hear her. With a few gestures, she instructed me to stay there. Then, she disappeared into the crowd.

I'd always been kind of socially awkward in this type of environment. In my college days, I'd hit all the bars. Once there, I would have a few drinks and maybe talk with someone. I was at a total loss when asking someone to dance. Chatting and flirting with someone in this atmosphere seemed out of the question due to the noise level.

Tatiana returned with a drink in each hand. She handed one to me. Then, she grabbed me by the arm and pulled me deeper inside the fray. I tried to avoid bumping into people, but that didn't work. Apologizing didn't work, either. I gave up and let my friend drag me through the crowd, bouncing off people like a loose pinball.

We stopped in front of a booth with three people in it. It was one of those long, curved booths restaurants had to accommodate larger groups. Marie sat at one end with two other women on her left side. I recognized them as a couple of nurses who worked with her. Tatiana shoved me into the booth next to Marie, forcing the doctor to move over to allow me to sit. Tatiana took a seat across from us. Her grin was positively mischievous. She then proceeded to ignore us and pulled one of the nurses in the general direction of the dance floor. The other one scooted her way around and out of the booth. If she said where she was going, I didn't hear it. All I could fathom was that Marie had not moved away from me when they left. Our legs touched under the table, and her elbow tucked itself firmly into my ribcage.

Marie put her mouth against my ear. "Isn't it too late for you to be out, Press?"

I turned my head and got as close to her ear as I dared. "My name is Nicole. Nicole Sheppard." Her breath in my ear caused a tickling sensation to run through my head and down my neck, stopping with a small explosion at the bottom of my spine.

"I know," she said. "I like calling you Press." As far as

nicknames went, I'd indeed been called worse. I nodded and took a sip of my drink to cover my awkwardness.

Marie shoved me out of the booth, "Come on, Press, let's dance."

She slid from the booth behind me, grabbed my hand, led me to the dance floor, and elbowed some other dancers out of the way. How she threw her body into the music was beautiful to watch. I closed my eyes briefly. I was self-conscious. People told me I had no rhythm. Marie didn't seem to care. Because of the lack of space, no one was doing any *Saturday Night Fever* moves anyway, so I hopped around like an erratic bunny.

One song melted into another. Some logical part of my brain kept telling me it was one continuous song that never ended. I didn't know how long we danced, but it seemed like hours. When Marie called it quits, I was hot, sweaty, and desperately needed another drink. We made a beeline for the bar.

"Let's get some air," she said, fanning herself with the drink menu. I grabbed our newly filled glasses and followed her out the back door.

The outdoor patio wasn't quite as crowded as inside. Marie pushed through the smaller group and found us an empty spot on a metal bench that probably used to be green before all the paint had peeled off. We sat, and I handed her one of the drinks. She drained half the glass in one gulp.

"Thank you, Press," she said, setting the empty glass on the railing.

"*Je m'appalle*, Nicole," I said. Maybe if I said it in French, she'd start calling me Nicole.

"I thought you couldn't speak French," she said, teasing.

When she smiled, the skin around her nose crinkled a little bit.

"Besides my name, I can say three phrases in French," I said in English.

"I'm intrigued. Let's hear them," she said. She leaned back, crossed her arms, and gave me an inquiring look.

I made sure I put an extra twang in my Texas accent. "*Donne moi in bierce.*"

"Bring me a beer. Nice," she said. "Next."

"*Où est la salle de bain?*"

"Where is the bathroom? Useful," she said.

"*Je suits une Americaine. Voici tout mon argent,*" I finished with a flourish and took a small bow.

Marie threw back her head and roared with laughter. I blushed because her reaction was incredible. It had been a while since I'd made anyone laugh like that. My final French phrase had been, "I'm an American. Here's all of my money."

"I find you completely delightful, Press," she said. For a second, I thought she was going to kiss me. Instead, she grabbed me by the arm and pulled me over to the outdoor bar where she ordered two bottles of beer.

The music wasn't as loud outside but still at a volume loud enough to make conversation difficult. The song ended, and a slow dance song came on. Even the people outside with us moved closer together. Marie stood, opened her arms, and pulled me close. I stepped up and took her hands.

As soon as we touched, the air raid siren went off. It was worse than if someone had thrown a bucket of cold water over us. My whole body ached for her to touch me, even if it was just for a slow dance. She jumped back as if a bomb had gone off in front of her.

"Damn!" I said aloud.

We heard the nearby explosions right before the DJ announced over the speaker system that everyone should proceed to the nearest bomb shelter. At least, that was what I assumed he said. Marie grabbed our two bottles of beer in one hand and held on to me with the other. She pulled me through the crowd and out a back gate. I looked around for Tatiana but didn't see her.

After we ran a few blocks, we came to the entrance of an abandoned subway. The city had repurposed it as a bomb shelter for this area of town. At this time of night, the only people out and about were the patrons of the bar. It still seemed like a lot of people cramming into a subway. We'd barely made it when another bomb dropped a few hundred yards across from the bar. Debris scattered over us, causing both of us to flinch. Frankly, I was scared shitless, but if I was going to die, at least I would die holding the hand of a beautiful woman.

Marie ran faster, pulling me along with her. The entrance was well marked. Patrons from the bar pushed their way in. When Marie started to enter, I pulled back a little. I did not want to be in an underground room with a high body count. I told her as much.

She nodded and pulled me over to the side near the door. "We'll just sit here on the stairs," she said. Patrons of the bar streamed past us. Tatiana went by with a tall blonde hanging on her arm.

"You okay, boss?" she asked. I nodded and gave her a thumbs-up.

"I'll catch up with you later." My fixer disappeared down

the stairway into the darkness of the tunnel below.

Marie and I were not the only ones sitting on the stairs. There were three or four other couples. A pair of young men next to us seemed locked together at the lips. They showed no concern for bombs or for the people still streaming by. I kept sneaking anxious glances up at the entrance of the subway, worried that it would collapse and we'd be trapped.

"Tell me about France," I asked Marie to distract myself from the kissing couple and the explosions outside. "Do you live in Paris?"

Marie laughed. "Not all French live in Paris. My parents have a villa in Saint-Malo." She described her hometown as a coastal city in northwest France. Tall granite walls surrounded the old town. It had once been a stronghold for pirates who had the king's blessing to pillage as long as they left his ships alone.

"Wait a second," I said, holding my hands out. "You're telling me that you're descended from pirates?"

"According to my mother, yes," Marie said, laughing. It was beautiful how she laughed so easily and how everything amused her. She told me more about where she lived. It was small compared to other cities in France. Only about fifty thousand people lived there. They'd come to romanticize the pirate life. During the summer months, the place swelled with tourists. Her hometown had long sandy beaches, a large aquarium, and a pirate fort.

"It's all very fun, with the recreations of great pirate battles," she said.

Her parents were both doctors. Her father was a general practitioner, and her mother was a pediatrician. Together, they ran a clinic for tourists during the summer months and offered free services to the locals in the off-season. When she was home, she worked with them. She had a younger brother in medical school.

"Did you ever want to be anything but a doctor?" I asked.

"I don't think I had any other choice," she said. "But no, I never wanted to be anything else. Well, except I wanted to be a cowgirl when I was five. I wanted a pony."

I had to laugh at that. When I was five, I wanted to drive a fire truck. I didn't want to be a fireman so much, but I wanted to drive that truck.

We talked long into the night. I tried to pay attention to her while keeping one ear open to the bombing. After a while, I gave up because all I wanted to do was listen to her talk. Eventually, she stopped talking and fell asleep with her head on my shoulder. I didn't want to move and wake her, but when the all-clear sounded, she started awake.

"I'm sorry, Press. Did I drool on your shoulder?"

"No," I said, laughing again. She made it so easy to laugh. I stood up and stretched, moaning at the cracking of my joints. She reached up her hand for me to boost her up. Just as I pulled her to her feet, someone bumped into me, and I plowed into Marie, and we both fell against the wall. The pressure of her body against mine made me want to wrap my arms around her and pull her even closer.

"If you wanted a kiss, you should have just said so, Press," she said. Her voice was husky, and she kissed me lightly on the lips. The explosions from falling bombs last night were nothing compared to the blast going off inside me, detonated by that tiny kiss. When Marie let go of me and ran up the stairs, I followed with my head spinning. She was gone when I pushed through the crowd to get outside.

Tatiana stood next to the Rover, waiting for me. "Did you have a good night?" she asked.

"It was magic," I said. I vowed to show Marie that I wasn't like other journalists. I was real, and I was falling for her.

CHAPTER FIVE

It wasn't entirely daylight when we set out a few days later. One of Inga Tupoleva's aides had caught up with us in the lobby and warned us about going out without her permission. The press secretary herself was nowhere to be found. Her normal routine didn't put her in our path this early. Somehow, Tatiana convinced the aide we were meeting up with the troops we were embedded with. His suspicious look made me wonder what would happen when he learned that was a lie.

None of the other journalists were up and about. I asked Tatiana about it. She shrugged and said it was her observation that most of them liked to go out later in the day and come back right at dusk curfew. Tupoleva liked it when they kept what we called bankers' hours in the States. The journalists would drink and tell stories all night once everyone was safely ensconced at the hotel. Tatiana said she didn't know how or when they wrote their stories. Starting at dawn would give me an edge, she explained. I would see the devastation before anyone had a chance to clean up. I would know the grief firsthand before it was replaced with the numbness sure to come.

When I had read war correspondent Marie Colvin's biography years earlier, she said the fear came later, after it was all over. I got that part. Sometimes, when I lay in bed at the hotel, listening to the distant mortar fire, the fear would overcome me, and my body would start to shake. Within seconds, it would be shaking so hard it was like an earthquake inside of me. Images from the death and destruction I'd seen played like a tape in my head. I had to focus on breathing evenly until the shaking and the images stopped.

Tatiana and I fell in behind a humanitarian convoy. Fortunately for us, this coincided with Tupoleva's idea of us participating in the coverage of troop movements. Tatiana explained the soldiers were looking for survivors on the outskirts of the city. The outlying citizens had been without electricity, heat, or water for a few days. We followed trucks filled with food, water, and other necessities.

At our first stop, a family of four huddled under their partially collapsed roof. They were cooking breakfast over a camp stove. The convoy moved on without us when I stopped in front of the home. Tatiana explained who I was and asked if we could interview them and take pictures. The woman nodded and offered us some of their meager porridge. Tatiana rapidly told me in English that to say no would be an insult, so I told her to tell them my stomach was full, but I would gladly have the coffee they offered. It was strong and bitter, and I drank every drop.

The family told me their stories through Tatiana's translation. The mother talked while the father sat on a nearby rock. His long arms dangled between his knees, and his eyes tried repeatedly to focus on something on the ground. It had happened a few days ago, on Tuesday, the mother thought. Maybe Wednesday. It wasn't easy to keep up with what day of the week it was. After the bombing stopped, the mother worried about how they would eat and where they would sleep if they could not get their roof fixed before the long, cold winter. The government had sent plastic sheeting to cover the broken windows, but it wasn't enough. It was never enough.

They had some food, canned goods, and grain for making porridge. But the children needed more. The boy, about four years old, played in the dirt, pushing a small car around, oblivious to us. He wore a pair of shorts, obviously cut down from a pair of pants that had belonged to someone much taller. The girl, about ten, eyed Tatiana and me suspiciously. She wore a faded yellow sundress and no shoes. Her warrior stance almost made me smile. She defiantly stood her ground.

The missiles had eventually found them, the mother continued. The bombs had started falling around three in the afternoon. It was drones, the father said, looking up from his misery. He remembered hearing a strange buzzing sound and the ground shaking as the explosions started. Before that day, most drones were silent. These made the sound like a million bees descending on them. Explosions followed. The explosions continued, each coming closer until a missile targeted their roof, destroying half their house.

They'd rushed into the street only to see the same thing happening to their neighbors. The shelling forced them to find shelter in a ditch across the way. Bomb after bomb fell, reducing their neighborhood to rubble. A neighbor had lost her husband and two children when their house caught fire and burned. That woman had sat in the yard and wailed until someone came and led her away.

"We don't know what happened to her," the mother said.

They had been lucky. Everyone in their family was still alive. Grabbing what few belongings they could find, they'd gone to the nearest bomb shelter. It was the basement of a local government building packed to the rafters with others bombed out of their homes. After spending one night there, the family decided they were better off anywhere else. With some apprehension, they'd made their way home. They'd salvaged what they could from their bombed-out home and camped in the remains. The next day, the Russian tanks and soldiers had come down the street. The family had hidden until they were gone.

"We have heard stories about the Russians raping women and killing men and the children," the mother said. "I was afraid for my family. I made them hide, even for hours after it appeared the soldiers left."

They weren't regular Russian soldiers. The woman told me they were the mercenaries hired by the Russian government. They had different uniforms, neater and cleaner than the ordinary soldiers. They wore patches with snarling wolf heads on them. The wolf's head had sharp teeth dripping with blood. These soldiers had dragged her other neighbor, an older man of seventy-five years, out into the street. She'd heard them screaming at the man. They were demanding he tell them where the troops were hiding.

The old man had begged for mercy but the mercenaries beat and kicked him until he lay still in the street. Then they'd shot him in the head. The soldiers had dragged the man's wife and daughter out. The mercenaries shot the mother and dragged the daughter away. The woman did not want to think about what had happened to her.

As the woman talked, she drew her two children closer. The fear and shame in her eyes told a story I had heard all too often. She'd gone to the city building that morning and made them give her a gun. The Ukrainian government was handing out weapons to anyone who wanted to fight. This woman would not allow the Russians to murder her family. If the mercenaries came back, she would shoot them.

"You go, and you tell them," she told me. "Tell the world what Russia is doing here. Tell them so they will come and help us."

I didn't see how the American government sending sixty billion dollars to Ukraine for more weapons would help this small family. Then again, if my stories recruited people like Marie to come help, maybe it was the right thing to do. I was having a crisis of conscience over my role here. Was I helping anyone? It was something I would have to take a long, hard look at.

At first, the family was uncomfortable with having their picture taken. It was almost impossible for someone to act naturally and go about their business while their pictures were taken. It was an instinct to pose. I squatted in the dirt beside the boy and got several shots of him playing with his one remaining toy. The girl refused to do anything but stand and glare at me. That was a statement, so I photographed her standing in her dirty dress, fists clenched at her sides, defiant and resilient.

I took many more pictures. I could not imagine living under these conditions, and I felt a deep sympathy for the bravery of these people. I took a picture of the mother coaxing a pot of porridge to boil over a camp stove. Another shot of her handing the meager meal to her husband in a broken bowl with a bent spoon. I wanted to give them money, but Tatiana warned me against offending their pride. As Tatiana and I walked away, I noticed she slipped some money into the woman's hand.

"I thought they would be too proud to accept money," I said.

Tatiana gave me a sad smile. "From you, yes. But from me, as the daughter of a government official, it is expected. They will need it. Sometimes, it can buy you out of trouble with men who join the war for money."

I didn't say what I was thinking. If these mercenaries were as bad as the woman had described, they would just take the money and rape, torture, and murder her and her family anyway.

"Tell me about these mercenaries," I asked.

Their local leader was a man named Yuri Kostov. He was a ruthless wannabe dictator. He lived in the back pocket of the Kremlin. Eavesdropping on her father's conversation, Tatiana had learned that Kostov was assigned to Kyiv as some sort of punishment for making officials at the Kremlin unhappy. Tatiana's father believed this had made him much more dangerous.

Instead of using the money to arm and equip the Russian troops, the Kremlin spent millions hiring mercenaries. It was well known that many of the Russian people did not want to go to war. There were dozens of stories of them running away from the country to avoid the draft. After such a poor response from the citizens, the government used mercenaries to carry out their bloody campaign for a price.

The Russian draftees didn't get paid regularly. Most days, they barely scraped by on one meal, sometimes even less. They had no bedding or protective clothing. Their uniforms were shoddy and ill-made. That was why they stole everything they could when they occupied a town. Russian soldiers had raided an office building in Tatiana's cousin's city of Bolhrad. They'd stolen everything in the building. They'd even removed the toilets. The mercenaries were well paid and could afford toilets.

Tatiana had overheard her father and uncles saying the Russians wanted to ensure the evacuated citizens had nothing to return to except heaps of rubble and useless dirt patches. It made her angry, I could tell. It made me angry. Tatiana thought the Russians did it because they had nothing. She felt sorry for those soldiers forced to participate in this war. I agreed but reminded her that it was also a tactic of war to remove all hope. When hope was gone, defeat was inevitable. She feared the hope was already gone from the poor Russians drafted and sent here. It was the first time she had expressed any sympathy for her country's invaders.

Tatiana had heard her father say Kostov spent a lot of time with the local mafia. The mob bosses supplied women, drugs, and weapons to the mercenaries. Dimitri had heard rumors that Kostov and his men also stayed with the mercenaries in an estate outside the city.

We went back to the Land Rover and drove around the area. Everywhere we stopped, we found a different kind of atrocity. I took pictures of older women and men rummaging through the debris of what had once been their homes, looking for anything salvageable. I took pictures of children playing in the street beside craters created by bombs and missiles. Another young mother washed her family's clothes in a ditch filled with dirty water. Any clean water was too valuable to waste on laundry.

We met up with a convoy of young Ukrainian soldiers hunting down Russian troops. There were about ten or fifteen of them. They all seemed so young, in their late teens and early twenties. Some of them spoke some English. One blond-haired, blue-eyed lad quoted Kiss to me, "Rock and Roll All Nite!"

They laughed and joked around. They told me their stories. Spending the rest of the day with them would fulfill our obligations to the press secretary and hopefully buy us a few days of going out on our own. One soldier was a student like Tatiana. When the Russians had invaded, he'd dropped everything and had gone to take up arms for his country. Another of the soldiers was much smaller than the others. They all looked the same in their uniforms, but upon closer inspection, this one was a female. Her boyfriend was a soldier, she told us. She'd enlisted to keep him company, but he'd died in the early days of the occupation. She pulled a much-handled photo from her pocket and held it out to me. He was a handsome lad, looking all splendid in his uniform. I told her so.

She wiped away a tear and placed the photo back in her pocket. Now, she was on a mission to wipe Russia off the face of the earth. If anyone could carry out such a monumental task, she and her fellow unit members believed they could. She would walk to the Kremlin if she had to and shoot everyone there. They would pay for his death and the thousands of others who'd died so pointlessly. Tears formed at the back of my eyes as I watched her wipe hers away.

Tatiana and I were walking with the group while one of the soldiers offered to follow in the Land Rover. They had a couple of vehicles carrying supplies, ammunition, and their wounded. I was about to ask if they thought they would see any action today when Tatiana grabbed me and shoved me to the ground.

"*Vkhidint!*" one of the soldiers at the front of the line shouted.

"Incoming," Tatiana shouted in my ear as the artillery started to fall around us. At first, a drone dropped a few bombs, then a few more, and finally, a downpour of bullets and missiles all headed in our direction.

"Come on," she yelled in my ear. "You can take pictures from behind the cover."

When I realized that missiles were heading in our direction, I felt my own explosion of fear. Missiles were different from bullets because missiles caused more widespread damage. At first, I panicked and ran in the wrong direction. I thought taking cover would be the most prudent action in this situation. One of the soldiers grabbed me by the shoulders and shoved me in the direction Tatiana was running. Running in a half crouch, we sprinted for a nearby drainage ditch, sliding in next to the soldier girl just as she unpinned a grenade and threw it as hard as she could toward a copse of trees on the opposite side of the road. The enemy soldiers had been hiding there and lying in wait for us.

"I was the star pitcher on the school baseball team," the girl said, grinning. The concussion from the blast made my ears pop and then ring.

Dust, smoke, and gunpowder filled the air. My protective sunglasses were the only thing keeping the debris away from my eyes. I twisted sideways in the ditch and took shot after shot of the young girl and two other soldiers as they tossed grenades in a launcher aimed at the other side of the road. The grenades started a fire in the tiny grove. Russian soldiers ran out of the cover, going in every different direction. Taking a chance and still scared shitless, I stood and took several photos of them running from the fire. The rest of the Ukrainian company fired bullets in endless staccatos of gunfire while three soldiers armed the grenade launcher. I caught a great shot of one of them juggling three grenades before tossing them, one at a time, to the soldier loading the launcher. They believed themselves to be young, ten feet tall, and bulletproof.

It seemed like we were in the ditch for hours and hours until the unit leader finally called for a ceasefire. I was surprised when my watch told me only a few minutes had passed. The following silence was even more deafening than the noise of the battle. The unit's leader performed a complicated series of hand gestures and whistles. Two teams ran off to check if any enemy soldiers were left alive.

After another eternity of waiting, the two scouts gave the all-clear signal. The others cheered and raced off to steal whatever valuables they could find on the dead Russians.

They came up with some loose change, a few rubles, a couple of tins of Spam, and two rifles that looked like they'd seen better days. These were typical of the booty they found on dead Russian soldiers. To the victor went the spoils.

We spent the rest of the day following the patrol. They told me their stories. It was my experience since becoming a journalist that everyone had a story. It might not have been huge or grand, but it was uniquely theirs. For the most part, they were ordinary people. They went to work. They were part of families. They laughed, lived, and loved. In times like this, they stepped up and became more than the sum of their lives. It made me take stock of my own life. So far, almost everyone I'd interviewed since arriving in Ukraine believed that people across the world cared about their plight.

When I had dreamed of becoming a war correspondent, I thought my goal was similar. It all seemed noble, but what was it I wanted? Did I want to make sure I was reporting so the people who could do something would? Or was I here for my own glory? I swore to myself that I would put more effort into making the notion that the rest of the world cared about their plight a reality.

Twice more, we came across Russian patrols. One member of the squad was wounded. The wound wasn't life-threatening, so after a brief discussion, they decided he should ride back to Kyiv with Tatiana and me. It would save them from sending a team and a vehicle they could ill afford to lose. It was time we headed back anyway. When we returned to the city, it would be almost dark. The Ukrainian soldiers warned us not to be caught this far on the outskirts after curfew. If we didn't return in time, we would have to spend the night in a subway station or the countryside, where Russian patrols might stumble upon us.

Tatiana drove back toward Kyiv in what I considered a reckless manner since she never knew where the craters were. Not to mention that the jostling could aggravate the Ukrainian soldier's wound. The soldier's name was Alec Suvorv. He came from Kyiv and had joined the fighting when the Russians first invaded. He was eighteen and spoke longingly of becoming a hero to his friends and family. He told me his high school had released the students. Most high schools and universities had shuttered when the war began. Students and teachers alike clamored to join the fighting.

When Tatiana hit another pothole, the wounded boy winced.

"How are you doing, Alec?" I asked. "Do we need to stop?"

"The pain will only strengthen me," he said through gritted teeth.

I admired his bravado. If I'd been shot by an invading enemy soldier when I was eighteen, I probably would never have left my room again.

We pulled up to the hotel just as the curfew alarm sounded. I told Tatiana she could stay in my room tonight and not have to try to rush home. She agreed and left me to unpack my things while she helped Alec inside where, hopefully, medical help was waiting. I'd noticed they were not at the Radisson every day. Of course, I paid attention when Marie was not there and they took their hospital on the road.

When I saw the hotel lobby filled with people dressed in scrubs, I felt a sigh of relief. It occurred to me that not knowing where medical personnel were going to be on any given day was a gross oversight on my part. When Marie materialized by my side to take a look at the young soldier, I felt a cramp of guilt. I was feeling elated that the wounded man gave me a reason to have her attention directed at me.

All the lights were out in the hotel. They had a generator and a backup generator, but electricity in the city was erratic since the Russians relentlessly bombed the power and water plants. Because of rolling blackouts, the staff often didn't bother firing the generators to save fuel. Waiting for fuel to be delivered was something else that was not very reliable.

"As if I don't have enough to do, you go out and find wounded to bring back to me," Marie said. Then she winked, as if to let me know she was teasing. My heart skipped a beat.

She had Alec sit on the table in front of her. It was a dining room table repurposed as a hospital bed. In one hand, she held a flashlight. She trained the beam on Alec's wound.

"Come here, Press. I need both hands," Marie said, thrusting the flashlight at me. "Point it there on the wound."

Elated to be noticed by her but cautious of what she wanted me to do, I dropped my gear on an ornate chair beside the lobby door. On better days, the chair offered a place for guests to sit while they waited for their cabs or tour buses. Today, piles of bandages, ointment tubes, and other medical supplies occupied the space. Dutifully, I held the flashlight while Marie tended to Alec's wound. When she finished, he hopped off the examining table.

"I go back to the unit now," Alec said in halting English after Marie made sure the bullet wasn't lodged in his body and that the wound was not life-threatening.

"No," said Marie. "You go find something to eat and someplace to rest. I'll look at your wound in the morning. If it seems okay, then and only then, can you go back to your unit."

Alec made his way to the door. He would go to his mother's home, he insisted. It wasn't far, and he wasn't worried about being caught out after curfew. After all, he was heavily armed. His mother would want to see that he was okay since he'd called her on the way to the hotel to let her know he was wounded. I couldn't help but hope he made it home without further incident. When I asked Marie about it, she shrugged and said he might or might not come back in the morning to have his wound checked.

"There is only so much we can do," she said.

She poured clean water from a pitcher by the table into a bowl and washed her hands. They'd boiled the water to fight lingering germs. Marie made even something as simple as washing her hands seem graceful and exotic. I'd been so engrossed in watching her movements, that I didn't notice I still stood there with the flashlight directed at the table where Alec had been. She reached over and took it from me and turned it off. I felt kind of stupid waiting for her to give me exact instructions. Being around her made me feel clumsy and oafish.

"Thanks for your help, Press," she said.

Tatiana reappeared holding a bottle of water and a Diet Coke. She handed me the Coke. I could only imagine what she had paid for it. I swear the kid was a miracle worker. The drink was ambrosia. She gave the bottle of water to Marie.

"I got the kitchen to prepare us some dinner," she said. "It won't be as good as my mother's cooking, but it will be filling."

Suddenly, I was starving. I realized neither of us had eaten since leaving that morning when I'd wolfed down the pastries Tatiana's mother had sent. I looked quizzically at Marie to see if she would be joining us. When she shook her head, my heart dropped a little bit.

"I had the borscht earlier," she said. "It wasn't too bad. I've got some cleaning before we head back to the villa."

Marie and her team were housed at a nearby villa belonging to one of Kyiv's elite families. They could have stayed at the hotel, which I fervently wished for, but the villa offered them more amenities than the hotel. Considering the Radisson was one of the ritziest places in Kyiv, I had some doubts about that. The family also made sure Marie and her team had transportation and security, which was something the hotel couldn't offer. I could see why the medical personnel would go for better accommodation. I did wonder how they fared since it was officially after curfew.

"Oh, we have a military escort," she said. "If they think it is safe, they will take us. If it is deemed unsafe, we usually bunk out here somewhere."

Since it didn't appear that tonight would be one of those nights her team stayed over, I bade her good night and followed Tatiana to the dining room, where a boisterous crowd of journalists had pushed most of the tables together. They treated the day's events like a party. No wonder Marie thought journalists were a bunch of low-moral louts. All she'd seen them do here was drink, hit on her, and share horrible images of war. Tatiana and I took two of the remaining seats next to Shawn Glass. He was regaling the others with a story about how he'd spent the day with the Russian mercenaries. He made it sound like they were the real heroes of the war.

He passed around his iPad, showing us some pictures and videos. Tatiana snorted in disgust when the tablet landed in front of us. It made me want to look away as I swallowed the bile rising in my throat. The footage showed two uniformed men. It was easy to spot the mercenaries. They were better armed and equipped than the average Russian conscript. Glass said they'd allowed him to tag along to film them while they hunted for Ukrainians.

That was the word he used: hunted. When the mercenaries couldn't find any Ukrainian soldiers, they dragged a young boy out of his hiding place in his bombed-out home. I only watched a few seconds of what happened next because it disgusted me. They secured the boy's hands behind his back with zip ties. Then they ripped off his shirt. He looked to be about fourteen or fifteen years old. I wondered what possible threat he could pose to these armed men. They outweighed him by about one hundred pounds each.

One of them lit a cigarette, and I knew what was coming. I passed the tablet back to Glass as the boy's frightened and painful screams played from its tiny speakers. Glass turned off the iPad and set it next to his plate.

"If you haven't got the stomach for war, what are you doing here?" he asked.

I leveled my gaze at him. "I'm looking for humanity," I said.

He roared with laughter. He'd had quite a bit to drink already. "Good luck finding it," he said. With that, he pushed back his chair, picked up his iPad, and strolled out the door. It made me wonder what the Ukrainian press office thought of his outings. For all I knew, they could have sanctioned Glass and encouraged him to go with the Wolf Pack. It would be an excellent way to determine what the mercenaries were doing.

"Don't mind him," Elizabeth, the newswoman from BBC, said. "He's a grade-A, number-one prick."

There was a general sense of agreement around the room. Elizabeth told me the only reason Glass was here was that the staff at his news agency couldn't stand him either. They kept hoping he would get killed if they continued sending him off to war zones.

It didn't seem that funny to me, but everyone else around the table laughed. The thought was morbid considering how many journalists the enemy kidnapped, tortured, and killed. It wasn't something one could dwell on, however. Dwelling on what might happen was an exercise in futility. Considering what a pain in the ass Glass was, though, I wondered how much of it might be true.

Tatiana and I finished our dinner. It was some broiled beef that was tough and horrible, a couple of limp green beans, two slices of bread, and borscht. I'd had borscht before, and it wasn't that bad if I could get past the fact that it was beet soup. Tatiana said beets made a dish better and shouldn't be underrated. This borscht was pretty good, and when she went to get a second helping, I handed her my bowl so she could refill mine as well. It wasn't as good as her mother's, she said. That went without saying.

The room had cleared out by the time we'd finished the second bowl. The electricity still hadn't returned, and I was glad for my solar-powered electronics charger. I wanted to write while the day's events were still fresh in my mind.

No electricity meant no internet, but that was a minor obstacle. If the Wi-Fi hadn't returned by morning, we would find someplace with an internet café. We could even find a private citizen who would lend us their Wi-Fi to transmit the articles back to the news desk at Titan.

I dug my flashlight out of my messenger bag so Tatiana and I could go up the stairs. Marie and her medical team were scrubbing down the triage area of the lobby. The smell of disinfectant chased down the other odious smells and wiped them out. Marie's team consisted of seven people: two doctors, two nurses, an EMT, and two support staff. Even though I was mentally and physically exhausted, I wanted to spend more time with her. Any excuse to be near her caused my pulse to quicken and my overactive imagination to kick into overdrive. I handed Tatiana the flashlight and my room key and told her I'd be up shortly. She glanced over at Marie and gave me a knowing look.

"Can I help?" I asked. Marie looked up at me with a puzzled expression. For a second, I had the horrible feeling that she couldn't remember who I was. Then she smiled.

"I don't know why I didn't notice before, but you look like you could use a cleaning yourself," she said. Then she squirted some of whatever was in the spray bottle in my general direction. I realized I was covered in dust from our earlier trek.

"I will still let you help me," she said. She handed me the spray bottle from her left hand and the cloth from her right. I went to work on a particularly nasty bloodstain on the gurney next to her. I started thinking about things we took for granted in everyday life. I rarely thought of hospitals, doctors, or medical and cleaning supplies. Back in Austin, there were twenty-four-hour emergency and trauma centers on practically every corner. They offered a less expensive and quicker alternative to the emergency room. My primary care physician was at my beck and call. I could make a quick phone call and have her or one of her staff on the phone less than twenty or thirty minutes later.

But here, halfway across the world, a doctor didn't just treat colds or sprains. They treated bullet wounds, missing limbs from explosions, and trauma from falling debris when a building came crashing down.

"What about the Ukrainians who need to get a prescription for an ear infection or something?" I asked Marie.

"Some of the members of Doctors Without Borders try to hold a mobile clinic at least twice a week," she said. "Sometimes, if fighting is happening in the region where we are scheduled, we are forced to postpone. Other times, we will trade the clinic in one town for another, counting on word of mouth to let the residents know the doctors are in. In many circumstances, parents opt to do whatever they can to treat any childhood maladies. Some of these home remedies are almost barbaric."

The doctors rotated the clinics, so no single person was going out every week. Her rotation was next week, and Tatiana and I were welcome to tag along. Marie thought it would make a human-interest story about how Ukrainians were trying to cope with daily things during a war. I agreed it was an excellent idea. The biggest obstacle to treating non-war-related ailments was the lack of medication. Things like insulin and antibiotics were in short supply.

"Maybe if your readers see the suffering of these civilians, they will be motivated to help," she said, scrubbing at a particularly stubborn stain.

The crew finished cleaning up. Marie bade me good night and left with her team and an armed escort of three Ukrainian soldiers. I collected my gear from where I'd left it in the dining room and headed upstairs.

Tatiana was already sound asleep. She'd made herself a pallet on the floor with the sleeping bag I'd brought. I would have given her the bed. Oh well, she was younger than me. She could probably handle resting on the floor better than I could. She'd helped herself to one of my T-shirts, and it reminded me of how young she was. She looked barely old enough to be in high school while asleep like this.

I sat at the cubbyhole the hotel brochure advertised as a "spacious and modern work area." It was a cut-out space that a desk chair could slide into. It was well past midnight when I finished writing. I quickly showered, changed into my sleeping attire, and went to bed.

CHAPTER SIX

During the next few days, I learned that if you spotted a drone, instead of running in a straight line, you should dodge and weave so the missile couldn't target you. It scared the shit out of me because I was generally a klutz, and I stumbled when I was trying to concentrate on not hauling ass for the nearest cover. After another long day of following troops, interviewing Ukrainian citizens, and dodging drones, Tatiana dropped me off at the hotel. I was exhausted. I'd tripped over my own feet and fallen several times, and at least once, I swear I felt the tailwind from the missile brush by me. I looked forward to a shower, food, and a chill evening.

When I entered the lobby, my first instinct was to look for Marie. She and a handful of nurses and aides were in the dining room drinking tea. For once, the lobby was clear of patients. The group was waiting for their escort to take them back to the villa where they stayed. My pulse raced a little bit faster when I realized that despite the hour, I hadn't missed seeing her.

When she spotted me in the doorway, she waved me over. I started that way but stopped when a car came screeching to a halt in front of the hotel. A middle-aged man jumped out of the driver's seat and rushed to the car's passenger side, yelling, "Somebody help me," in Ukrainian.

Two nurses from Marie's table raced outside and pulled a woman out of the back seat. She was limp and showed no signs of consciousness as they carried her into the lobby. The driver of the car had a small, dirty bundle that soon revealed itself to be a screaming baby. Marie ordered the men to put the woman on the gurney. The driver thrust the baby into Marie's arms and ran out again. He'd done his duty and brought the baby in for help. From my perspective across the room, it appeared the mother was already dead. It was pretty obvious to me that the last thing the good Samaritan who had brought them in wanted was to get stuck with a kid.

A brief panic flashed across Marie's face as she scanned the room. Everyone else appeared occupied with some important tasks, or they had all simply vanished. Her eyes locked on mine, and a moment of fear shot through me. Surely, she was not going to give me that baby. After a brief consideration, she practically tossed me the kid.

"Press, take the baby," she said. She didn't even wait for a response, and I was the only person in the room standing still. Although it seemed like it was too late to do anything for the mother, Marie tried anyway.

Now, I had a tiny screaming human in my arms. I held the kid out like it had the plague and quickly searched the room. Everyone else appeared to be occupied while ignoring me and the wailing banshee I held at arm's length. I have very little experience with babies. Anytime someone gave me one to hold, I passed them right back as soon as the screaming started.

There was no one here to pass the kid to and nothing I could do except try to calm it down. Frantically, I racked my brain trying to remember what to do with a screaming baby. Food! I didn't see a diaper bag anywhere, so no bottle.

I swung my camera over to my side so it wouldn't hit the kid and pulled it closer, thinking maybe it wanted to be comforted. I wasn't sure if it was a boy or a girl. I unwrapped the blanket and peeked. It was a baby boy. Since he didn't have that hey-I-was-born-a-few-minutes-ago look, I estimated he was about a month old. He weighed about nine or ten pounds, so he didn't seem to be malnourished. His diaper was soaking and smelled like he'd recently dropped a load. Otherwise, the kid seemed to be unharmed. Okay, so we'd find a clean diaper first, then some food.

The blanket the kid was wrapped in did have a lot of blood on it, but it appeared to belong to the woman they'd brought in with the kid. He had a few scrapes and scratches but no apparent wounds to account for that much blood. Marie and her staff had their attention on the mother. I wouldn't be getting any help there.

"Well, kid," I said, "I don't suppose you know where they keep the diapers." His response was to scream louder.

No one sat at the front desk, and I didn't see any hotel personnel around whom I could ask for help. I headed in the general direction of the dining room. It was empty, so I made my way into the kitchen. There were a few people; some were cooking, and some were cleaning. I could only hope that at least one of them spoke English. I didn't have the first clue about the Ukrainian words for diapers or formula. If I tried to dig my iPad out of my bag to activate the universal translator, I'd have to put the kid down. There didn't seem to be any space in the kitchen to put a dirty kid with a soiled diaper. Fortunately for me, babies screamed in a universal language. A large, matronly woman took one look at my situation and beckoned me to follow.

She didn't say anything but led me to a small pantry where she took several large napkins from one of the shelves. Holding it by the corners, she shook one out and held it up. It appeared to be a square foot in diameter. It would have to do. She tossed me the napkin and dug around in a desk drawer. The metallic sound of stuff shifting around in a junk drawer barely made it through the kid's wails. With a cry of triumph, the woman held out two large safety pins. Otherwise, we might have had to tape the clean diaper on.

When the woman said something to me, I shook my head to indicate I didn't understand. The one Ukrainian phrase I'd learned was, "I don't speak the language." She frowned and looked thoughtful for a few seconds. "Not your baby?" she asked in broken English. I shook my head.

She pointed to herself and said, "Mischka."

"Nicole," I said. I didn't shake her hand because I was afraid I would drop the baby if I did.

"Come, Nicole," she ordered. I followed her into another room with a small table and a few chairs. There were no windows, so it was dark and gloomy. When Mischka turned on a lamp, it didn't do much for the gloom or improve the décor. She shoved a bunch of papers off the table, and I laid the baby on top of it and started unwrapping the blanket.

Quite a few scratches covered his tiny face, but none appeared to be life-threatening. He wore a filthy yellow onesie with a cartoon cat on it. I stripped it off and removed his diaper. Sure enough, there was a whole pile of shit waiting for me. The smell made me gag. Changing diapers wasn't something I would have listed on my resume. I'd done it a few times when my cousins were having babies, but that was years ago. Babysitting was not what I'd expected when going to cover a war zone. I knew there would be bad smells, but this was beyond smelly.

Mischka chuckled at my reaction and tossed the dirty diaper in a nearby trash bin. She indicated I should follow her again. Gingerly, I picked up the baby to get the least amount of his mess on me as possible. Mischka led us to a large, galvanized sink at one end of the kitchen. Putting a plug in the bottom, she turned on the water, waited a few seconds, and tested the temperature with her fingers. After a few adjustments, she seemed satisfied. She nodded at the baby and then the sink, letting me understand she wanted me to bathe him. I plopped the kid in the water and gently began removing the multilayered grime. He was a slippery little thing. The screaming didn't stop as I clutched him in a death grip. I feared he would slide right out of my arms and go under, never to surface again. A tap on my arm and Mischka mimed how to prop the baby up in the crook of my elbow so I could wash him with one hand. Once she seemed reassured I wouldn't drown him, she said something else I didn't understand and walked away.

I liked kids. I did. I only wanted them to belong to someone else. I couldn't help but feel a mixture of emotions about this screaming bundle of joy. My overactive imagination concocted an entire scenario around what had happened to him. He was an unwitting pawn in a high-stakes game. Poor little guy didn't even know what was happening.

He was with his mom, at least I supposed she was his mom, and then suddenly, he was on the ground. His mom had probably dropped him when she was wounded; that would account for the scrapes and scratches. It had hurt, so he'd cried to let Mom know. When she didn't respond, he cried louder. That should get her attention. Then he was jerked around by a bunch of strangers, and there was no telling when he would be safe, warm, and happy again. He couldn't find Mama anywhere, and wailing didn't bring her running to his rescue like before. There were loud noises he didn't recognize. I'd once read somewhere that babies could sense their mothers' emotions. God only knew what this poor little guy felt. If I'd gone through something like that, I'd be screaming my head off too.

"I think I'll call you Max," I told him. The bath seemed to soothe him, and the screaming went down a notch. When I had him as clean as I thought possible, I lifted him out of the tub and wrapped him in a dish towel. We sat on a stool beside the sink, where I dried him off.

Mischka returned with more napkins and a plastic bottle she'd rigged with a nipple-like contraption. The bottle had what appeared to be milk in it, though it was watery and thin. It was probably powdered milk, but beggars couldn't be choosers.

Diapering Max proved another challenge to my skill. It took three tries to get the napkin secure enough that it wouldn't fall off. Then, Max gave me the honor of peeing halfway through our third attempt, causing me to start all over.

The blanket he had arrived in disappeared into another trash bin. Mischka replaced it with a hotel blanket she'd torn into three or four pieces so it wouldn't swallow him. I wondered where, if anywhere, one could buy baby supplies in Kyiv. It wasn't something I'd found in the guide for journalists. Hopefully, our makeshift care would be sufficient until I could find someone to take him off my hands. I refused to see this as a bad omen. We returned to the empty dining room where I could sit and try to feed him.

It took me, Max, and Mischka working together to get the milk into the right place. Once we had the makeshift bottle in his mouth, Max settled down and drained it like a cowboy on dollar beer night in a Texas bar. Mischka came up with another bottle. The mixture in this one appeared thicker, but it still resembled watery gruel. She produced a bag. She opened the top so I could see she'd filled it with napkins, a box of porridge mix, and a container of powdered milk. If I understood her miming correctly, this second bottle contained a mixture of powdered milk and porridge.

Part of me felt like jumping up and running in circles with my arms triumphantly raised in the air. I had successfully bathed and fed a baby. Nothing could stop me now.

Max's mouth concentrated on the bottle, but his eyes started closing. After the adrenaline rush wore off, my body sympathized. I'd have loved to go somewhere I could sit and chill for a few minutes. I thanked Mischka as best as possible in my simple Ukrainian. She'd done her best, considering the circumstances. Little had I realized diapers and baby formula would be a concern when I came here.

Using my bag and a couple of cushions from one of the chairs, I wedged Max into the seat next to me. Getting his good side in my photos was easy. He was cute. I made sure some pictures focused on the makeshift diapers and bottles. I wanted to ensure my readers understood this innocent little guy's predicament when I wrote the story. He blinked at me a couple of times, then nodded off. I was envious of his ability to fall asleep in the chaos.

It wasn't until then that I realized I still wore my helmet and tactical vest. Although the manufacturers had designed the gear not to be uncomfortable, removing it was still like getting home and changing out of work clothes into pajamas. I removed my gear and piled it on a chair on the other side of the baby.

A picture of Max dressed in a baby-sized tactical vest and helmet flashed through my head. The image was so ridiculous, it made me laugh. Out of the corner of my eye, I noticed Marie enter the dining room. She looked around, then approached my table and sat.

When she saw the diaper, blanket, and bottle, she smiled. "I knew you would find a way to manage," she said. She unwrapped my little burrito and checked him for any wounds more severe than the superficial cuts and bruises. She pulled some ointment, swabs, and a couple of bandages from her smock pocket and deftly applied them to the worst of his injuries.

"I'm afraid his mother never had a chance," she said sadly. "She was already dead when they brought her in." At my startled expression, she gave another small smile. "Oh, don't worry, Press, we've got someone trying to locate his other relatives now. I'm not going to saddle you with a baby."

"If you give me a baby, you must marry me," I teased. "It's a Texas law."

She laughed, which was the reaction I was shooting for.

"What will happen to him?" I asked, changing the subject.

"If we cannot find any relatives, he will go to a local foster home," Marie said. "The best-case scenario would be for someone out of the country to sponsor him. The logistics of that option can be a nightmare, though."

A scathingly brilliant idea began forming in the back of my mind. If I wrote a series of stories about Max and his plight, childless couples across the United States would line up to take this baby off the Ukrainian government's hands.

"Maybe I can help," I said. "Give my card to whoever picks the baby up, and I'll make sure his story goes out."

"That is an excellent idea, Press," she said. "We can keep tabs on him, and you can follow his story."

She smiled at me, and after glancing at the card long enough to memorize the information, she pocketed it in her white lab coat. I noticed her clothes had blood and dirt stains. It had been a long day for her as well. She looked like she could curl up and drift off to sleep herself.

A server brought her a bowl of stew, and when she smiled her thanks, the sun had to shield itself from the brightness. I would have floated away if she had cast that smile in my direction. Since our night in the bomb shelter, she'd acted aloof and distant. I'd racked my brain to remember if I'd done something to offend her. I couldn't think of anything, but the nagging feeling prevailed. I'd tried to make those thoughts go away. First, I wasn't here for romance. I was here to cover a war. Maybe she regretted our flirtation. After all, she was here to provide medical help, not kisses. But I couldn't stop my imagination from remembering what those lips had felt like against mine.

A group of volunteers arrived, forcing my wayward thoughts to change the subject. They were there to take charge of Max. My first reaction was to tell them, no, they couldn't have him. He was mine! Then sanity once again asserted itself, and I grabbed my camera so I could record the event. At least they came prepared, bringing in baby clothes and a diaper bag stuffed with bottles and diapers. They removed my makeshift diaper and put him in some clean clothes. I asked a lot of questions.

"Where are you taking him?" I asked, hoping they understood English. Fortunately, one of them did and answered my question.

"We will take him to a safe house," he said. "We have a designated place to gather lost children. It makes it easier for parents to find them."

"But his mother is dead," I said, looking at Marie for confirmation. She nodded.

"We will try to find other relatives. If we cannot, then he will stay with us until such a time that someone might want to adopt him."

They had food, water, shelter, and most of the time, electricity. I made them promise to notify me the second someone claimed him. They were to tell Marie or me if no one came for him. I made a mental note to arrange a full-blown set of stories on the group and their work. Marie had one of her assistants bring the mother's things to help identify him and find some relatives. They weren't very hopeful about the chances of someone claiming him or adopting him. Since the war began, thousands of Ukrainian children had gone missing.

A soldier came in and beckoned Marie. "That's my ride," she said. "Thank you for stepping up, Press. I'll see you tomorrow." She put her hand on my shoulder and kissed me on my forehead. My heart fluttered at the contact. Out of the corner of my eye, I saw the soldier frown. Ukraine had some severe misgivings about gays and lesbians. I was spoiled. Even in Texas, where many of the laws are archaic and bigoted, we had a fair amount of freedom of expression.

As the group from the orphanage was leaving, Glass and some other journalists were coming in from their daily coverage. "Come on, Doc," Glass said. "Have a drink with us."

Marie deftly stepped past him. "Some other time, perhaps."

He shrugged. "Your loss." Marie ignored him and continued out the door. Bringing my attention back to the newcomers proved a bit difficult.

"How about you, Sheppard? You going to have a drink with us?"

Why not? I sat at the table and reached for one of the lukewarm beers.

CHAPTER SEVEN

Tatiana dropped me off at the hotel long after curfew a few days later. I was kind of worried that we would be stopped and detained. She didn't seem to be overly concerned. Many of the city's police force knew her father, and they knew her car. I asked if she wanted to stay at the hotel, but she turned me down.

"My Mama kind of freaked out a little bit the other night when I didn't come home," she said. "I tried calling, but the bombing damaged the cell towers. She's already stressed with worrying about my brothers' fighting, and my sister lives farther south, where the war is more intense. I promised I'd be home."

I could see her point and admonished her to be careful. I wanted to tell her to text me when she arrived safely. That was something Hannah and other friends always insisted I do when I was out late at night. But with all the shelling and bombing of infrastructure, cell towers had taken their fair share of hits. I'd discovered texting and calling were luxuries these days. Sometimes, days passed before I could get a call in to Pamela back in Austin.

Just thinking about home made me long for home and my best friend, Hannah. I missed talking to her. I realized that even with all the hustle going on around me, I was lonely. I wanted to talk to someone about what I'd seen and felt this day. I wondered if Hannah would have time to talk. It was about midafternoon back in Austin.

It was quiet at the hotel's location in the city center. The lights from the front of the hotel chased the shadows, daring any enemy soldiers to try to storm the fortress. One could almost imagine it was an ordinary weeknight with the kids turning in early and the parents preparing for tomorrow's workday.

The dimly lit lobby illuminated one or two people. The desk clerk sat behind the counter, watching a news program on a small TV. He had the sound turned down low and the closed captions on. It was kind of strange and surreal to me to see the Ukrainian words crawl across the screen. When was the last time I sat down and watched TV? I hadn't even turned on the set in my room.

One of the housekeepers was mopping the lobby floor. The only immediate sounds were the swish of her mop and the water trickling back into the bucket when she squeezed it out. In the distance, a radio was playing something almost but not quite rock and roll. The medical people were gone, and I was about to admit my disappointment when I noticed

Marie sitting on top of a gurney with her legs pulled up to her chest and one arm slung across her knees.

"Hey, Press," she said tiredly.

"Hey, Doc. You look beat."

"Rough day," she said. "I didn't finish up until after curfew. I didn't want to make the rest of the team wait, so I just stayed. Except, there doesn't seem to be any room at the inn."

My mouth had the words out before my mind even considered it. "Why don't you come up to my room?" I offered. "You can shower. I'll lend you some clean clothes. You can sleep in the bed. I've got a comfortable sleeping bag."

For a second, I thought she would turn me down, but perhaps her fatigue didn't leave enough energy for her to argue. She jumped off the gurney and joined me at the foot of the stairs.

"That sounds wonderful," she said.

We climbed the stairs to my fourth-floor room. I noticed it took a little longer to reach the top of each flight, but I was in no hurry. When we got to my room, Marie headed to the bathroom and turned on the shower. I loved the way she just made herself at home.

"Thank God, there's hot water," she said over the running water.

That was a miracle. Since coming to Kyiv, I'd almost become accustomed to cold showers. I opened one of the dresser drawers and removed one of my favorite T-shirts, the one I got at a Pat Benatar concert years ago. It was from her *Get Nervous* album. Pat was on the front of the shirt with her hair all teased out in an afro, the kind you see in cartoons caused by electric shock. Her eyes were wide and wild, and she wore a straitjacket. It was weird, but I thought the shirt was excellent social commentary, not to mention a perfect metaphor for our times. It pleased me to think Marie would sleep in it.

I hesitated over the underwear. Some people were skittish about that sort of thing. Then I remembered I had a package of new panties I'd stashed for emergencies. I removed the entire unopened package and laid it on the T-shirt. I was nervous as hell at asking Marie for a sleepover and imagined myself looking a bit like I needed a straitjacket. I added a pair of gym shorts to the pile of clothes. They weren't regular pajamas but the most comfortable thing to sleep in. I gathered the stack, cracked the bathroom door, and laid the clothes on the counter next to the sink.

While she showered, I pulled out my iPad and reviewed my notes. A full-length article formed on my screen as my fingers tapped away at the keyboard. I loaded up the pictures from my camera, did a few quick edits, and emailed it to the news desk back at Titan while the internet connection was still good. Not a bad day's work, I thought to myself.

I heard Marie laughing in the bathroom. "This shirt is exactly how I feel," she said.

She looked adorable in that shirt when she came out of the bathroom. Lusty thoughts rushed through my brain. I could feel myself blushing. My mind kept going back to our night in the bomb shelter. She was flirting with me then but had been distant since. I kept my mouth shut and told my galloping libido to settle down. Maybe she was one of those women who couldn't help but flirt with everyone. God, I hoped that if she was, it didn't make me look like a lovesick puppy following her around begging for attention. The thought made me almost physically ill.

I'd had my share of relationships, but I'd never instigated one. I usually hung around the woman I was interested in until she noticed me and said something. Since going to work for Titan, I'd spent more time focusing on my career than dating. I seriously doubted becoming involved with a French doctor was a good idea. Especially if she didn't feel the same way about me. I mentally forced myself into the friend zone.

"That was wonderful," Marie said, towel-drying her hair. "Thank you." She could still flash that smile at me anytime.

"You're welcome," I said. I told her to make herself at home while I showered.

"I don't know if I left you any hot water," she said.

I didn't say that a cold shower would do me much better anyway. I just smiled and mumbled something about being used to it.

She was fast asleep when I exited the bathroom a short time later because cold showers were less time-consuming than hot ones. She hadn't bothered to get under the covers. An open bottle of water sat next to her on the nightstand.

With the tension and fierce concentration she normally displayed when she was working missing from her face in her sleep, it struck me again how beautiful she was. Her skin was soft and smooth. A slight whistle came through the end of her pert little upturned nose. Standing there watching her sleep, I felt what the Italians called a lightning strike. It hit me hard and left me a bit dazed. I was falling for the doctor and falling hard.

"Friend zone," I whispered to myself. "Friend zone. Friend zone." I gently tugged the blanket and bedspread from underneath her and tucked her in. Then I slid into my sleeping bag and pulled it over my head so the temptation to make out Marie's profile in the dark disappeared.

When Tatiana banged on my door the following morning, Marie was already dressed and gone. She'd left my shorts neatly folded on the bed with a note saying thanks, and she wanted to keep the shirt. I tucked the paper in my pocket, knowing I would read it repeatedly to picture her standing in my room with that smile on her face. Damn! She could have had the shirt just for the price of that smile.

Forcing myself to refocus on something other than Marie wearing my favorite T-shirt, I headed down the stairs to the press office. I supposed I could discuss everything with Tatiana. The kid was smart, and she was a good listener. But some warning bells about giving away too much information about myself kept going off in my brain. Tatiana was great, and I liked her, but she was so damn young. Plus, she worked for me. If working for Pamela at Titan had taught me anything, it was that you don't confide in your employees. I put the thought out of my head and lined up to receive my assignments from the press secretary's aide.

Tatiana and I received permission from the press office and set out for Kherson, where the fighting was intense. I didn't know why the press secretary decided to let us go. Maybe she was hoping we'd get killed, and then we would be out of her hair. None of the other press corps were given assignments that close to the front. Still, it was better not to ask questions that might cause Madame Tupoleva to rethink letting us go. Tatiana had overheard her father say the Ukrainians were gaining ground there, and she thought it would make a good story.

The ride there was uneventful. When we reached the city, sentries blocked the road. Most citizens had evacuated as the Ukrainian army prepared to engage the incoming Russians. One of the sentries told us to turn around. Tatiana explained that we were press and were there to cover the fighting. She handed him the pass Tupoleva's aide gave us.

While she convinced the sentries to let us in the city, I had to stop myself from chewing on my fingernails. It was a bad nervous habit I had. I didn't want the sentry to notice, so I forced myself to stay still. That pass could easily have been a fake.

One of the young men took my press pass and passport and examined them with the intensity of a scientist studying bacteria under a microscope. I wondered if he even read English. He returned my documentation and told us we could enter the city, but no one could be responsible for our safety. Both Tatiana and I assured him we were aware of the danger and would be careful. Reluctantly, he let us go.

Tatiana drove slowly, a first for her. We stopped in the center of town where the evidence of the fighting lay in the broken glass and rubble. We stopped one harried-looking man. He told us the government had provided them with plastic sheeting and other supplies to help cover the holes where their windows used to be. He told us he'd also salvaged pieces of wood, metal, nails, or anything else he could use to patch the holes. Today's bombings had leveled his home and business, making his repairs futile. They were leaving for Poland as soon as he could gather his wife and children. Until then, he had to do something to protect his family from the elements since he couldn't protect them from bullets and missiles.

We got back in the car and drove through the streets until we came upon a relatively undamaged neighborhood. Tatiana parked the car, and we got out and walked around. Few of the houses were inhabited. It looked like any suburban American neighborhood with similar-looking houses, lawns, and driveways. What struck me as odd, though, was no evidence of children. Some toys and a couple of bikes lay scattered here and there. I asked Tatiana about it, and she said the children had been evacuated first. Having the children away from the bombing helped the adults cope. Still, it had to be hard to be separated from their children like that.

Later, she would take me to the children's shelter. A story about the children of Ukraine had been on my back burner since I arrived. It kept coming up, especially after my experience with Max. Other stories and events pushed it back to its soon-but-not-now status. A momentary rush of excitement that maybe we would find Max brought the idea up again. I would have loved to see him and find out how he was doing. Since we were already here in Kherson, I decided to go ahead and see if there was anything newsworthy left.

We saw a couple loading things into a late-model Russian-made UAZ Patriot. The car was a bright blue. That color would stand out on the road if this couple evacuated. They'd dressed casually, each wearing jeans and a polo shirt. To my untrained eye, nothing about them looked unusual. Tatiana, however, narrowed her eyes. Something about this couple was not right in her estimation. We stopped at the edge of their driveway and parked behind a burnt-out vehicle partially blocking the road. Tatiana called out to them. They looked at one another in surprise and turned back to us. The man's answer made Tatiana frown.

"He says he and his wife are evacuating. He says they are going to Poland until it is safe for them to come home. But I don't think that is correct."

"What is it?" I asked.

"Their accent is not right," she said. The couple continued to watch us. Tatiana kept her voice low, and I followed suit.

"What do you mean, not right?" I asked.

"They don't sound like they are from this area," she said.

"Maybe it's because they're yelling at us from a distance," I said hopefully.

"Maybe," Tatiana said. She sounded uncertain. Her gaze kept going back to the couple. I was picking up on her anxiety. From where I stood, seeing it from her point of view, it seemed like their clothes were too clean and too new looking. Even the car looked new. The fear she felt jumped out of her voice and went straight into my veins. I shivered.

I asked myself why there would be Russians inside the town when they were surrounded by Ukrainian soldiers at the city limits. I wasn't an expert on war like Titan's former war correspondent. Even though some of my colleagues back at the hotel were more familiar with battle plans and tactics, I still didn't get the logic of the Russians. Maybe there wasn't any. Maybe they weren't following any rhyme or reason; maybe they were grabbing the spoils of war and getting out when they thought they could.

The couple stopped loading items in the car. They seemed to confer with one another. The woman looked over at us, then turned back to the man. Tatiana and I had not moved closer, so it was impossible to hear what they were saying. It looked like they were arguing. The man's face twisted in anger. He shoved the woman aside and reached behind his back and pulled out a gun. I froze in disbelief.

Tatiana cursed loudly and grabbed me by the arm. She swung me around the nearby burned-out car. We almost made it before they started firing. The pops sounded like a hammer pounding nails into a board. Some of the bullets pinged off the car. Before I made it to cover, I felt something hit my upper arm with the impact of a sledgehammer. I stumbled and fell forward, cutting my hands on the broken glass strewn around the street.

In the distance, I heard tires squealing as the couple jumped in their car and raced away. My first thought was the couple was going to chase and kill us, but the car was going in the opposite direction. I crouched even farther behind the wreck we hid behind. I think I would have crawled under it if I could. Even as the car took off in the other direction, my flight reflex was still in full gear.

Every sound seemed far away. Something else didn't seem right. My ears rang, and I gradually became aware that my shirt was wet. I put my left hand up and touched the place on my right arm where I'd felt the hit. It came away covered with blood. The palms of my hands were also bleeding from where I'd landed on the broken glass covering the street. My jeans were ripped, and a small cut on my knee leaked bright red.

"*Laino*," Tatiana muttered. The Ukrainian word for shit. She pulled my messenger bag off my shoulders and rummaged through it until she came up with my extra shirt. She took a small knife out of her pants pocket and used it to rip the shirt into strips. Then, she tied one of the strips around my arm and knotted it tightly.

"Come on," she said, pulling me to my feet. "We've got to get you to the doctor."

Doctor? Marie? I liked that idea. She pulled me to my feet and half dragged, half carried me back to her car. I felt kind of woozy and wondered if I was going to faint. Tatiana swung me into the Range Rover with a strength that belied her size. Stuffing me in the passenger seat, she buckled my seat belt and rushed to get behind the wheel. My left arm seemed useless and limp. Blood poured from the wound in defiance of the makeshift bandage. Since I'd never been shot before, I didn't know if it was supposed to be like that. I must have passed out because the next thing I remember was her lightly slapping my face to try to get me to wake up.

Then Marie was there, waving something in front of my face. A sharp ammonia odor assaulted my nostrils, and I jerked into consciousness. That was when my arm started to hurt. Marie and Tatiana dragged me inside the hotel. Tatiana was explaining what happened.

"They were Russians posing as Ukrainian citizens," she spat. Unshed tears dangled on the edge of her voice. "One minute we were standing there watching them load up their car, then the next they're shooting at us."

From a distance, I heard Marie say she heard Russians were going in to occupy homes in Kherson, posing as citizens. First, the Russians stripped the houses bare of anything of value. Their primary motivation, however, was propaganda. When the fighting began, the Russians would use these plants to try to trick people into believing Ukraine was attacking its own citizens.

"That's heinous," I said with a slight slur. I still felt woozy but was proud of myself for using the word heinous in a sentence.

"Yes, it is," Marie said. I felt a pinch near where the bullet went in as Marie gave me a shot. She barked out some orders in French, and a nurse rushed over to set up an IV.

They rolled me onto a gurney. Tatiana stepped back to watch as the nurse ripped my shirt sleeve and Tatiana's makeshift bandage off and swabbed my upper arms with some foul-smelling, rust-colored concoction. That made two shirts I was down now.

"It's not that bad," I said, trying to sit up. "I'm sure you have other patients who need help more than me." Marie pushed me back down.

"It's a good thing you were wearing your vest," she said, ignoring my protests as she pulled the vest over my head. My helmet lay on the floor next to the gurney, and I couldn't remember taking it off.

"It didn't help my arm much," I slurred. Marie held the bloody body armor up before my face. The front of it was pocked in at least two places. I gulped, abashed. The damn thing had saved my life.

"You were lucky we are not very busy at the moment, and the bullet went right through," Marie said. "Otherwise, I would be forced to let you bleed to death on the hotel lobby floor."

A small hole in the front of my arm gave way to a slightly bigger hole in the back. I was also lucky that the Russians had been firing an MP-443 Grace pistol instead of one of their automatic AK-12s. The automatic would have blown my arm off and probably taken half my head. I gave a silent word of thanks to my colleague Kevin for making me memorize Russian guns before I left Texas.

I kept trying to turn my head to see what Marie was doing. Whatever it was, involved a lot of stinging up and down my arm.

"Hold still, Press, or I'm going to stitch your arm to your side," Marie said. I was momentarily distracted by the sound of her voice. She finally called over one of her nurses and rattled off something in French. The nurse hurried through a door off to the side of the lobby and came back carrying a hypodermic. Marie took it from her and unceremoniously jabbed it in my arm just above the wound. The first shot she'd given me was a local anesthetic. This one was meant to make me calm down. Everything around me, except Marie, faded away into the distance.

"You're beautiful," I said, trying to smile seductively at her.

"You're delirious," she said.

"Yeah, but I'm going to come out of it, and you're still going to be beautiful," I said, slurring my words a bit. I was feeling better. Nothing hurt, but my head felt like it was full of air, and I was about to float away like a balloon. Then, I remembered something. "Wait! Where's my bag?" I jerked around to try to find Tatiana. While doing so, I pulled away from Marie, accidentally wrenching my arm out of her hands. She let out a few French curses and pulled my arm back. I needed my stuff before I passed out, or Marie put me under. I tried to explain. I had to record my thoughts before I forgot everything.

Tatiana came into my range of vision and held up my messenger bag. "I got your stuff right here, boss."

That bag went everywhere with me. I'd had it since college. It was a brown leather bag that had cost me much more than a poor student could afford. It was more than luggage; it was part of me. My blood spattered all over it along with two distinct bullet holes. Exactly how many bullets had they fired at us? Thank God, Tatiana wasn't hit. I would never forgive myself if something happened to her while she was working as my fixer, no matter how much she told me she knew the dangers of the job.

I had Tatiana open the bag and pull out my iPad. When she opened the case holding the device, a spider web of cracks was spread across the surface of the tablet. A casualty of war. It would never work again.

"I don't suppose Amazon delivers here," I said glumly.

Marie took the iPad from me and glanced at it before setting it on the table next to me. "This iPad probably saved your life," she said. "If your bag was empty, the bullets most likely would have gone right through the openings in your vest, and I'd be locked in a desperate attempt to save your life right now. You have been very lucky today, Press."

She picked up my messenger bag off the floor where Tatiana had dropped it and set it on the gurney next to my damaged iPad. I stared at the holes in the bag made by the Russian bullets. It was one of those moments when my brain had to stop and take a minute to process what had happened. Staring at those holes, all I could think of was how much the bag had cost, how much I loved it, and whether I would have to get rid of it now. My overtaxed brain slowly comprehended that I'd almost died.

Once I comprehended that this bag had saved my life, I decided I would never go anywhere without it again. Hell, I might even wear the damned tactical vest for the rest of my life. Together, they'd kept me from being a corpse.

The iPad was another story. It was a nifty device, and I'd had it neatly tucked into its protective case. After telling Marge I'd ruined it by getting shot, I was sure I'd get an "I told you so."

Tatiana tucked the iPad back into the side pocket of the bag. My laptop was in my room, so I wasn't out of commission. I decided I could make do. After all, this was a war zone. Carrying around a tablet was a lot easier than carrying my laptop everywhere. I would have to find a way to get another device to write on and to file my stories and photos from the field. That thought led me to make sure my camera was okay. I tried pulling it out of the bag. Marie slapped my hand away and had Tatiana take my things and put them out of my reach.

"I'm warning you, Press. Stay still, or I'll knock you out so I can tend to your wound," Marie warned. "Your things will still be there when I'm finished, and they'll still be in the same condition."

Tatiana seemed to be a little more sympathetic to my concerns. Maybe she knew that without the tools of my trade, I would be rendered useless. Removing the camera from my bag, she held it up to show me it was undamaged except for being covered with my blood. I'd been wearing it around my neck when the shooting had started. Tatiana must have taken it off and put it in my bag. Relieved, I sat still long enough for Marie to finish.

After Tatiana put the camera away, she jammed her fists into the pockets of her jeans, and her shoulders slumped over like a condemned prisoner. She couldn't be blaming herself. Or could she? So I asked.

"I am not a good fixer," she said. The unshed tears in her eyes caught me off guard. I thought she was one of those kids who got mad instead of hurt. "I didn't protect you. We walked right into that situation. I will be a laughingstock among the other fixers. I will give you my resignation and help you find someone else."

"Are you nuts?" I asked loudly. "You saved my life. You're undoubtedly the greatest fixer in Ukraine, and if anyone says any different, they'll get an earful from me." I tried to reach out to her, but the movement hurt my arm so much that I settled for vehemently shaking my head.

There was no way I'd let anyone tarnish her performance as a fixer. The organization Fixers in Ukraine was a whole new business that came with the war. They were akin to the Teamsters union back home in the way they closed ranks around anyone they deemed unworthy. Fixers had turned Tatiana down solely because she was a woman. It was their loss. Ukraine supposedly had equal rights laws to prevent that from happening. No one seemed to enforce those laws. I imagined that all over the country, men and women were more interested in basic survival than whether they got hired or fired from a job because of their gender.

I felt outraged on Tatiana's behalf because the kid was damn good at what she did. I was willing to bet she was more knowledgeable about what was happening here than any of their stable of people. Besides, Fixers in Ukraine focused more on the on-air news media. Coordinating a crew of three or four people allowed the fixers to multitask assignments, thereby increasing profits. We lowly print and internet journalists were considered unworthy of their time. It was because they thought we paid less.

It did not escape my notice that when it came to recruiting soldiers to fight this war, gender had become a nonissue. After all, I'd seen many women stand up and fight beside men in my short time here. Maybe I could do a story to promote change in other professions. Women did the same jobs as men. The women in this country did things I could never in my wildest dreams imagine American women doing.

"Don't give it another thought," I said to Tatiana. "You are the absolute best. Did you have the doc here check you out?"

I looked at Marie, who had been stitching up the hole in my arm. "She wouldn't let me until I took care of you. She says she isn't hurt, but I prescribe some rest and maybe a little TLC."

I looked back at Tatiana, "There you have it, doctor's orders. Go home, rest, and let your mom fuss over you. We'll start fresh in the morning."

"Oh no, you won't," Marie said. "You need at least a couple of days to recuperate. You lost a lot of blood, and since our supplies are low, I didn't give you a transfusion. Your body needs some time to get your level back up. You won't report anything if you pass out from anemia."

"You heard the doctor," Tatiana said. "Take a couple of days off. She told you to rest also. I will come tomorrow and bring you food. My mother is a much better cook than hotel chefs."

That sounded like a good plan. I realized I was starving. Marie told one of her team she would help me up to my room. Perhaps they would be so kind as to get me a tray and bring it up. She slipped the IV off its stand and laid it on the gurney next to my stuff. I slid off the gurney right into her waiting arms. It felt so nice. We stood like that for a beat or two longer than necessary.

"Easy there, Press," she said. "Come on. I'll help you." She gathered up my things along with the IV bag, wrapped an arm around my waist, and led me toward the elevator. She decided taking the elevator was worth the risk. Walking up four flights of stairs might be too much of a strain on my poor, shocked system. Not to mention, the majority of my one hundred and forty pounds depended on her holding me up. Touching her almost made me forget how much pain I was in.

I half expected Marie to prop me against a wall while we waited for the elevator, but she didn't. Being this close to her made all of my senses go into hyperdrive. Usually, I was not a forward person. I tended to be insecure and often thought other women couldn't possibly be interested in me, so I let them make the first move.

She smelled like mint, and her underlying womanly scent was irresistible. I wondered if it was pheromones. I had observed many situations, especially with my best friend, Hannah, when I couldn't precisely smell it when someone felt an attraction, but something made the air around them spark. If Hannah was here now, I wondered if she could sense that I was definitely into the good doctor. I wanted to kiss Marie so much that I licked my dry lips in anticipation. I thought better of it because if I missed, we would both go tumbling to the floor.

"Will you have dinner with me?" I asked, slipping and sliding over the words.

"I've already eaten," she said. "But I will stay with you until your IV is finished."

"No, I meant like a date," I clarified. "I mean, will you go out with me?"

She laughed, and my heart sank like a rock for a second. "I doubt we could go to a restaurant, have dinner and a movie, and follow up with a nightcap and a second date in a war zone."

She must have noticed my disappointment and perhaps my humiliation. Maybe I could blame my faux pas on being delirious from a loss of blood. She tapped me on the nose. "Don't look so heartbroken, Press. We'll have to make our own dating rules. You're a creative person. You'll think of something."

That my heart was soaring now wasn't the result of the elevator shaking and rattling. We reached my floor, and Marie dug around in my bag until she found my key card and let us in. Once inside, she dumped me on the bed.

She went to the bathroom, and I heard the shower turn on. Luckily, it was a good water day. When she emerged a few minutes later, she went to the dresser and pulled out some clean clothes. With her help, I stripped off my bloody and torn shirt and tossed it towards the garbage can. My jeans, covered in dirt, grime, and blood, were salvageable. Marie bent to help unlace my boots, removed them, and neatly stacked them in a corner. I was in my underwear in front of a woman I was wildly hot to kiss. Usually, this would have been an awkward moment for me, but right now, under the influence of whatever was in that shot, I felt almost empowered.

When she leaned in, I bent in with my lips ready. I thought my dream would come true, but she reached around my shoulder and wrapped me in my bathrobe. Then, she discreetly helped me remove my underwear. She marched me into the bathroom, where she dug a plastic bag out of the trash, deftly wrapped it around my wounded arm, and told me to get in the shower.

It was awkward at best, trying to shower when I could only use one arm. Not to mention, I was trying gamely to hold on to the handicap bars along the side of the stall to keep from falling. Handy things, those bars. It wasn't the best cleansing I'd ever done, but I made a passable attempt to remove the grime. Marie pulled the shower curtain back a few inches, turned off the water, and held out my robe. She did a masterful job of not looking at my naked body.

With a sigh, I let her help me back to bed and into a pair of boxers and a T-shirt to sleep in. She dug around in a couple of her pockets and came up with a tube of anesthetic and some bandages. I'd noticed those were some of the things she always had on her. She cleaned the cuts and scrapes on my hands from where I'd fallen on the broken glass. Then she cleaned my scraped knee. When she finished putting the Band-Aid on, she leaned over and gave it a little kiss. I almost fell off the bed.

While she was doing that, her aide knocked on the door. He entered with a tray, set it on the desk, and asked if she needed anything else. When she said no, he reminded her their ride would be there soon. Frowning in my direction, he said he'd see her downstairs and left. Part of me was hoping she'd stay the night, but her assistant had made it clear they were waiting for her. She shut off the IV and removed the needle from my arm, putting another Band-Aid on the mark there.

Digging into the tray, I barely tasted the food. It was as bland as usual, but I didn't care. While I ate, Marie watched me closely. Under normal conditions, the scrutiny would have made me uncomfortable. A few bites later, my stomach protested. Marie grabbed the nearby trash can and placed it at my feet. Luckily, it was there when everything I had just eaten came right back up. Great, she wasn't watching me calculating how she could kiss me, she was waiting for me to puke. She went to the bathroom and returned with a wet washcloth, my toothbrush, and toothpaste.

"Here you go," she said, wiping my face with the cloth. "Sometimes the sedative has that effect. You go to sleep, and I'll come to check on you in the morning."

It didn't seem very smart of me to attempt to kiss her right after I'd tossed my cookies. I mumbled something silly about not being very attractive right now. After assuring me my reaction was normal, she picked my feet up off the floor and swung them around. She dropped another kiss on my forehead, and then, she was gone.

CHAPTER EIGHT

Two things were acutely obvious when I woke up the following day. Marie was nowhere to be found, and my arm hurt like hell. I stumbled to the small fridge on the other side of the room and downed a bottle of water. It was lukewarm, but that didn't matter because my body felt like its moisture had evaporated into a cloud of dust.

Marie had left a Post-it note stuck to the top of the fridge. Press, I've left you medication for the pain and an antibiotic to keep out any infections. Rest and see me when you feel up to it. The handwriting was more like calligraphy than letters on a page. That amused me because it had been my experience that all doctors had atrocious handwriting. I had a theory that Bad Handwriting 101 was one of the first courses they taught in medical school.

115

There was also a sling folded neatly underneath the note with instructions for me to wear it. These words were in all caps, so I assumed that meant I was expected to obey. Slipping my sore arm into it, I vaguely wondered how I was going to operate my camera or type up my articles. Then I remembered I was supposed to be taking a couple of days off.

I rummaged around until I found the pills and downed a couple. Marie hadn't said how many to take, so I decided two were better than one, tossed them to the back of my throat, and chased them down with the last gulp of water.

I wasn't the sort of person who did well with idle time on my hands. First of all, someone had tried to kill me yesterday, and my brain was trying to process that. I paced the length of the room several times, thinking I had to get out of there. Which, when I thought about it, was kind of crazy because I was relatively safe here in this room. Outside, with the bombs and guns and people shooting in my direction, wasn't safe. It dawned on me that I was afraid. Not terrified afraid, but the kind of fear that started like a small seed, and the more nutrition you gave it, the more it grew. If I didn't do something, I was going to have a full-blown panic attack.

I know Marie had told me to take it easy for a few days, but I grew bored trying to sort out the mess in my hotel room. It annoyed me that I couldn't do laundry. Sure, there was a war going on, and I got that the hotel was short-staffed and everything. I thought with the fortune Titan paid to keep this room open, getting some clean clothes once in a while would have been possible. This line of thinking made me realize what a privilege it was to live in America, and honestly, I was ashamed of myself for allowing a few dirty clothes to put me off. These people were doing the best they could under the circumstances.

I could have lain there and fantasized about Marie some more, but that seemed a bit pointless as well. I'd just be getting myself worked up for nothing. I might as well see if I could do something about my clothes situation.

I took a quick inventory of my clothes. I had one clean pair of jeans left and a couple of shirts. I was okay with socks and underwear. The rest of my wardrobe required a good washing. Everything was covered in blood or dirt. I went to the bathroom and filled the tub with water. I dumped a travel-sized bottle of shampoo in for good measure. Next, I tossed in the jeans I'd worn yesterday and swished the mess around with my good arm. Bribing the staff to throw my clothes in the wash was possible, but knowing the hotel was short-staffed made me reluctant to ask. I could hop in the tub and stomp around on the clothes, but the fear of slipping and falling changed my mind about that. I decided the effort wasn't worth it and left the clothes to soak.

I scattered everything else from my bag across the bed. My essentials included my damaged iPad in the protective case that had failed in its duties. There was my camera, some toiletries, a small first aid kit, my passport, and papers for traveling abroad. I dumped everything out on the bed, then I dampened a towel from the bathroom and scrubbed the outside of the bag to clean it up. Most of the grime came off, but the bloodstains were there to stay. I decided it would be a great conversation starter when I returned to Texas. "Here's where I got shot by a Russian impersonating a Ukrainian citizen."

It hit me hard at that moment. I'd been shot. Another human being tried to kill me. Not only that, but the fact that it wasn't personal tumbled around in my head. A perfect stranger, not knowing anything about me at all, had attempted to end my life. I dropped heavily onto the bed. My whole body shook with aftershocks. Would I even be able to go back out there and do my job? At this point, I didn't know for sure.

None of my female war correspondent heroes ever gave up. Hell, Marie Colvin went back to the front lines after she lost an eye. "We always have to ask ourselves whether the level of risk is worth the story." That was one of her most famous quotes. This was the question I now asked myself as I curled up in a fetal position on the bed.

Then I thought of Mila Kiryanova, camping out in the back of her coffee shop with two of her employees. I thought of the watermelon farmer, rummaging through his destroyed fields searching for every intact melon. I thought of the family cooking their breakfast on a rusty barbecue grill in front of their destroyed home. I thought about the baby I called Max lying in the street next to his dead mother.

Another Marie Colvin quote reverberated in my head: "We can and do make a difference by exposing the horrors of war and especially the atrocities that befall civilians." I would get up and get back out there. I would make a difference.

My laptop beckoned me from across the room. Many times, I had promised myself I would keep a journal, but I'd never followed through with any regularity. If I could bleed this fear out of my system and onto a page, I thought I might be able to function. The words were all but jumping out of my head, and my fingers flexed, anxious to get them written. Unfortunately, the electricity kept flickering on and off. Not to mention the hassles of trying to type with one arm immobilized in a sling. I gave up trying to put my feelings into words and drafted an email to Pamela. After a third attempt at that endeavor, I gave up. I didn't want to tell her I'd been shot over an email. That was almost as bad as breaking up with someone via text. If I used the satellite phone to call her, could I tell her I needed a new iPad without telling her I'd been shot? If she found out from someone else, she'd be pissed.

Pamela might be tempted to bring me home if she knew I'd been wounded. Even as terror hopped around my brain like a bunny, I still didn't want to be recalled to the States. Maybe I could talk her out of bringing me home. It was only a flesh wound, I told myself. Maybe I wouldn't tell her at all.

Instead of contacting my editor, I decided I was hungry and more than a little cranky. The drugs Marie had given me had dulled the worst pain in my arm. I'd go downstairs and see if she was on duty to thank her for patching me up. Then, I'd see if the dining room had any food. Tatiana's promise of bringing me some of her mother's cooking loomed large in my mind. I'd call Tatiana and get her back out there with me. Together, we'd get right back on that horse.

Vaguely, I remembered I'd told Tatiana to take a couple of days off. Hopefully, she was handling the stress of someone trying to kill us better than I was. Of course, she lived in the middle of a country that had been at war for more than two years now. Maybe getting shot at was passé to her. *I'd better check in with her just in case.* I felt an overwhelming sense of amazement and affection for the kid as I realized what she'd been living with. I couldn't just call her up and tell her we were going to get back to work.

I wasn't expecting anyone, so the knock at the door surprised me. For a brief second, my heart jumped in excitement thinking it might be Marie. I glanced through the peephole to see Tatiana standing in the hallway with a bag in hand.

"You read my mind," I said, throwing open the door and snatching the bag out of her hands.

She grinned. "Sure, boss. Mama thought you might be hungry." Tatiana set the bag down on the desk. She unpacked a thermos. If it were coffee, I'd kiss her. Then she unloaded a couple of paper plates with her mom's pastries. She went to the bathroom while I wolfed down the delicious pies.

"I was thinking, boss," she said, coming out of the bathroom and sitting on the edge of the bed. I tore my attention away from the food and focused on her. "The doctor said you need to rest, so why don't you come home with me for a few days? Mama would love to take care of you. You wouldn't have to worry about how you will eat or how you can take care of yourself. She would even do your laundry for you." She waved a hand in the general direction of the bathroom.

I had to admit, the idea was highly tempting. But this country was in a crisis, and most families were stretched thin regarding food and supplies. I didn't want to put her family out. I said as much to her as I continued to eat the food her mother sent. My stomach had no qualms about taking her family's food.

"We're not millionaires by any means," Tatiana said matter-of-factly after I voiced my concerns about being a drain on her family. "But with the connections of my dad and uncles, we are doing okay. Besides, I've already run the idea past my parents and the doctor. They all think it's a great idea."

Her sister was married and lived two hundred miles south in Odesa. Her brothers were out of the house. They had joined the fighting in other parts of the country, leaving the big house feeling oddly empty with only Tatiana remaining at home. Pasha would welcome the opportunity to fuss over someone else, and Tatiana said she could stand not being the center of her mother's attention for a few days.

"What if your brothers come home?" I asked. Even worse, what if they didn't come home? I hesitated to impose on the family's grief that hadn't even happened yet.

"Even if either of them comes home, we will make room," Tatiana said cheerfully. "Mama told me not to take no for an answer." It was a matter of pride for older Ukrainians to offer hospitality.

I certainly didn't want to offend Tatiana's parents. Honestly, it sounded like a great idea to me. They had a generator and a well, so they had electricity and water. Hopefully, the internet stayed connected. Best of all, I wouldn't be alone in this hotel room with nothing but my thoughts driving me crazy. I agreed to come with her and packed my smaller duffel bag with a few of the essentials. While I packed, Tatiana stuffed my dirty wet clothes from the bathtub into a couple of pillowcases she shook free from the bed. She helped me dress. I told her that my stay with her family would only be until I was well enough to care for myself. She dismissed this as unimportant.

It took her less than five minutes to pack the stuff I needed after she took over from my fumbling. There were some clothes, my camera, my laptop, and my protective gear. I threw in a bunch of toiletries and candy I'd brought from home. My mother had taught me to never go to someone's house without taking a gift. Tatiana heaved the suitcase off the bed, and we headed out the door.

"The doctor told us to stop on our way out so she can check you out," Tatiana said.

Before I could agree to stop by triage, one of Tupoleva's aides materialized in front of me. He said something in Ukrainian. I looked at Tatiana. Although she tried hard to hide it, whatever this guy said caused her some concern.

"Madame Tupoleva wants to see us," she said. "He says they know you were wounded yesterday." Could Tupoleva send me home? Just the thought of being deported caused my cheeks to flush. She wouldn't dare send me home after she'd permitted us to go, albeit reluctantly, to Khershon. Even if she didn't send me packing, Madame Press Secretary could make my stay here a lot more difficult. It was already a struggle with all the foreign journalists jostling for assignments. If Tupoleva decided to cut me off, even with Tatiana's sources, I could be screwed. I hadn't been this anxious since I'd been called into the principal's office in high school for water bombing the marching band.

I needed to suck it up and see what Tupoleva wanted before I saw Marie. I signaled to the aide to lead us to her. He took us to a tiny office behind the check-in desk. Tupoleva sat at one of the workstations there. I couldn't very well hide the fact that my arm was injured, although I was tempted to pull it out and hide the sling. Tupoleva was not a tall woman. I'd have eaten one of her high heels if she were five feet. Despite her diminutive stature, she exuded authority. It practically seeped from her pores. When she spoke, she expected obedience.

She didn't look up from her tablet until she finished what she was doing. Once satisfied, she put the tablet on the desk and gazed at me with a thoughtful glance, like she wasn't quite sure what she wanted to do with me.

"I just spoke to your editor," she said. "I told her you were wounded." Had she called Pamela, or had Pamela been the one to reach out? I didn't think my editor would call the Ukrainian press secretary without trying to reach me first, and I had no missed calls. Therefore, Tupoleva must have thought to see what my boss thought of my thoughtlessness in getting shot. I swallowed my nerves and put what I hoped was a neutral look on my face. Tupoleva kept looking at me as if she expected an explanation.

"I apologize, Madame Tupoleva," I said with as much sincerity as I could muster. "We were careless and didn't recognize the danger until it was too late."

"You were lucky to have been chosen to visit the front line," Tupoleva said. She acted like my getting shot was my fault. "This is why we only allow a few journalists to go near the fighting."

The red zones were where the action was, but the fighting was not the only story of the war. I wanted to go to the red zones, but with the competition for those assignments so fierce among the journalists here to cover the war, I'd found the human side much easier to get to. Almost anyone could tell you how many soldiers had died in a particular battle, but not everyone could tell you how the civilians coped with it.

"I understand," I said with what I hoped was consternation. "I will be more careful in the future."

"I should hope so," Tupoleva said. Her tone dripped with disbelief at my assertion that I hadn't intended to get shot. "Since this was your first offense, I will not send you back to America today. You will stick to stories away from the front lines. If you cross that line again, you and your news service will be barred from Kyiv. You will also file a report either with me or one of my aides, giving me your destination for the day before you and your fixer head out. Consider yourself on probation."

After glaring at Tatiana as if she were also responsible for my behavior, Tupoleva turned away and picked up her tablet. We were dismissed. I thanked her as profusely as I could and pulled Tatiana out of the room. I didn't want her to get barred from doing her job.

"Sorry, boss," Tatiana said when we were safely back in the lobby.

"Don't be sorry. We got the scoop on the Russians impersonating Ukrainian citizens. We will have to be more careful in the future, though."

We went from Tupoleva's temporary office to Marie's temporary triage. Hopefully, she wasn't tied up with patients. I wanted to make myself scarce after Tupoleva's dressing down. It did cross my mind, however, that if I wasn't in the hotel, how would I get to see Marie daily? She'd already turned down my request for a date. How would I see her if Tupoleva threw me out of the country? The thought of being unable to see her reinforced my decision to stay on the press secretary's good side. Tatiana, as if she knew what I was thinking, told me not to worry.

"We will stay away from trouble. At least for a few days," she said, grinning. "You will see the doctor again. If you and the doctor are meant to be an item, love will find a way." Normally, I hated platitudes like that one, but love finding a way to Marie and me seemed like the best thing I'd heard today.

We found Marie in a glassed-in alcove off the main lobby. Before it became an examination room, it had served as a business office for the hotel. A young soldier sat on the desk while Marie looked into his eyes using a penlight. She spoke to him in French and a spattering of English, with some Ukrainian words thrown in. Tatiana left to bring around the car. I patiently waited in silence while Marie finished up with the soldier. I wondered if Ukraine had anything like HIPPA and if I should excuse myself. I decided it didn't matter since I couldn't understand most of what they were saying anyway, and since we were in a hotel lobby, such things as privacy took a back seat to more critical issues.

Marie finished her examination and put her small penlight back in the pocket of her white smock. The young man hopped off the desk, thanked Marie, and left with the barest glance at me. Marie wrote something on her tablet, then set it on the table and turned her full attention to me. That smile was like the sun coming from behind a cloud on an overcast day. My heart started beating a little faster. Suddenly, I couldn't think of anything to say.

"Sit here," she said, pointing to a chair on the side of the desk. I obediently sat. She touched my arm to remove the bandage. Her finger left a trail of fire along my spine that had nothing to do with the gunshot wound. The ache of not being able to cup her face and kiss those beautiful, full lips was much more intense than the sharp sting I received from her poking around the bullet hole in my arm.

She didn't speak while she examined my arm. Once satisfied that I wasn't going to contract gangrene and have my limb amputated, she bandaged it again and handed me a small plastic bag of medical supplies. The bag held bandaging material, some of her ever-present antibiotic cream, and a small bottle of pills. She instructed me on how to clean and care for the wound. Then, she told me to use the medications sparingly. Good drugs were hard to get.

"I'm glad you're going with Tatiana," she said. "I'll feel better knowing you aren't on your own. I won't tell you to be careful. Somehow, I don't think you would even if I warned you. I will come by Tatiana's tonight to see you if possible."

The prospect of seeing her later made me giddy. I thanked her, which didn't seem nearly adequate and seemed even less than appropriate when all I wanted to do was kiss her. I expected, if I tried, she would give me a friendly pat on the arm and tell me she was doing her job. Imagine my surprise when she leaned in and lightly kissed me on the lips.

"I'm afraid my motivation is purely selfish," she said. "You owe me a date."

It took all my self-control not to grab her and extend that kiss. Just as I was about to do it, she gave a little exclamation of surprise and turned away. One of her colleagues stood at the door, frowning at us. He threw out some rapid French in an angry tone. She responded in kind. Between their gestures and the rising inflection, they were both passionate about whatever subject they were discussing. I vowed to study more French. The other doctor fired a parting shot, at least that was what I gleaned from his tone, and left. Marie glared after him for a second. When she turned her attention back to me, she was smiling again.

"I almost forgot," she said. She reached into a large tote sitting on a chair behind her and pulled out a box about the size of an average picture frame. I took it and opened it. Inside was a brand-new iPad.

"How?" I started to ask.

"Let's just say our office manager agreed not to notice some of her missing supplies," she said.

"Is that what that little heated exchange was about?" I jerked my head in the direction of the door.

Marie shook her head. "No, that was something else entirely. Now get out of here. I have real patients to see. When you win your Pulitzer Prize, you can thank me in your acceptance speech."

The words gave me hope for the promise of a future with her in it. I'd never believed in love at first sight, but she might have made me a convert. Her offhanded certainty that I'd win a Pulitzer also elated me. I'd never bragged about it as many colleagues did, but the aim was a burning hope in the back of my wishes. It wasn't a bonfire, more of a birthday candle. Her faith in my ability made me realize it was possible. If that ass Shawn Glass could win two, surely there was one with my name on it.

I thanked her again and left to find Tatiana waiting patiently in the lobby. She led me to the car and helped me climb in. Land Rovers were high off the ground, and I usually had to grab the handle inside the door and propel myself inside. It was awkward and challenging with two good arms. With one arm primarily out of commission, it was damn near impossible. It took us a few minutes, but I was finally in. Tatiana buckled the seat belt around me and trotted to the driver's side. When my satellite phone buzzed, I decided I'd better answer it. My reckoning was at hand.

"Hey, Pamela," I said, keeping my tone upbeat and lying as smoothly as I could. "I was just about to call you."

"What the hell, Sheppard?" she asked. "The press secretary called me last night. She said you wandered into a red zone and got shot. She threatened to throw you out of the country if you got out of line again." When Pamela said last night, I was momentarily confused until I remembered there was an eight-hour time difference between here and Austin.

"Why didn't you call me immediately?" Pamela demanded. "If you're hurt, I need to pull you out of there."

My heart stopped at hearing those words come out of her mouth. I'd had my existential crisis over getting shot, and as far as I was concerned, that was the end of it. Not to my editor, though.

"Honestly, Pamela, it's barely a scratch," I said projecting more confidence in my voice than I was feeling. The real threat of being sent home cast a pall over me. "I've had more damaging paper cuts. Tupoleva is acting like I did it on purpose, and she's the one who permitted us to go there."

"I took a chance on you, Sheppard," Pamela said. "I did it because I like you, and you're good at what you do. If you piss off Tupoleva, it's going to be next to impossible for me to send anyone else. That will piss off the big brass here, and I don't need the aggravation."

It took most of the drive to Tatiana's house for my editor to vent her feelings. For any future adventures into red zones, we would exhibit extreme caution. She wasn't mad because Madame Press Secretary had called her in the middle of the night, it was because I hadn't told her first.

"I was kind of preoccupied," I said. "You know, with getting shot and all."

"Don't be a smartass," she said. "It's bad enough dealing with Kevin's PTSD. No story is worth that kind of risk."

"Marie Colvin would disagree," I said quietly. Marie Colvin had been shot twice while covering the war in Bosnia. The first time, she'd lost an eye. The second time, she'd lost her life. That was how important getting the story was to her.

"And where is Marie Colvin now? She's dead!" Pamela said in a tight voice. Since she couldn't slam the receiver of a cell phone down like she could in the old days, using that loud bang followed closely by silence to make her point, I had to imagine the process when she disconnected the call.

"That went well," I said to Tatiana.

Maybe Pamela was right. It wasn't worth dying over. I shut off the phone to preserve its battery and sighed. Tatiana was watching me out of the corner of her eye while weaving in and out of traffic. Ending the call on that note made me feel like I'd dodged another bullet. I smiled reassuringly at my fixer.

"Don't worry, kiddo. We'll try to keep out of the red zone for a few days. This will all blow over." I wasn't so sure.

Despite the difficulty of getting around the city, we made it to Tatiana's place in record time. Pasha greeted us warmly when we came in through the kitchen door. She sat at the table and served us the last quass. This pitcher would be her last batch until she found some fresh fruit. I mentally cursed the Russians for this latest atrocity. I knew that in the grand scheme of war, it wasn't the biggest or worst thing that could happen, but it felt personal. It was like my grandma couldn't make cookies anymore because some evil villain had stolen all the chocolate chips.

My inquisitive nature took over, and I asked Pasha many questions about what fruits she used, where they were grown, and what was happening to them. She didn't mind when I pulled out my new iPad and began taking notes, typing one-handed and cursing the sling. Pasha patiently reviewed the ingredients needed to make the quass and where they were grown. Different fruits produced different flavors, but inflation had tripled the price of fresh fruit since the war started. Some fruits, such as watermelons, were almost nonexistent. Pasha wouldn't give me her exact recipe. Saying it was a family secret she planned to leave as an inheritance for her children, made me laugh, and it made Pasha seem much more warm and friendly. She gave me enough material to write a good feature story.

"We are lucky," Pasha said with a sigh. "We have what is sufficient to meet our needs and some above that. So many in the country are without even the basics. I can live without fresh fruit if it gets the Russians out of our country."

War was hell, and not just for the soldiers doing the fighting but also for everyone who loved them, she said sadly. She confessed her worry about her other children who were off fighting. Her older daughter, Galina, and her grandchildren lived in the southern region where the fighting was intense. Galina called when she could get through to let

Pasha know they were safe and well. Sometimes, when she couldn't call, Pasha waited anxiously, never letting her phone out of sight. She jumped at each little noise that felt magnified a hundred times and checked the phone every few minutes.

Since the war started, the university where she taught, Taras Shevchenko National University of Kyiv, had closed. At the same time, most students and a significant number of faculty and staff had joined in the fighting. Since the closure, Pasha had devoted her time to helping her husband and organizing local groups accepting aid from other countries and distributing supplies.

Her expression grew sadder as she described the living conditions of many Ukrainians. Bombing forced even some of the most affluent families to accept shelter, food, clothing, and other necessities. Pride had no place in their new world order. When I asked if we could visit the distribution center and interview some volunteers, and hopefully some of those needing aid, she wholeheartedly agreed.

I'd been typing up my notes, and the bullet hole in my upper arm was beginning to ache. Pasha must have noticed my sagging energy and insisted on showing me to my room and helping me put my things away. I sat on the bed, listening to her talk. Her voice's lilt and tone faded into something almost like a lullaby. As my eyes closed of their own accord, her voice faded away. Vaguely, I recalled her removing my shoes and covering me with a blanket. I thought how nice it must have been to have a mother. My mother had been gone so long that I barely remembered her.

I slept through most of the day. Tatiana came in around dusk and shook me awake so I could come to dinner. I sat with Tatiana, Pasha, Dimitri, and one of his aides. Tatiana's father was about a foot shorter than his wife. He also had a bit of a potbelly, but his clothes were a loose fit, indicating he'd lost weight recently. Despite their physical differences, the love and devotion they shared for one another was obvious. I'd always hoped and dreamed of finding a love like that.

A knock on the door startled us. Fear touched down on my heart like a jet coming in for a landing. For a few brief seconds, I imagined the Russians who'd shot at us yesterday had found us and were going to finish the job. Then, Pasha laughed. The Russians would not knock on the door. They would knock the door down. Still, with an abundance of caution, she picked up a golf club sitting by the door. She opened it slightly and then flung it open. Marie entered carrying a bag of medical supplies in one hand and a basket of food and drink in the other.

Ever the gracious hostess, Pasha offered Marie some quass and invited her to join us for dinner, and she gratefully accepted. When Pasha tried to apologize for the sparseness of the meal, Marie and I were quick to reassure her that it was excellent and perfectly acceptable.

"My impression of the French was they always ate rich, heavy meals, thick with cream and sugar, and drank gallons of wine," Pasha said.

"That would be the interpretation one would get based on the movies." Marie laughed. "The truth is, most French people try to eat lighter meals. Especially for lunch, as it slows us down in the afternoons."

While they talked more about cultural and culinary differences worldwide, I watched Marie. Her face and gestures became more animated when she spoke of something she was passionate about, like Doctors Without Borders or French cuisine. Her voice had a rising and falling lilt without changing volume the way some people did when they talked.

Tatiana kicked me under the table. It startled me out of my musings of pulling Marie into my arms and giving her a genuine display of passion. Then, I realized the object of my attention had asked me a question.

"I'm sorry, what?" I asked dumbly.

"I asked if you were ready for me to look at your arm," Marie said. Her bemusement at my sputtering had put a twinkle in her eye.

"Yes." I'd take any excuse to have some actual contact with her.

Pasha led us to a small bathroom off the central part of the house. She instructed Tatiana to tidy up the kitchen while we were gone. Once Pasha had shown us the way, she left us alone. I sat on the closed toilet seat while Marie ministered to my wounds. The bathroom had a definite feminine vibe. Everything was pink. The shower curtain. The wallpaper had pink roses. The pink soap dish held tiny, rose-shaped pink soaps. The rug on the floor and the toilet seat cover were all pink. It calmed my rapid heartbeat to stare at something besides Marie.

"Take off your shirt," she ordered. I fumbled with the buttons a bit, wondering how I'd fastened them this morning. After a couple of minutes of me twisting and turning, trying to unbutton it one-handed, Marie grabbed the hem of the garment and pulled it over my head. While I fantasized about reciprocating, she unwrapped the last bandage she'd applied this morning and closely examined the wound.

She didn't speak, nor did I. I sat there and breathed in her scent. When she finished her examination, she generously applied her foul-smelling antibiotic cream to the hole in my arm and wrapped it in a fresh bandage. Then, she handed me my shirt and helped me slip it back over my head. For a few seconds, we gazed at each other. Her expression was thoughtful.

"Were you serious about taking me on a date?" she asked.

It wasn't the question I was expecting. "Uh, yeah, I was."

My confession caused her to frown. My thoughts jumped to the premise that she was straight and trying to figure out how to let me down easily. Our kiss the other night had to be her going through her experimental phase, I thought. While I appreciated her concern, my disappointment went far beyond whatever humiliation I was about to endure.

"The thing is," she said finally, "we're in a war zone. A date where you pick me up at a predetermined time, bring me flowers, take me out to dinner, and leave me at my doorstep with a brief kiss, wanting more...." She paused, thinking for a minute. "Well, that is not an option for us. Is it?"

"I get that," I said. "Honestly, I expected you to turn me down. Women like you normally aren't interested in me."

My confession seemed to puzzle her. She cocked her head and looked at me with a quizzical expression. "What do you mean, women like me?"

I could feel my cheeks turning red. "You know, beautiful, smart, funny."

She laughed, "Oh, Press, any woman should count herself lucky to be the object of your affection. I'm concerned about us drawing too much attention to ourselves. Ukraine is not like the United States or France."

"Did something happen?" I asked.

She sighed and sat on the edge of the tub. Having her so close but so far away was maddening. "That doctor who came in this morning and interrupted our kiss," she said. "He reported me to our superior. The doctor is extremely homophobic. I knew this and still let my guard down."

"Are you in danger of losing your job?" I cursed myself for not being more careful. My real anger focused on the narrow-mindedness of her coworker. How could they even think of sending her back to France when the need for doctors was so great?

"No, of course not. My superior is an ally. He did warn me of the danger of being out in a country where being gay is still considered criminal, even if the law says it is not. He told me I have an important job here, and we should not court unnecessary danger. Unfortunately, as an organization, Doctors Without Borders is also rather conservative."

It seemed to me that a desperate need for doctors would cancel out any concern over someone's sexuality. Once again, the differences between cultures came home for me. I wondered if heterosexual members of Doctors Without Borders ran into the same sort of issues if they happened to get into romantic entanglements while in foreign countries.

Marie stood and walked to the door, then back again. Agitation came off her in waves. "When I'm around you, I find it hard to concentrate," she said. "I have seen the photos you take for your news organization. I see how close you get in the way of bombs and guns. When Tatiana brought you in yesterday and you'd been shot, my heart almost stopped with fear and worry for you. I came here to save lives, but I don't want to have to save yours. I am not sure this is the time and place for romance."

I wanted to sweep her up into my arms and give her passionate kisses while telling her who knew what tomorrow would bring. Getting shot made me realize that we shouldn't take love for granted and that we should reach for the stars. Instead, I sat on the toilet and glumly looked at the floor.

She was right. We both came here to do a job. If we let our emotions run away with us, then it could jeopardize our careers. Maybe the Ukrainian government wouldn't send me home for being caught with a woman, but I'm not sure I wanted to find out. A few years ago, I watched a documentary about gays and lesbians in Ukraine. Granted, it was before the war, but the treatment of homosexuals in this country was almost as much of an atrocity as this war.

She was right. It would be challenging to hide part of who I was, but it could also save our lives in a country that ignored gay bashing. Being out and proud like we were in our home countries was one thing. Here, it was too risky. We could be ourselves if we were alone or around people like Tatiana, but in public, it was dangerous. Could it be that the one homophobic doctor was an enigma? After all, most of Marie's colleagues and staff came from the more progressive countries.

"What I'm saying is that, as much as I would love to see where this might go, we will not be able to go out on an actual date," Marie said with a sigh. "We must stop flirting with one another in public, and I will stop teasing you."

My heart made its final drop to the bottom of the world and stayed there this time. We'd been acting like a couple of lovesick teenagers in a place where people like us were beaten and imprisoned for such actions. As sympathetic as we were to Ukraine for being the underdog in this fight, we could not lose sight that the nation's human rights still had a way to go.

I nodded and tried to hide my disappointment. I'd never been good at keeping my emotions off my face. It was a struggle now. She placed her hands on both sides of my face. I hoped she intended to kiss me, but I doubted it, considering our conversation.

"Don't look so glum, Press," she said. "We can remain friends." The hoped-for kiss ended up on my forehead. Something I would give someone I'd just pushed into the Friend Zone. The moment hung in the balance, lasting forever and over in an instant. Then, she stood and waved me toward the bathroom door.

Marie stopped briefly on her way out to say goodbye to Pasha and Tatiana. She promised Pasha she would see her at the clinic later. I watched her go, sliding into my regret. I wanted to kiss her again, but discretion was the new behavior. My eyes locked on the door long after it shut behind her.

Tatiana elbowed me. "The doctor is not going to be your girlfriend?"

"What? No! I mean…" I sputtered. The question startled me. I didn't know whether to deny everything or admit I felt rejected. Tatiana, my willing accomplice in pursuing the lovely doctor, deserved to know the truth. "No, she doesn't think this is the time or the place for romance. She reminded me there is a very different culture here," I said. "I'm hoping it is temporary insanity on her part."

"When you and the doctor are in the same room, your attraction is so thick, like a dense cloud surrounding everything," Tatiana said. "When you came out of the bathroom, you both had sad faces."

"War tends to exaggerate emotions," Pasha said. She gently smacked Tatiana across the head. "As I am constantly telling this one here, the danger, the uncertainty of it all. It makes people do crazy things. You all must be careful not to show your feelings. It is for the best."

That was what I was afraid of.

CHAPTER NINE

When I entered the kitchen the following morning, Tatiana and her mother were in a heated discussion. Even if I didn't understand the words, their tone and demeanor spoke volumes. "Is everything okay?" I asked.

"Yes," Pasha said. She didn't seem like the sort of person who wanted to air any family issues in public. As welcoming as she'd made me feel, I was still an outsider. Tatiana, on the other hand, had no such qualms.

"She thinks we are not being careful," Tatiana retorted. "She is afraid we are getting too close to the fighting."

Pasha looked at me, not unkindly. I gulped uncertainly. How could I tell a worried mother that I was taking her child, no matter if the child was technically an adult, into a war zone? If people were shooting at me, then surely, they were shooting at her daughter as well. Dammit! I wanted to try to console Pasha, but Tatiana had proved invaluable to me. I needed her.

"Not only did she save my life, but she has been an invaluable resource in my work. I wouldn't want any other fixer," I finally said. "She is way more careful than I am."

Pasha still didn't look convinced. She already had two sons fighting as soldiers, and her other daughter was living in an area where the fighting was intense. No wonder she wanted to keep Tatiana safe. I could only imagine that she felt she had no control. She couldn't keep her children safe. Even as someone who had no children, I could understand the fear and worry she was going through. With that thought in mind, I told her passionately how much I depended on her daughter, but I also promised to do everything I could to make sure Tatiana was not harmed.

"I suppose that will have to be good enough," Pasha sighed. "Her father says we must let them find their way. But it is hard." Pasha glanced fondly at her daughter and brushed a stray lock of hair off the girl's forehead.

"As long as you both promise me you will be more careful," Pasha conceded. Since I agreed, the matter seemed settled. Pasha quickly washed the breakfast dishes and left for the distribution center with Tatiana and me close behind.

Even before Pasha opened the door, a line was waiting to get in. With Tatiana translating, I spoke with the people waiting for supplies. We heard stories about devastation, hunger, and loss. We heard so many stories of lost loved ones. Sons, daughters, brothers, sisters, fathers, and cousins. Many grieved the loss of their homes. The local shelters were overcrowded, leaving a vast majority homeless and wandering.

As someone who grew up poor in rural Texas, I understood about waiting for the food to be distributed. How many times have I been forced to go to the food bank back home? I remembered standing there, hoping I didn't see anyone we knew, and that no parents of my classmates were volunteers. I remembered the shame and humiliation I felt holding an empty tote bag, praying when they called our number, all the good stuff wouldn't be gone.

I remembered what it was like pretending not to be at home when the bill collectors came to the door. If they caught us and we didn't have their money, we'd be out on the streets. Of course, that didn't compare with being bombed out of your home, but I still felt like I could relate, if only just a little bit.

Pasha went about her usual business of coordinating the distribution. When we finally took a break, she pulled me over and tilted her head at a beautiful young girl sitting alone on a pallet of grain sacks. Her clothes looked new and meant for a night out on the town rather than standing in line waiting for a food allotment. Despite the fancy clothes, her face looked tired, and defeat surrounded her like a well-worn coat.

"She is asking about a baby," Pasha said. "A boy about a month old. He is her nephew. Her sister's body was at the Radisson hotel where you are staying. The baby was nowhere to be found."

It had to be Max. What a lucky break for me. Although it would change my story about Americans who wanted to adopt war orphans, if it reunited Max with his family, that would be an even better scoop.

I caught Tatiana's attention and jerked my head in the direction of the girl. Tatiana walked over to me and spoke in a low voice. Since most of the people around us didn't speak English, I thought she was a bit dodgy about the whole thing.

"Are you sure you want to tell her where the baby is?" Tatiana asked.

"Why wouldn't I want to?" I was puzzled she would even ask.

"She was a *nobeio,* a prostitute," Tatiana whispered. "A baby would be better off finding new parents."

"How can you think that?" I demanded. "If she's asking about him, obviously she's worried. Isn't being wanted by someone better than being an orphan?"

"I wouldn't be so sure," Tatiana retorted. "Maybe she thinks she can get money for him."

I had to admit that was possible, but I refused to be that cynical. While I thought it over, I chewed on my bottom lip. It wouldn't hurt to talk to her. We didn't have to tell her where Max was. In all honesty, I hadn't gotten around to finding out where the misplaced children were being held yet.

Child custody laws here were different than they were in the States. Growing up in an overcrowded orphanage didn't seem like the lesser of two evils. At the very least, this girl could probably tell us where to find Max's father. Wouldn't it be up to the social workers to let this woman have him or not? Tatiana stood by stubbornly while I decided what to do. I'd discovered that even if my fixer didn't agree with me, she would abide by my decision. After all, I was the boss.

If I was being totally honest with myself, I wondered if the prostitution business was good during wars. When I insisted on at least speaking to the girl, Tatiana sighed and made her way over. After an animated conversation, they glanced in my direction, and Tatiana waved me over.

Her name was Lidiya Gribkora. She'd grown up in Kyiv. She swore she was nineteen years old. If she was even eighteen, I'd eat the candles on her last birthday cake.

"The baby's name is Akim," she said. "Akim Garifullin. His father is my employer." I wrote the name Akim in my notebook, but honestly, I still called him Max in my head.

"The authorities called me when they identified my sister, Okasana." Upon saying her sister's name, Lidiya's voice cracked, and she struggled with her tears. I put my pen aside and waited. I wanted to comfort her, but really, what could I say? Being sorry her sister was dead seemed woefully inadequate under the circumstances.

When Lidiya had herself under control, she continued. "When I arrived at the hotel, the staff swore they knew nothing of Akim. Finally, one of the nurses there told me the doctor had given the baby to an American journalist. The nurse did not know what happened to the baby after that."

Lidiya had spent the rest of yesterday and today searching for me because I was the only American journalist staying at the Kyiv hotel. No one seemed to want to talk to her. She was shunned by everyone she tried to question about the baby's whereabouts.

"How do you Americans say it?" she asked. "Oh yes, they look down their noses at me."

Finally, one of the staff attached to the press secretary's office had told her where he thought I might be today. Lidiya admitted she had to bribe him to give her the information.

"Bribe him? How much?" I asked. I was curious to know what information like that cost. Did she pay him in Ukrainian hryvnia, Russian rubles, or American dollars?

Tatiana's face turned bright red before she translated Lidiya's answer. "She paid him in sexual favors," she mumbled.

"Oh," I responded. My fixer didn't seem to want to elaborate, but I could imagine what those sexual favors entailed. A momentary flash of guilt struck me as I imagined this girl giving one of the press secretary's minions a blowjob in the hotel bathroom. My face turned hot as I tried to wipe that image out of my head.

"What about Akim's father?" I asked. I'd heard the name somewhere before. I searched my brain trying to remember where I'd heard it.

"He is my employer," Lidiya repeated. "My sister and I went to work for him last year. Our father owes him a debt. As a way for Papa to repay him, he offered Okasana and me jobs."

"He's a gangster," I blurted. That was where I'd heard his name. Makar Garifullin. He was the crook who had control over the local mercenaries. I looked at Tatiana for confirmation. She nodded. Lidiya's command of English was good enough for her to catch the phrase.

"Most people see him as a legitimate businessman," she said. Her tone suggested I'd offended her with my term. "He owns several restaurants and bars in Kyiv. We thought we were going to work for him there. Instead, he told us we would be working for his escort service."

I refrained from scoffing at the term escort service. A side question to Tatiana confirmed Lidiya said *suprovid*, the word for escorts, and not *nobeio*, the word for prostitute. I gave her a slight shrug. If Lidiya wanted to call herself an escort, who was I to argue? I didn't apologize for my use of the word gangster. Lidiya waited briefly, then continued with her story.

From the beginning, Garifullin had taken a liking to Okasana. At her insistence, Lidiya was offered a place on the escort team as well.

"It made me uncomfortable," she said. "All of these older men pawing at me, expecting favors. At first, I resisted, but Garifullin told me I had to play along or he would collect our father's debt."

She paused in her story while I contemplated what that collection would entail. Granted, my knowledge of mob bosses collecting debts came from movies like *The Godfather* and *Goodfellas*, but a single questioning glance at Lidiya told me that wasn't far from the truth.

"If we refused to work for him, Garifullin would send his soldiers, the Wolf Pack, to our home. They would beat my father and rape my mother," she said, confirming my suspicions. "If I continued to refuse, he would kill them both."

"Why are you telling me this?" I asked. Surely, she wasn't so naïve that she didn't know I wrote stories for the American press. Stories that would be made public.

"Maybe you can save Akim," she said. "Maybe you can save me and my parents."

A lone tear slid down Lidiya's cheek. She babbled about how the Americans came to Kyiv and the surrounding area. They tossed money around like they were all millionaires. In her mind, it was only fair that some of that money be thrown their way.

Was that how they saw us? As wealthy parasites, living off their misery? It made me ashamed. It also made me want to hand over all my available cash and tell her to get the hell out of Ukraine. When I questioned Tatiana about it in English, my fixer shrugged.

"She would probably end up giving the money to Garifullin anyway," Tatiana said.

"When Oksana told Garifullin she was pregnant, he was very happy," Lidiya continued. "His wife is barren. More than anything, he wanted an heir. When Akim was born, his wife punished Oksana. She beat her and made her stand outside in the snow with no shoes and hardly any clothes."

"She didn't hurt the baby?" I asked.

"No. Garifullin would never allow it. After Akim was born, he lost all interest in my sister," Lidiya said. "All he cared about was having a son and an heir."

"Typical," I muttered under my breath as I struggled to write all this down.

"Oksana knew she had to save Akim from these people," Lidiya continued. "She planned for them to flee. She did not tell me about the plan. I fear she didn't want to tell me she could not take me with her."

"Didn't that bother you?" I asked. She shrugged.

"Oksana knew her priority must be Akim," she said. "When they disappeared, Garifullin was furious. He raged on for days and beat me several times, demanding to know where she had gone." Her voice broke again as she described how she'd told him over and over that she did not know.

Garifullin enlisted the mercenary, Kostov, an expert in torture, to interrogate her and the other escorts, all to find out where his son was hiding. None of them knew, so none of them could tell him. Even Lidiya herself did not know.

"I found out today that Oksana and Akim had been at a refugee center for people who are waiting to escape to Poland," she said. "Many of those hiding there ran when the Russians attacked the facility. Oksana ran from the gunfire, holding Akim close to her body to protect him from the bullets. She was gunned down, leaving Akim lying in the street. They told me she was already dead when some stranger brought them to the hotel where the doctors were. Her body was taken away to be cremated."

At this point, Lidiya could no longer control her tears. Whether it was the loss of her sister or the fact that if she didn't find the kid and return him, her own life would be in danger, was unclear. I hated myself for being so cynical, but surely there was a reason her sister had not included Lidiya in her plans.

"Please, you must tell me where Akim is," she begged. "Markar will kill me if I return without him."

It was apparent her terror was absolute. She believed that Garifullin would kill her if she didn't return his son. I stopped writing and looked at Tatiana. She suggested we take a break and called one of Pasha's assistants to see if Lidiya needed anything. I followed Tatiana outside. We stood beside the Land Rover while she asked me what I wanted to do.

"You were right," I said. "I positively do not want to return that kid to his father. Is there any way we can get them both out of the country?"

Tatiana gave it some thought. "I could ask my father. He often talks about having Garifullin arrested as a war criminal."

"I don't see how that would help Lidiya and the baby," I said.

"It would keep him out of his father's grasp," she said. "But, you're right. It would not help the baby or her." She tossed her head in Lidiya's general direction.

Tatiana had eavesdropped on her father's conversation with some of his colleagues when they came to their house for dinner one night a few days ago. According to Dimitri, several members of the Wolf Pack had moved into barracks on Garifullin's estate just last week. Garifullin had several outbuildings he used as barracks for his staff and others as bedrooms for the girls who worked for him. The mercenaries had taken over some of the buildings, giving them quick access to Ukrainian citizens. The threat of the Wolf Pack being at a mobster's disposal was more concerning than the mobster himself.

Dimitri was outraged that Garifullin armed the mercenaries, knowing that each time they went out to patrol, they used those weapons against Ukrainian citizens. In Dimitri's eyes, the man was not only a traitor to his country but a war profiteer as well. The villain charged outrageous sums for other goods and services. A few days ago, Dimitri said he heard Garifullin sold a pleading woman a partial toilet paper roll for 184.00 hryvnias. That seemed like a lot to me. I asked Tatiana for clarification.

"Five US dollars," she said.

That was outrageous. As my anger against this man increased, I felt a sudden yearning to take him down. Hatred for him and people like him flooded me. People were starving and living in what was left of their homes, cooking over campfires. Knowing that every war had its profiteers didn't make the actions of a notorious gangster acceptable. Things like drugs, alcohol, and women flowed like water at Garifullin's establishments during peace. To force people to pay outrageous sums for the necessities they couldn't get elsewhere during wartime made his actions even more deplorable. The federal police were too busy trying to keep the city from falling around their ears to do anything about it. The ones that didn't accept Garifullin's bribes, that is.

"We can't let that man get his hands on Max," I said finally, making my decision. Calling him Akim would take some getting used to. Of course, if his father was that well off, the kid would want for nothing. Nothing but love, I thought.

"What can we do?" Tatiana asked. "The law is clear. If Garifullin is the boy's father, he has a right to claim him."

"Can we get him and Lidiya out of the country?'

"It would be difficult and costly. Poland is already bursting at the seams with refugees."

We decided to take Lidiya somewhere away from her employer's spying eyes while we sought information on how to get them somewhere safe. Tatiana would ask Dimitri, and I would see if Pamela could pull some strings.

Why did this story seem so personal to me? Why didn't I feel the same burning desire to get the other people I'd interviewed out of the country? Maybe I couldn't save everyone in the whole damn country, but if it was possible to save this one child, I wanted to try. Was it because in the short time I'd been entrusted with his care, I'd developed an affection for the boy? Maybe, just maybe, it was because the other people I'd seen and spoken to since I'd arrived here in Ukraine didn't have a choice. They showed resolve and the courage to pull themselves out of the ashes. Akim didn't have that luxury. Neither, it appeared, did Lidiya.

We went back inside, where Tatiana pulled her mother aside and explained the situation. A string of Ukrainian curses poured out of Pasha's mouth. Even without speaking the language, I understood what she was saying. There was no way in hell she would allow her daughter to get mixed up in a plot to double-cross the Ukrainian mafia.

"We'll take her back to the hotel," I said. "She can stay in my room."

Lidiya protested. Garifullin would find her, she said. He had spies everywhere. He would find her, and he would kill her and everyone around her. Of course, she was right. The first place he would look would be an American reporter's hotel room. She begged me to please take her to the baby. The irony was, I wasn't sure of the exact location of the orphanage. That was something we had scheduled for another day. I told her as much.

"We must find him," Lidiya cried. "I must take him back to his father." The despair in her voice hit me hard. She was begging for her life. I didn't think she understood I was trying to help her.

"Where can we take her?" I asked.

Pasha thought it over. "There are several refugee camps on the outskirts of the city," she said. "We can take her to one of those. If we move her every few days, it will be harder for Garifullin and his mercenaries to find her."

That might be our best option. If Garifullin and his men searched one refugee camp, we could move Lidiya to the camp they'd already searched. The best place to hide someone was where their hunters already looked.

Lidiya didn't interrupt again while we discussed her fate. The look of fear didn't disappear from her face, either. I had the feeling that she was listening to what we were saying, but when the time came, she would make up her own mind.

"Give me your phone," Pasha ordered Lidiya. She held out her hand and firmly insisted. When Lidiya asked why, Pasha told her. "So your employer cannot track you. This is the last known location."

Reluctantly, the girl pulled a slim, older-model phone from inside her dress and handed it over. Pasha turned it off and tossed it into a bin behind her. It was good thinking on her part, but since at least a couple hundred people were present, it wouldn't take long for Garifullin to figure out we had taken Lidiya. I hoped we had enough of a head start to get Akim out of the country before his crook of a father could get his hands on him.

My satellite phone chirped loudly in the brief silence, causing me to just about jump out of my skin. I looked at the caller ID and saw Pamela's number. If my math was correct, it was about four in the afternoon in Austin. I stepped outside the big double doors to the warehouse to take the call.

Pamela didn't hesitate to get right to the point. "Dammit. Sheppard, I just got off the phone with the hotel management. They said a small group of Russian mercenaries burst into the hotel and trashed the place looking for you. The manager said they searched your room and roughed him up, trying to get information out of him."

A jolt of panic rushed through me. "Was he hurt?" I asked.

"Nothing serious," Pamela told me. "But it is going to cost us a lot of money to keep a roof over your head. The Titan CFO is all up my ass about expenses. And why the hell do you have Russian mercenaries, who have a very nasty reputation, looking for you?"

Garifullin must have sent them. It sounded to me like the mobster didn't trust Lidiya to get the kid, and Garifullin had sent them in as backup. The point was, they had homed in on me as their lead to Akim. It seemed unlikely they would just give up and go home if they didn't find me at the hotel. I explained the situation to Pamela, reminding her I'd done one story on Akim already. I tried to make it sound like my recent activities were a part of that story.

Pamela wasn't buying it. Kids in Ukraine were disappearing in droves every day, she told me. The government had cracked down on foreigners adopting Ukrainian children. Especially children who still had parents alive. Even if the said parent was a notorious gangster.

It seemed no one would let us save even one tiny baby boy. It was crazy. Pamela told me I could write the story and not be a part of it. Part of me knew the story wasn't all Pamela cared about. Another part of me knew that she had to care about the story, or she'd never be able to justify my being here. I felt panic flow from the bottom of my gut right up into my brain. Pamela could pull me out of here in a heartbeat if she thought I'd lost my focus. Two phone calls in a single day meant it might be more trouble than it was worth to keep me here. Between crushing on Marie and interfering with a parent's right to his child, I knew I was on thin ice.

Hopefully, Pamela trusted me enough to give me enough string to fly this kite. If she couldn't make things right with the hotel, I'd have to find somewhere else to stay. If that happened, she might just yank me back home. Sheesh! Anyone would think I was an aging rock star who'd gotten drunk or high and trashed my room. Belatedly, I told her that I was staying at Tatiana's for a few days while I healed from the gunshot wound. Maybe that would take some of the heat off my employer.

She acknowledged my absence from the room my employers were paying a small fortune to keep open for me. She also laid down the rules. Either I stayed at the hotel to justify the expense, or I checked out and saved Titan from having to pay the hotel's jacked-up, albeit legitimate, charges. My second order was that I report back to her every day whether I was sleeping at the hotel or not. This was a direct order. Going rogue was not an option.

"I swear to God, Sheppard, if the mafia puts a hit out on you, I will kill you myself," Pamela said and slammed the phone down, cutting me off again.

I went back inside to ask Lidiya about her passport. I suspected that if Garifullin was smart, he wouldn't allow her to have it. With the number of refugees leaving the country, it shouldn't have been impossible to get one woman and one baby out. Hell! At this point, I was willing to cough up the money for a fake passport for Lidiya. I'd heard that was another booming business in Kyiv.

"Where's Lidiya?" I asked Pasha and Tatiana when I got back inside.

"She said she was going to the restroom," Pasha said. "Come to think of it, she has been gone awhile."

153

I ran to the corridor where the bathroom was located. The building was an old, abandoned warehouse with one large room where the supplies were stored. There was a large overhead door leading to the outside. That was where I'd been standing while I'd spoken to Pamela. Off to the side of the large room was a hallway leading to several smaller rooms. These were offices, a small breakroom, and restrooms. There was an exit door at the end of the hallway leading in the opposite direction of the storeroom where Pasha and Tatiana were waiting. The hallway and adjoining offices were all empty.

I checked the ladies' room first, startling a young woman holding a toddler up to the sink to wash her hands. I asked her if she'd seen anyone else in the restroom. She shook her head and said something in Ukrainian. I got the gist of it. No one had been in there except her and her child.

I checked the men's room next. Since most of the people here at the distribution center were women, sometimes the line for the bathroom could get long. Some women weren't above using the men's room in an emergency. Unfortunately, Lidiya was not there either.

"She's not there," I said, coming back to the storeroom. "She probably left by the front door." I pounded the wall in frustration.

Tatiana looked horrified at my outburst. "I'm sorry, boss. I should have gone with her."

Ashamed of myself, I apologized to my fixer. "It's not your fault, kiddo. I underestimated how scared she was."

If she was that scared, where would she go? If she went back to Garifullin without Akim, even if he didn't kill her, he would punish her. Lidiya had said as much. What if he killed her parents instead? This was a nightmare. I had taken care of a baby at the request of a pretty girl, and now the whole thing had turned into this shitshow.

"Okay, so what's our next move?" I said, talking to myself.

I wasn't certain I wanted to get Tatiana and her family involved in this caper. Hell, if I had any sense, I wouldn't have been involved in it myself. Undoubtedly, my best option was to give Lidiya directions to the orphanage where we'd stashed Akim and let his thug of a father have him. My conscience would not let me do that, however. I'd seen what growing up with a lack of love could do to kids.

Pasha stood watching me, her expression unreadable. Dammit! If I was going to do this, I'd need her help, and I didn't even know if it was the right thing to do or not. I needed some sound advice bordering on motherly. In a few days, I'd developed a deep respect for this woman and her family. I couldn't go off half-cocked and bring the mob down on their heads.

I pulled Tatiana over to her mother's side and asked Pasha, "Is it worth it for us to find the kid, hide him somewhere until we can get him out of the country? Lidiya, too, if we can find her?" I asked. Pasha looked at me with her startling blue eyes. She must have been something of a beauty back in her youth. I stammered out what I thought was an explanation: "I don't want to be that 'American Journalist' who comes over here and tries to tell people how to live. But Pasha, if you could have seen that kid…"

I trailed off uncertainly. This was a compassionate woman I was appealing to. If she told me to forget the whole thing, I knew it would not be because she didn't care. Her very presence here in the clinic and distribution center told me she cared. Very much so.

"You are very passionate, Nicole," she said, offering me a slight smile. "It is hard to see the children suffer. Especially during war, when everything happening to them is an atrocity."

She sat down on a pile of sixty-pound bags of potatoes piled haphazardly on a pallet. The weight of her compassion seemed to drag her down. Tatiana sat next to her. Pasha reached over and patted her hand. "Because of my position at the university, and of course, Dimitri's position as a city leader, we are what could be considered the upper-class society of Kyiv," she said.

"When we are not at war, my colleagues, friends, and I play tennis. We meet once a week to play cards. We have lunch at nice restaurants. We volunteer at libraries and food kitchens. When the Russians invaded, the university shut down so the students could go to war with all the passion of the young, and some of my friends and colleagues left the city. Some even left the country. They went as far away as they could from the fighting. I stay here to help the ones who are displaced. Why do I do it? Because *dammit*! We live here! If we can save only one child, I say yes."

It was quite a stirring speech. Inwardly I cheered her on. Pasha pulled out a notepad and wrote down the directions to the three local shelters that she knew of where displaced children were taken. If we found Akim, we could bring him to her house after dark. By the time we got there, she and Dimitri would see if they could find a place to stash him until we could get him, and possibly Lidiya, out of the country.

Dimitri, on the other hand, had a different point of view. Pasha had called him while I was being read the riot act by my editor. He called Tatiana and implored her to talk some sense into me. He told us to leave this alone for our safety. I understood that. He was a father who loved his wife and daughter and did not want to see them involved. I had to wonder again if I was doing the wrong thing by asking them for their help.

When Tatiana told Dimitri I was determined and that Pasha had a different perspective than her husband, he resigned himself to do what he could to help. He would try to use his connections to get them to Poland, but he wasn't hopeful. There were too many people trying to get out of the country already. He advised Tatiana to warn me not to get my hopes up.

This whole discussion might have been a moot point now that Lidiya had disappeared. With or without her, I was determined to get Akim away from his father and into the safe, loving arms of some childless couple. Hopefully, my hubris wouldn't come back to haunt me.

CHAPTER TEN

Tatiana and I spent the next few hours circling the neighborhood around the distribution center, hoping we would spot Lidiya and convince her to come with us. When it became obvious we weren't going to find her, we returned to the center. Curfew was fast approaching. We would go back to the house, and when Dimitri came home, we could discuss some options. It was the most sensible plan so far. I was already in enough hot water with the Ukrainian government for allowing the Wolf Pack to trash my hotel room. Another black mark for violating curfew wouldn't look good.

Pasha shooed the few remaining stragglers out of the distribution center. Tatiana and I helped load her car with items Pasha had deemed too important to leave unguarded overnight. This included the antiquated computer she used to keep track of everything, boxes of paper records for when the computer failed, and a few of the more precious items, such as toilet paper, baby formula, and diapers.

The distribution center had been subjected to several break-ins during the past few weeks. Since security everywhere in the city was stretched so thin, Pasha and her assistants tried to be proactive about keeping what they could manage safe and intact. What did it matter if someone broke in and stole a few pounds of potatoes and flour? But having someone break in and steal all the baby formula to sell on the black market could be disastrous for some young mothers.

After loading what we could in the back of Pasha's car and the Land Rover, my arm ached where the bullet had hit me. A couple of spots of blood dotted the bandage Marie had put on…was it just this morning? It seemed like it was a lifetime ago. I hoped I hadn't reopened the wound.

Later, when Dimitri joined us in the kitchen for supper, his news was not hopeful. Without the proper paperwork, filed with the correct office—and reviewed by three other offices—the only way we would get a baby out of the country would be if we kidnapped him. I wasn't quite ready to go that far yet, but I mentally filed it away as a Plan B.

We were finishing supper when we heard a car pull up outside. It was unusual because it was way past curfew, and there was little or no street traffic. A car door slammed, and then there was the sound of the car driving away. Although Tatiana and her parents lived in a suburb of Kyiv, they were on the western side of the city, as far away from the invading Russians as possible. Nighttime visitors were rare these days, even in this semi-safe environment. The bombing and fighting had been minimal in this area. I wondered how long that could last. A knock on the door after curfew could only be bad news.

Dimitri picked up the golf club leaning next to the door. There was a timid knock. Maybe I was stereotyping the mercenaries, but I didn't think a golf club would slow them down, and I didn't think their knock would be timid. Dimitri peeked out the window. He didn't turn on the outside lights. That could attract a lot of unwanted attention.

"Who's there?" he called in Ukrainian.

"It's me, Doctor Marie Dubois."

Dimitri dropped the golf club, unlocked the door, and pulled Marie inside. He quickly shut the door behind her. Pasha went to the two of them and wrapped a friendly arm around Marie's shoulder. At the sight of her, I could feel the heat rising throughout my entire body. Even with her hair pulled back in a sloppy ponytail and her scrubs wrinkled and dirty, she was still beautiful. She had her doctor's bag in one hand and my large duffel bag in the other.

"Come, Doctor," Pasha said. "Have some tea and a bite to eat. Tell us, what brings you out so late?"

Marie thanked her and allowed herself to be led to the kitchen. I'd been sitting there, patiently, waiting for Marie to notice me. She was here for me, my heart cried joyfully while my brain told me to stop being ridiculous. Maybe she was there to see Dimitri or Pasha.

Shut up, my heart replied. She was there because she hadn't seen me for a couple of days, and she needed to make sure I was okay. She cared.

She cares about doing her job, my head muttered.

Pasha turned on the burner under the teapot. She pulled the slices of meat and cheese that she'd only just put away out of the refrigerator. She arranged everything nicely on a serving platter and set another plate in front of Marie.

"I heard about soldiers coming to the hotel," Marie said. "The staff told me they were looking for a baby." Her curious gaze fell on me.

As briefly as I could, I stammered out an explanation. Marie's frown deepened.

"That is unfortunate," she said. "The group that took the baby from the hotel moved when the fighting came too close. They could be anywhere by now. Our normal channels of communication have been cut off."

That meant she didn't know exactly where Akim was either. It seemed crazy that a whole organization could just up and disappear like that, but I'd come to realize that during times of war, people got lost. Things went missing. It was not unheard of.

While Marie ate, we discussed options. Dimitri and Pasha agreed that until the organization could be located, our time would be better spent assuring that Akim and his aunt had a way out of the country when we did find them. Of course, that also meant finding her. I had a feeling finding her would be a lot more difficult.

"I also need to check on Nicole's wound," Marie said.

My face turned bright red at the suggestion while my heart did a double backflip. She had risked violating curfew just to see me.

"Of course," Pasha said dryly. "I'm sure Nicole will live another few minutes while you rest and have something to eat."

After Marie sipped some tea and ate a couple of bites, she looked at me. "I went back to the hotel to pick up a few things for you," she said. "The manager asked me if I'd seen you today. When I told him no, he said he had to find you. He seemed particularly anxious."

"Did he happen to say why he needed to find me?" I asked.

"Not exactly, but I'm sure it had something to do with the place swarming with soldiers," she said. "And I am afraid."

"Ukrainian soldiers," Dimitri asked, "or Russians?"

"When I got there, they were Ukrainians, but I got the distinct impression that the Russian mercenaries had just left and tried their best to destroy the place." She looked at me with some concern. "I'm afraid your room was trashed."

I tried to shrug off my concern. I had brought my most important possessions with me yesterday when Tatiana invited me to come home with her. Most of my clothes, my electronics, and my protective gear were all stashed away in her bedroom. For that much, I was grateful.

Another area of concern, however, was what if everyone in the city knew I'd talked to Lidiya and that I might know where Akim was? Had Lidiya gone back to the hotel looking for me? Was that why my whereabouts were such a hot ticket item? I mumbled something about explaining it later.

A new fear popped up inside me. It wouldn't take long for the mercenaries and whoever else was looking for me to trace my whereabouts here. Once again, I had put my fixer and her family in danger. Tatiana was registered with the press secretary's office. Somehow, I doubted even the ice maiden, Tupoleva, would give Ukrainian citizens up to Russian mercenaries. On the other hand, if one of her aides could be persuaded to reveal my location for a few minutes of pleasure then it wouldn't be a stretch to believe they would sell Tatiana and her whole family out.

"It is too late to do anything about it tonight," Dimitri said. "Doctor, you will have to spend the night." A look passed between him and his wife.

Pasha gave a curt nod. "You cannot go back out tonight," she agreed.

"I don't want to be a bother." Dimitri and Pasha brushed away her protests. Marie sighed and looked at me. "Let's take a look at that wound."

"I'll get you something to sleep in, Doctor," Pasha said. "I'm afraid you'll have to share a room with Tatiana and Nicole. We've been using the other bedrooms to store the overflow from the distribution center."

Surely, Marie could see my stomach doing somersaults at the thought of being that close to her all night. I should have probably offered to bunk with Tatiana since there were only two beds in the room. I should have offered, but I didn't want to. It wasn't necessarily that I wanted to have sex. I wanted to know what holding her in my arms felt like. I wanted to breathe in her scent and hear the rhythm of her breath while she slept. The desire to just touch Marie was so overwhelming that I had to force my one good arm down to my side. The muscles in the other arm tightened against the sling, causing a sharp pain to shoot through the wound.

Pasha headed down the hallway. Tatiana gestured for us to follow, and she led us to her bedroom. Before her sister had married and moved away, they'd shared this room. Posters of pop singers I'd never heard of graced one side of the room, while the side Tatiana claimed as hers was decorated more with motivational posters. The kind someone might have seen in corporate break rooms. Her bed was also covered with an entire circus of stuffed animals. It gave me a pretty good idea of my young fixer's seemingly double persona.

"The doctor better sleep with you," Tatiana said loudly. A wicked grin plastered across her face. "I'm a light sleeper, and I toss and turn all night."

I smacked her on the arm. She rubbed the spot, and if anything, her grin widened. Pasha brought in a small bundle of clothes and some toiletries. "It's a slumber party now," Tatiana said, still grinning.

"Yes, but don't keep the doctor and Nicole up all night with your talking. You all have work to do tomorrow." Pasha said good night and smiled indulgently.

Marie gave me one of those bright sunshine smiles when Pasha moved aside to let her into the room. Marie dumped her things on the bed that held my iPad and some of my clothes. She rescued a new toothbrush from the pile of clothes Pasha had given her. Then, she took the pajamas and headed toward the bathroom.

"I want to check that arm before we go to bed," she said, looking back at me before she left. I stripped to my boxers and T-shirt as quickly as I could and sat on the bed, waiting for her. Tatiana had changed into a long T-shirt that reached her knees and did a crowd-surfing move on top of the stuffed animals covering her bed.

"You look like you're waiting for the headmistress to come back and punish you for doing something bad, boss," she teased.

I'd never been so conscious of my entire body as I was at that exact moment. I sat, and it felt awkward. I stood, and it looked like it was posed. I lay down and imagined that instead of looking seductive, I looked like I was at my funeral. Having Tatiana snickering on the other side of the room didn't help. Marie let herself back in. She had folded her scrubs and laid them carefully on top of the dresser in the middle of the room. She retrieved some supplies from the medical bag she always carried and came over to the bed.

She shoved my legs apart with her knee and stepped between them. Carefully, she pulled my injured arm from the sling. Her arm accidentally slid across my breast, causing a sharp intake of breath on my part.

"Did that hurt?" she asked. A worried frown creased her forehead.

"No, it's just a little tender, that's all," I stammered, hoping to cover up why she'd taken my breath away.

She unwrapped the bandage she'd put over the wound a couple of days ago. "It's not infected, so that's good. It looks like you aggravated it, though."

"Maybe I overdid it a little bit today," I mumbled.

"I'm going to clean it and rebandage it," she said. "If you can resist using the arm for a few more days, you can lose the sling." I didn't tell her I had ditched the sling about five minutes after she'd given it to me. I only retrieved it this evening when the wound started to ache. She stared intently into my eyes as if waiting for me to say something. When I didn't, she turned away, packing her supplies back up and wiping her hands with an antiseptic cloth.

"Do you prefer sleeping on the inside or the outside?" she asked.

"Um." I didn't seem to have a vocabulary.

With an impatient huff, she crawled around me, pushed her legs under the covers, and wiggled in. I tried to follow suit without kicking or hitting her or even touching her in any way. If any part of my body happened to touch any part of hers, I was a goner. I lay rigidly under the covers with my back turned to her. My arm wasn't the only part of my body that seemed tender.

"Relax, Press," she said and wrapped her arms around me. Her breath tickled my neck, and I shivered. I couldn't get the thought of her kissing the back of my neck out of my mind. When it didn't happen, I chided myself for being ridiculous. We were grown-ups. No way would we be groping one another in the dark, in a strange teenager's bedroom as if we were a couple of teenagers ourselves.

"Americans are so uptight about sharing sleeping arrangements," Marie said sleepily.

I was sure I wouldn't get a wink of sleep that night. Marie's proximity seemed both exhilarating and terrifying. When her breathing evened out a few minutes later and she seemed to be asleep, I forced my body to relax, and it wasn't long before I dropped off myself.

It was way too early when I felt Marie struggle out of my arms and crawl out of bed. Sometime during the night, I had turned toward her and embraced her. If it had been up to me, we would have stayed there, wrapped up in one another, even for just a little while longer. If we had been somewhere else, we could have planned on spending the day together. As it was, we both had other things besides one another making demands on our time.

Marie dressed quickly and quietly. When she'd gathered her things, she leaned over and gave me a quick kiss on the lips. It set my whole body on fire and was over much too quickly. For someone who said we couldn't pursue a romantic relationship, she certainly was making it difficult to resist.

"I'm going to ask Dimitri to give me a ride into the city," she said. "I will be at the distribution center later holding a clinic. Will I see you there?"

I nodded, not trusting myself to speak. With a curt nod, she slipped out the door. There was no chance of me going back to sleep, so I crawled out of bed and dressed quietly. Dimitri had already left, taking Marie with him. Pasha sat at the kitchen table going over some spreadsheets. She started to get up when I entered the room, but I motioned her to sit back down. Ukrainians had different views about hospitality, but it made me feel uncomfortable to have someone wait on me. I was perfectly capable of pouring myself a cup of coffee. When I had my cup, I sat across from her.

"The doctor gave me the last known contact information of the people who took Akim," Pasha said. "With so many people moving in and out of the city, it is difficult to keep track of them all." She shoved a sheet of paper across the table at me. It was written in English and had the name, phone number, and address of a local refugee camp that took in infants. It was useless information now that they'd moved on, but it could work as a diversion if we had to give up some information. Hopefully, Garifullin's information wouldn't be any better than ours when it came to tracking down refugee camps.

If we couldn't find Lidiya, and if we had no way of getting Akim out of the country, I wasn't sure what good this information would be to me. I looked at Pasha, hoping she could tell me what to do. She shook her head slightly as if she'd heard my thoughts.

"Probably, it would be best if you waited to see if anything happens," she finally said.

Before I could ask her to elaborate, Tatiana joined us. When she asked what our plan for the day was, I was lost. Finally, I took the paper and shoved it into the pocket of my jeans.

"Since we're already on the press secretary's shit list, we should probably go back to work as if nothing happened," I said. It didn't feel right to say it, but what else could I do? I couldn't go get Akim and carry him around with me while I worked. He was better off staying where he was until we could either find some way of getting him out of the country, or until his father found him. If that happened, the whole situation would be out of my hands.

"That's probably best," Tatiana said, nodding.

Tatiana and I left for the hotel to check in with the press secretary's office. Her aide told us she wanted me to meet with a local group doing their part in the war by making uniforms for women. The press secretary had told her aide to tell me it was something she wanted me to cover. To get on her good side, the best thing we could do was to carry on with our assignment.

Though there was not a precise number of women in the Ukrainian military, an estimated 32,000 had signed up by March of 2022. The majority were assigned men's uniforms. Often, the uniforms were too big. The boots didn't fit, causing painful blisters. The flak jackets, even when tightened to the maximum, were loose-fitting on most females. In some cases, the loose fit negated the protection the jackets were designed to give.

It was an excellent story for my "Women in War" series. As a bonus, Madame Secretary Tupoleva approved the content. Pamela had agreed when I submitted the idea to her at our weekly planning call a few days ago. Titan's target audience was primarily women between nineteen and fifty-five. They loved female success stories.

When we arrived at the warehouse, recently converted to a tailor's shop, I took dozens of photos, knowing Titan would only use one, but I couldn't help it. The female soldiers fawned over the boots and clothes like they were at a Paris fashion show. When I commented on that, they took it as their cue to model their new gear and equipment for me. They walked in front of my camera individually, stood still for a pose, twirled, and walked away. It was the most fun I'd had in a long time. Even if Titan didn't use these pictures, I could sell them as a package on the open market. Titan didn't own the rights to my photos, only to those they used.

One of the soldiers who came in while we were waiting was three months pregnant. I spent a long time with her, with Tatiana translating. Yes, she was concerned about being pregnant, but she was more concerned about what kind of world her baby would grow up in if Russia succeeded in winning this war. She was sure that there were other pregnant soldiers. Knowing that she would finally get a uniform that fit was a relief. It's hard to concentrate on fighting when your boots don't fit.

Once I'd finished with the photos and made sure I had everything spelled correctly, it took us a while to extract ourselves from the group. Each woman wanted a copy of her photo to send to friends and family, and of course, to post on her social media pages. Tatiana made herself indispensable by writing down everyone's email addresses and promising them we'd get the pictures out to them in due course. When we finally got to leave, it was already past noon.

We decided to head to the distribution center to see if Lidiya had resurfaced or if anything else had transpired in our absence. The thought of seeing Marie caused my stomach to do little somersaults. I didn't know where we were heading. It seemed like I was getting mixed signals from her. On one hand, she kept telling me we couldn't, but when her lips touched mine, I couldn't care less about where we were and who we offended. It was like I was on an inner city bus and couldn't pull the cord to request a stop.

CHAPTER ELEVEN

When we pulled up outside the distribution center, the place was already packed. Although there weren't many cars in the dirt parking lot outside, I could see two separate lines of people queuing up just outside the double doors.

One line was for the clinic Marie and her team had set up for the day. From what injuries I could see, they ranged from a woman holding a bloody rag against a small boy's forehead to an old man leaning heavily on a cane and coughing loudly into a handkerchief held up to his mouth. I remember Marie telling me that when they held community clinics, most of the ailments they saw were not associated with some type of war trauma.

We found Marie inside, patching up a young woman with a nasty-looking gash trailing down her upper arm, ending almost to her elbow. While Marie stitched, a nurse held a tray of instruments within reach. I knew better than to

171

bother her while she concentrated on her patient. Her eyes briefly met mine when I entered, then she turned her attention back to the young woman.

We found Pasha standing beside a table where the second line of people had formed. They were there for supplies to get them through another few days. The air practically fogged up with their despair and helplessness. As each one stepped to the front of the line, for a few seconds, they looked hopeful that somehow they would be able to get what they needed to get on with their lives. When that failed, they took what meager supplies Pasha's group could offer them and left with their shoulders slumped and any hope they might have had left behind.

Marie finally finished up with the young woman. As I moved closer, I heard her telling the woman to take care to keep the wound clean and to come back and see her in a few days. She smiled at me, but that was all I got. She signaled for the next patient in line. When she said she'd see me at the distribution center, I didn't realize that she meant exactly that and nothing more. She saw me.

Lidiya had not made an appearance, Pasha told us. Neither she nor any of her volunteer staff had seen or heard anything different from the regular line of citizens hoping to get enough food to keep starvation at bay. Some part of me was secretly glad that Lidiya had not returned to beg for us to give up her nephew.

Since we had no other pressing stories to pursue and the distribution center seemed to have a good internet connection for the moment, I decided to go ahead and write up my story on the female uniforms. Directing me to one of the vacant offices, Pasha told me to feel free to use it. She could use

Tatiana's help since one of her volunteers was a no-show this morning.

The look on Tatiana's face told me exactly how she felt about helping her mom pass out soap and cans of beans. She wanted to be out there dodging bullets and chasing down exciting stories about heroes and evil Russians. If I hadn't known exactly how she felt, I would have laughed at her expression of mortification.

Since my uniform story practically wrote itself, it didn't take me long to type up the words. Choosing what photo to include with it was a lot harder. They were some of the best pictures I'd taken so far. I could send the whole batch to Pamela and let her decide. Doing so would take forever with the slow internet connection in this part of Kyiv. The photo I finally decided to use was of the pregnant soldier. With her hands resting gently on top of her bulging waistline, she looked down lovingly while at her feet, the tailor worked on adjusting the hem of her pants. The contrast between the uniform made for war and the young mother-to-be's pregnancy seemed a perfect representation of good and evil.

I'd just wrapped up the story, attached the photo, and sent it off to Pamela when Marie stepped into the room. I stood to greet her but found myself pushed up against the wall with her mouth clamped over mine in an almost desperate kiss. It was everything I could do not to allow my hands and lips to caress every part of her body I could reach. When we finally broke apart, she shoved herself away.

"What brought this on?" I asked her, not surprised to find my voice was a little bit shaky.

"I've been thinking about you all day," she said. It pleased me to note that her voice was not too steady either.

"When you walked through that door, I was so pleased and relieved to see you. Then I thought, what if something had happened to you?"

She let out a long sigh and sat in the chair I had vacated what seemed like only a few seconds before. I started to reach for her but thought better of it. It almost seemed like she was close to tears.

"Every day, I must push thoughts of you out of my head so I can concentrate on my patients. Every night, as I lie down to sleep, I replay every second of when I saw you during the day. I see your smile. I hear your voice. My heart beats a little faster. My head tells me to leave you alone. My heart demands I take you in my arms and kiss you until you are dizzy. I do not worry about the danger for myself. I fear for you. What am I to do the next time Tatiana drags you in covered in blood? Or even worse, she tells me you are dead?"

She stood and walked in small circles, waving her hands. I loved the way she always talked with her hands. The declaration that she thought about me as much as I thought about her floored me. Both of us were afraid to admit we had feelings for one another. We were only here together for a short time. We lived on different sides of the planet, for God's sake! There was no way we could have any kind of lasting relationship. Neither one of us was the type to engage in a situational fling. Unfortunately, we also couldn't keep our hands off one another.

For a few seconds, everything else faded into background noise. What if we did throw caution to the wind and just got as wrapped up in one another as we could despite our circumstances? We were both adults. Surely, we could have a no-strings romance. Even as I considered it, I felt the horrible truth gnawing away at my resolve. No. We probably couldn't because that wasn't who we were. I'd never been any good as a fuck buddy.

Just as I was about to tell her I felt the same, commotion in the warehouse caught our attention. Were those gunshots? We spared a fleeting glance at one another and rushed back into the main room. The door to the center burst open, and six heavily armed men crashed through. They wore the uniforms of the mercenaries, the Wolf Pack: the snarling wolf with the blood dripping from its fangs. They were unmistakable. One carried a bundle over his shoulder. A body-shaped bundle.

The mercenary who had a few different patches and insignia on his uniform, marking him as their leader, had his pistol pointed up in the air. The noise that had prompted Marie and I to rush back into the warehouse had come from the two shots he fired into the ceiling to get everyone's attention. He was a tall man, well over six feet. He had black hair and a bushy mustache. When he removed the aviator glasses covering his eyes, I saw nothing but calculating coldness. The sight of him turned my whole body to ice with fear.

"I am Colonel Yuri Kostov of the Russian Army," he said, first in Ukrainian, then in English. "Do as I say, and we will spare your lives."

After a nod and a wave from Kostov, the soldier with the body over his shoulder dumped it unceremoniously in the middle of the room. He bent and tore off the bag covering the body's head. Bile rose in my throat, and I had to swallow it to keep from vomiting. My heart plummeted to the floor.

Fear, despair, and guilt all dumped a shitload of emotions on me all at once, and Marie had to grab me to keep me from fainting. It was Lidiya.

There were about fifty to sixty people left in the warehouse. Since Pasha oversaw the distribution center, she told everyone to do as Kostov said and not to resist. Her face remained unreadable, and she gave no sign of recognizing the poor dead girl they'd dumped at her feet. Acknowledging Pasha's authority, Kostov walked to her and demanded to see her identification. She handed it to him.

Standing closer to her mother than me, Tatiana took two tentative steps in my direction. Her expression was a combination of fear and horror. I silently willed her to be still and not give Kostov or his men any reason to single her out. Pasha dared to take her eyes off the mercenary long enough to catch her daughter's attention and shake her head slightly. Tatiana stopped mid-step. When Kostov looked up, Pasha's eyes were steadily focused on him again. Tatiana stilled her steps but could not hide the fear in her eyes.

"I am looking for the American journalist and the French doctor," Kostov said loud enough for everyone in the warehouse to hear.

All eyes in the warehouse, including those of Kostov and his unit, turned in my direction. Fear shot through me again. He was looking for me. Since the word PRESS stood out like a neon sign in two-inch red letters over my flak jacket and helmet, it was apparent I was an American journalist. The person I had my arms around, who was wearing scrubs and a white lab coat that announced Doctors Without Borders, could only be the French doctor. Kostov's look practically pinned us to the wall.

I tightened my grip on Marie, thinking she would try to run to her staff and patients, and Kostov would order her shot. I was in flight mode, and she was in fight mode. I could feel her trembling, or maybe it was both of us. But we stood our ground. There wasn't anywhere we could run or hide. I planted my feet and looked Kostov directly in the eye. My fear screamed at me to be reasonable and beg for mercy. I told it to shut up and tried to pretend it didn't exist.

He took his time looking us over, surely not missing any detail. A fake smile touched his lips but never reached his eyes. He walked over to where we stood and stopped. The man towered over me, so he had to bend to be able to look directly into my eyes.

"You," he said softly. "You are the American journalist?" He spoke in Russian. When I didn't respond, he asked again in English.

Yes," I answered. "I am an American journalist. What do you want of me?"

"You are the one who told this unfortunate young woman you did not know where her nephew is being held?"

"I didn't know where he was being held," I said, then realized my error. I said I didn't know where he was being held, which could mean that I now did know where Akim was. Silently, I prayed Kostov wouldn't notice.

"And do you know where he is now?" He stepped so close, I could smell the onions he'd had for lunch on his breath.

"No," I said firmly. My fear screamed out again, and I'm sure he heard it. He nodded toward Marie. "And the doctor here, did she not know where the boy was taken?"

"Even if I did, I wouldn't tell you," Marie said defiantly. My arms tightened around her again, but she struggled to break free. Surely, she was just as terrified as I was. Maybe she was trembling in anger and not fear.

"No. She had nothing to do with it. It was all me. I acted alone," I said.

Kostov shook his head and clicked his tongue. The noise was obscenely loud in the almost silent warehouse as everyone watched him play out his terrifying scenario. I forced myself to keep my eyes on him and kept my arms tightened around Marie.

"Now, now, American journalist, what is your name?" he asked.

"Nicole Sheppard." I had the oddest desire to stick my hand out for him to shake.

He walked around us in a tight circle, and when he stood in front of us again, he reached out with his finger and lifted Marie's chin to where he could look her in the eyes.

She let out a stream of French curses that would have made any French sailor proud and spat directly into Kostov's face. The fake smile faltered, then readjusted itself back into place. He pulled a handkerchief from his pocket and wiped off the spit. Then, like a pitcher winding up to throw a fastball across the plate, he pulled back his arm and slapped her hard enough to send us both tumbling to the floor.

Giving in to my fear with a sick kind of resignation, I thought this was it. This is where we both die. With strengthened resolve, I untangled myself from Marie and stood. I reached for her hand and helped her stand beside me. She didn't let go of my hand.

"You are lucky that I need you, Doctor, or I would kill you right here," Kostov said. "Mr. Garifullin has suffered a traumatic injury at the hands of this unfortunate girl. When he questioned her on the whereabouts of his son, she brutally attacked him with a kitchen knife. He requires medical assistance. Specifically, he has requested you. No doubt that once you have seen to the healing of his injuries, he will want to discuss the location of his son."

Kostov turned and barked orders to one of his men. The other man stepped forward and pulled a bundle of plastic zip ties from his belt. He jerked Marie away from me and deftly wrapped one of the zip ties around her wrists. When he pulled it tight, she winced a bit but stayed silent. Another soldier ran over, and Kostov spoke to him in rapid Russian. Then, he shoved Marie toward his underling.

"No!" It came out of me before I could stop it, and I took a step forward. Kostov put his hand against my chest to prevent me from going further.

"Don't worry, my American friend," he said. "You are going with her. Mr. Garifullin also requests that we bring you along. He has plans for you."

He took another zip tie from the soldier, jerked my arms in front of me, and tightly secured my wrists. He barked another order, and about half of his crew ran through the door to the office where Marie and I were when they first entered the warehouse. A few minutes later, one of them rushed back, triumphantly carrying my messenger bag, laptop, and camera.

Kostov took my bag and rummaged through it until he found my phone; he shoved the bag and camera toward the young man at his side. With a jerk of his leader's head toward the door, the soldier ran out with my things.

Kostov then dropped my costly satellite phone to the ground. He brought the butt of his rifle down with enough force to smash the small screen. Again and again, he slammed the rifle down until nothing was left but shards. He picked up a couple of the pieces and shook out the SIM card. He ground that into the dust with the heel of his boot. No one would be able to track me now. Thoughts and feelings engulfed me. There was more fear. It had taken up permanent residence inside my brain now. But guilt and regret had packed their bags and were moving in next door as I watched him destroy my outside connection to the world.

"Tell me, Nicole Sheppard, American journalist, who else helped you?" he asked.

"No one," I said. "No one else."

"What about your…" He snapped his fingers. "What do you call them?"

"Fixer," the soldier next to Kostov said.

"Yes, your fixer. Where is he?" Kostov asked. It took every bit of self-control available to me not to risk a glance in Tatiana's direction. If Kostov thought my fixer was a man, I could still save her.

"He's dead," I lied. "He was shot and killed in Kozlyov two days ago."

"Pity," Kostov said. "My employer had hoped to complete that task himself. Oh well, he will have to settle for you and the doctor."

"I'm telling you, the doctor had nothing to do with it. She tried to talk me out of it."

Without Borders

"It's a shame she didn't," he said. "However, your little stunt with Lidiya has had some serious consequences, and the doctor is needed. Now, she will have to pay for not being more persistent. And you, my friend, are coming along because Mr. Garifullin wants to hear of his son's location personally from you."

Kostov started barking orders in Russian. Then, he turned to me as if to ensure I was paying attention and told his men in English, "Burn the place to the ground."

"No," I screamed as the fear for these innocent people leaped back into the forefront of my heart and mind. As the soldier tried to restrain me, I screamed and cursed. I fought like a wildcat. There were so many stories circulating of the cruelty and brutality of these men. Would he keep everyone inside and let them burn to death? Or would he bring them out so his men could rape the women and kill the men and children? Hiding my feelings didn't matter anymore. I wailed in despair. If I had to stand there and endure what these monsters might do to these innocent people, I might go mad. Without another coherent thought, I sagged uselessly. The soldier restraining me stumbled but quickly regained his footing and viciously twisted my head to make sure I watched as his fellow soldiers whooped and hollered and systematically began setting fire to the piles of goods stacked along the warehouse walls. I took several deep breaths so I wouldn't throw up. Dear God, this couldn't be happening.

Among the rest of the hostages, many were now crying. Some were praying aloud for God to save them. Others pleaded with the mercenaries to have mercy on them. Most stared at the floor, the ceiling, or anywhere else they could focus their attention rather than on their executioners. My brain struggled to take it all in as Kostov's man held me so tightly, that it was hard to breathe.

Kostov returned to where Pasha stood with her fists clenched so tight, I expected to see blood dripping from them any second. I didn't understand what he said to her, but he made sure I saw what was happening. If he killed my friend's mom right before us, I would never forgive myself. I forced myself to watch because I wanted to witness his inhumanity so that when I killed him, it would be justifiable. Anger pushed the fear aside and demanded a place up front.

"Take one good last look, Nicole Sheppard, and see what your actions have brought down upon this community," Kostov said.

The blood rushed to my head, and adrenaline pumped into my veins like a firehose was on the other end. Out of the corner of my eye, I saw Tatiana take a couple of steps in my direction. Pasha grabbed her and pulled her close. I appreciated my fixer wanting to fix this, but even more so, I was grateful her mother grabbed her and held her back. Tatiana hid her face in her mother's shirt, just as I was sure she used to do when she was a child, and something scared her.

"Now. If you would be so kind as to come with me, American journalist," the mercenary said. He was almost polite as his minion dragged me out of the building. The mercenary opened the back door of the second SUV and shoved me inside. I fell face-first right into Marie's lap. She clumsily helped me sit up but held on to me once I was prone again.

With apparent glee, Kostov's men ran back inside. If only I could close my ears as easily as I closed my eyes. We heard screaming, crying, and confused shouts. There were a few random shots, and I wondered with sick dismay who they'd killed first.

They loaded themselves into the SUVs afterward. Kostov climbed into the front passenger seat. One of his men slid behind the wheel and started the vehicle. Another one slid into the back seat next to me, and a fourth took a seat between Marie and the door.

The rest of them took shelter behind the other SUV. One stopped at the door of the distribution center and tossed in a grenade. *Dear God, please let the people be away from the door.* I heard the explosion behind us, as the driver of our car floored the accelerator, and we sped away from the scene.

Tatiana was surely dead, along with her mother and many others. I thought I might faint and would have welcomed the relief of unconsciousness. I felt sure the mercenaries in the other car would wait outside the warehouse and gun down anyone who tried to escape. I tried to add up the number of people I'd just gotten killed and almost prayed for unconsciousness to get away from the heartache and guilt. A sob escaped my throat, and Marie murmured something to me in French. I didn't understand what it was.

The soldier on the other side of Marie rummaged in the pockets of her lab coat until he came up with her phone. He handed it over the seat to Kostov. As we crossed the bridge, Kostov rolled down his window and tossed the device over the side.

"We can't have anyone tracking you now, can we?" he asked.

I turned toward Marie and whispered, "I'm sorry."

She shrugged. Her face was impassive. When I started to say something else, she shook her head. Right now, more than anything else, I wanted to touch her. Not to reassure her but to reassure myself that she didn't blame me. With great effort, I pushed those feelings aside and tried to pretend I was as stoic as she appeared.

The man sitting in the back with us reached down and pulled something out of a bag at his feet. I panicked again when I realized he had two smaller black bags and he intended to cover our heads. I was not the kind of person who liked her head covered. It made me claustrophobic, and I couldn't breathe.

I had to force myself to take long, deep breaths. Even then, I could feel my heart pounding away in my chest, and my body was shaking like an earthquake was happening inside my muscles. I felt Marie take my bound hands in hers and squeeze.

CHAPTER TWELVE

We drove for what seemed like hours. Time stood still as fear and panic pushed every other emotion out of the way to make room for them to expand.

The car finally stopped, and rough hands dragged me out of the vehicle. When I tripped and almost fell, those same rough hands steadied me. I stumbled along as my captor pulled me to our destination. I heard men shouting, and somewhere, a woman was crying. A door opened, and someone pulled me through. My heart was pounding so hard, I was surprised my captors couldn't hear it.

When we entered the house, Kostov ordered his men to take Marie to Garifullin. I hoped the bastard would be dead. Then, I realized if Garifullin was dead, Kostov would probably kill me and Marie since he no longer had any use for us.

185

The house where they had taken us smelled like garlic and cheap cigars. There was another underlying odor I couldn't quite place at first. I realized it was the smell of death and decay buried under the odor of a shit-ton of lemon-scented furniture polish. Someone shoved me through another door and pushed me down on a chair. The bag was ripped off my head. Harsh light hit my eyes, and I blinked. Kostov's minion pulled a knife out from a sheath on his belt, and with a quick jerk, cut the plastic ties binding my wrists.

When things finally came into focus, I saw we were in a large room that served as an office. Bookcases lined the walls, and a glance showed the shelves packed with the classics. It looked like most of the titles were in Russian or Ukrainian, but some were in other languages. I recognized the works of Shakespeare because they were in English. Snidely, I thought they were probably just for show because I was such a snob that I didn't think a gangster would be able to read, much less read the classics.

Kostov seated himself behind a large wooden desk and helped himself to a fat cigar from a humidor. Instead of lighting it, for which I was grateful, he put it in his mouth and chewed on it. He stared at me for a long minute without saying anything. My first thought was I probably should have paid a lot more attention to that survival manual Pamela had given me back at Titan headquarters. I specifically should have concentrated on the chapters about the interrogation techniques of kidnappers. One more thing to regret, I thought glumly.

"What do you want with me?" I asked, finally, to break the silence.

Kostov stood up and came around the desk. He took the cigar out of his mouth and leaned down until our faces were even. His breath still smelled like dead animals. I refrained from saying anything about it.

"You insist that you do not know where Akim Garifullin is?" he asked.

"No. I don't have any idea. I kept an eye on him for a couple of hours until someone came from one of the refugee camps to pick him up. I don't have any idea who they were or where they were from." This was all technically, if not completely the truth.

"And what about the doctor?" Kostov demanded. "Did she call the authorities?"

"I doubt it," I said. "She was busy trying to save lives. It could have been anyone on her staff or at the hotel or even the stranger who brought in the kid and his mother."

This also technically was the truth.

"If the good doctor can save Mr. Garifullin's life, perhaps I might be merciful and let her go. I might even let you live if you tell me where the boy is."

"I'm telling you I don't know where he is," I said. "Some social workers took him. I don't know who they are or where they went. That's all I know." That earned me a hard slap across the face.

"My superiors have ordered me to obey Mr. Garifullin. Therefore, your fate is in his hands. Otherwise, I would kill you now." He bent down again, making sure his face was less than two inches from mine. "Pray that he survives your doctor friend's ministrations."

What possible plans could a gangster have for me? Maybe he was going to try to turn me into a hooker. It gave me pause to consider the option. Would I do it to save Marie's life? Sure, but I would hate myself for it. I would want to die.

"Mr. Garifullin believes others have shown him in an unfair light," Kostov said.

"He wants to prove to you he will be a good father. If it were up to me, I would torture you until you told me everything. But I am duty-bound to obey Mr. Garifullin's orders. He will allow you to tell his side of the story. The story of a businessman trying to keep afloat while his country is at war with his biggest client."

I didn't show how relieved I was at not being blackmailed into being a prostitute. However, writing an article about Garifullin as a legitimate businessman would be equivalent to selling my soul. It made me wonder where all those lofty ideals I had in grad school had disappeared.

"What is Mr. Garifullin's legitimate business?" I asked, not even bothering to keep the sarcasm out of my voice.

"He is an importer, exporter," Kostov said.

"What does he import and export? Teenage girls?" That earned me another slap. This one was so hard, I would have flown across the room if I hadn't been sitting down. My face stung from the blow. It would be bruised by tomorrow morning.

"You will show Mr. Garifullin respect while you are a guest in his home," Kostov said. "Or you will deal with the consequences. I won't kill you, but I can make you long for the release of death."

Of that, I had no doubt. Once Kostov determined I wouldn't make more wisecracks, he returned to behind the desk and sat down. Mrs. Garifullin, Sonja, he told me, ran a legitimate escort service. If Garifullin could convince me that Oksana's life had not been so bad, maybe I would believe his only interest was finding the son he loved. I refrained from snorting in disbelief when Kostov gave me this information. From his tone, I could tell he didn't believe it himself.

Garifullin wanted me to tell stories about him helping his country and his fellow Ukrainians by supplying goods and services that had become hard to find when the war disrupted the supply chain. In other words, he wanted me to gloss over his black-market contraband and lie about his five-hundred percent markup on hard-to-find items. We'd make no mention of the fact that a whole platoon of Russian mercenaries seemed to be at his beck and call.

Sonja Garifullin wanted me to help her with marketing the escort service. That threw me for a loop. They were in the middle of one of the worst wars this country had ever been engaged in, and she wanted me to hype her stable of call girls. I was flabbergasted at the gall of the woman. I hadn't even met her, and she disgusted me.

When I was in college, a local man called himself a legitimate businessman and dropped off a catalog and brochures for his business. It was a Russian mail-order bride service. It had made me sick. These people wanted me to put an acceptable public face on their illegal dealings. Bile rose again in my throat, and I thought maybe I was just going to have to surrender and vomit.

"I tried to explain to him that you would be more forthcoming about Akim's location if we tortured you or the doctor, but he insists we try it his way first." I could tell from how Kostov ground his teeth that he thought Garifullin was a fool. If being a fool kept Marie and me alive, I was all for it.

It was better than being tied to a chair in a damp, dirty basement.

I would do it, I decided. Even if it killed my soul, and went against every journalistic value I possessed, I would do it. Because being alive and compromised was better than being dead and on high moral ground. Some things are worth dying for. This was not.

When he heard that I would agree, Kostov told me that before Garifullin was injured, he'd left instructions that I would be granted access to the grounds and the employees. I could take all the pictures I wanted, but Kostov would approve them before either of the Garifullins saw them. I couldn't send any emails or make any phone calls. I had no access to the internet or phones. If I asked any staff member to reach out for help, that staff member faced instant execution, whether they helped me or not. It was Kostov's way of keeping me from gaining sympathy from anyone I encountered. At all times, I would have an armed guard as an escort.

The thought of asking someone to help and watching them die filled me with sick despair. I couldn't see a way out for us. I tried to listen to what Kostov said, but my mind cried in agony and grief at the thought of every death I was responsible for today. I vowed to do whatever I could to destroy the man sitting across the desk from me.

I'd often wondered if I could kill another human being, even at the threat of losing my own life. I hadn't thought I could. But if I'd had a gun in my hands right then, I believed I could have pulled the trigger and blown the smug look off his face.

"You will write what we tell you," Kostov said.

"Okay, let's start with you," I said. "What is a group of Russian mercenaries doing working for a two-bit gangster like Garifullin?" It was like I couldn't stop myself from provoking him. He could make me forget my ethics, and he could keep me on the edge of fear with his threats of torture and death, but he couldn't stop my smartass mouth.

Kostov laughed harshly, then shrugged. "Mr. Garifullin has multiple interests in Russia and Ukraine and a few in some other countries. My employer was concerned about his Russian assets since Garifullin is a major investor and supplier. I am here to protect those assets."

"He provides your boss with guns and artillery, and your boss sends you and some other thugs to Ukraine to cover Garifullin's assets."

That made Kostov laugh even harder. "Yes, but don't ever call Mr. Garifullin, how did you say it, a 'two-bit gangster' in his presence. You would not like his reaction. You may call me and my men 'thugs' on this occasion, but your articles will reflect us as protectors and soldiers."

He stood, walked to the door, and shouted something in Russian. One of his men came in carrying my camera and messenger bag. Kostov handed them to me. "I will have someone escort you to your room," he said. "The doctor will join you when she is finished ministering to Mr. Garifullin. Let me once again remind you that any attempt on your part to escape will be met with immediate death."

The threat was made so matter-of-factly, it struck more fear in me than if he had used his menacing voice. Someone who could speak so casually of killing me and Marie had no conscience at all. I'd already seen him and some of his unit murder without hesitation. Why would I think he would act any differently when it came to us?

Being a war correspondent was dangerous. Every biography I'd read or documentary I'd watched emphasized that part. On a certain intellectual level, being kidnapped, tortured, or even killed were possibilities I accepted when I had begged for this job, but I'd glossed over the facts. Yes, some war correspondents died. Others experienced torture, and still others were kidnapped. Even the correspondents who escaped personal harm suffered from varying degrees of post-traumatic stress disorder. Now I knew why. Mental torture was still torture.

While I'd daydreamed about bringing the war news to the world, I'd focused on the glamour. I'd pinpointed the camaraderie between journalists from all over the world. We'd rush out every morning to do assignments together. We'd watch each other's backs and share our stories. None of the cutthroat competition would keep us from banding together. We'd sit around the hotel every night, drinking beer and exchanging stories of close calls.

It hadn't worked out that way, but I'd met Marie, who might turn out to be the love of my life. I'd made some good friends with Tatiana and her family. I'd written good stories about Ukraine, its people, and the war. I knew I'd been lucky and should count my blessings. I'd been kidnapped, but instead of being tied up, tortured, and starved, I was staying in the equivalent of a five-star hotel. It could have been worse.

The second myth I'd created was imagining myself as a hero to the locals. I was here to tell the world of their plight and save them from evil oppressors, making sure I secured myself a Pulitzer while doing so. Things hadn't worked out that way, either. Not yet, anyway. I couldn't even save one defenseless baby from this ruthless maniac.

I'd sustained a flesh wound. I unexpectedly might be falling in love. At least, I thought it might be love if I ever had a chance to find out. I'd managed to get kidnapped by ruthless men who would likely kill us before letting us go. A great sense of failure dropped on me like a sudden rainstorm.

"Can I see Marie?" I asked.

"She is operating on Mr. Garifullin," Kostov said. "Pray that he does not die. My man will take you to your room now. You will stay there until I am satisfied that this location is secure enough for any escape attempt to fail."

With a barked command and a jerk of his head, Kostov summoned one of his soldiers. The young man must have been waiting just outside the door. He pulled me to my feet and dragged me toward the door, expecting me to follow. Kostov watched me go. The look in his eyes was made of pure contempt and hatred. It made me shudder.

I followed the young man up a flight of stairs. Although I tried to commit the path to memory, this place was huge. It would take days to find my way around, even if I was free to wander. When we reached the third floor, we went down a nondescript hallway with doors on each side. When we came to the last door, he removed a key from his pocket, unlocked the door, and waved me in.

I removed my flak jacket and helmet and laid them aside on the bed along with my messenger bag and camera. Inside the room was one window covered by outside bars, with a queen-size bed positioned directly under the window. A large dresser and a wardrobe stood against one wall. There was another door along the other wall that the soldier indicated with gestures and some broken English was a bathroom. Next to the bathroom door was a mid-sized desk. The desk was the only modern furnishing in the room. Everything else looked elegant and old. Someone had perfectly color-coordinated the room in soft blue tones. Garifullin had an excellent decorator.

The soldier grunted something at me, did a quick about-face, and walked out the door. I heard the key turn in the lock and realized I was a prisoner. Maybe I wasn't as free to wander about as I'd assumed. I did wonder how they expected me to take pictures or write stories if I couldn't leave this room. I almost laughed at myself because anything I wrote saying Garifullin was a legitimate businessman was fiction anyway. I could make stuff up from this room as well as anywhere else.

A quick exploration of the bathroom showed it connected to another room. I turned the knob, not expecting it to open. When it did, I found another bedroom, identical to mine, except its color scheme was yellow instead of blue.

The bathroom had everything a person needed for cleanliness and good grooming. Toothbrushes, toothpaste, hair products, loofahs, and washcloths filled the shelves. Several fluffy, neatly folded white towels lined another shelf. An oversized white bathrobe hung on the back of each door. At least we'd be clean during our captivity. I couldn't help but marvel at the sheer volume of products when the majority of Kyiv struggled to buy toilet paper.

Returning to my room, I examined the wardrobe and closet. There were lots of clothes, primarily girly dresses. A small shoe tree held mainly high heels. I'd keep my boots on, thank you very much. The dresser had more of the same, some frilly underwear. There were some jeans and T-shirts neatly folded. If these guys thought I would wear dresses and heels while they held me at gunpoint, they were even crazier than I thought. I wondered if any of the girls in Garifullin's employ had occupied these two rooms. Or were they housed somewhere else? My imagination put them in stables, just out of sight of the main house. These rooms had the impersonal touches of hotel rooms. They were for guests.

There was a knock on the door, and I shouted for them to come in before I realized the door was locked from the outside, and I couldn't let anyone in. Whoever it was had wasted their time by knocking. Unless they were just trying to be polite, which was something I didn't expect in a house run by thugs and crooks.

The key rattled in the lock, and a short but stout middle-aged woman entered. She wore an outfit that sort of resembled a maid's uniform. A scarf around her hair let just a few brown strands escape. The expression on her face made her appear stressed, but I could have imagined it. She was older than I expected someone working for Garifullins to be. Maybe she took care of all his kidnap victims. These people certainly were polite, considering they were murderers, thieves, and kidnappers.

"I am Svetlana," she said, using reasonably good English. "I will care for you and the doctor while you are here. I came to see if you needed anything."

"Yeah, a car to take us away from here."

She smiled. "Colonel Kostov told me about your American sense of humor. The master of the house does not want you to feel like a prisoner. He prefers for you to consider yourselves as guests."

"Does he keep all of his guests locked in their rooms?" I asked. She smiled again and ignored the question. I started asking her other questions to see if I could get a response and try to determine if she might be sympathetic.

"How old are you, Svetlana?" I asked

"Please, call me Lana," she said.

"How old are you, Lana?" I asked again. I know it was probably considered rude, but I was a journalist, and a lot of people expected me to be rude.

"I am forty-five years old."

"How long have you worked for Mr. Garifullin?"

A slight smile briefly touched her lips. "I started working for him when I was just a girl. I was about fifteen." That answered my question of whether this lowlife was involved in prostituting teenage girls. I could have been wrong, though. Lana could have come to him to work as a maid when she was barely a teenager and not as one of his escorts. If I still held on to the tatters of my journalistic reputation, I'd better clarify.

"Were you a prostitute?" I asked.

She turned a shade of red I didn't think I'd ever actually seen before. "When I was much younger and prettier, I did entertain some of Mr. Garifullin's frequent callers," she said, carefully choosing her words. "When I was nineteen, a young man came to call. He was very handsome and so confident, I couldn't help but fall in love with him."

Her eyes took on a faraway look as she remembered what had to be in her mind, a fairy-tale romance. She laughed quietly at herself and shook her head. "Mr. Garifullin was so impressed with him that he agreed to let us marry. I became a housekeeper, and throughout the years, I have risen to the position of head of the house." This last was said with no small amount of pride, and I swear, she raised herself to make herself just a little bit taller.

"We are still married to this day," she said proudly. "We have three children and four wonderful grandchildren."

I didn't quite know how to respond, so I changed the subject and asked if she'd ever witnessed her employer committing any crimes. With that, she became tight-lipped and started pacing, looking for something to clean. Her boss's activities were a touchy line of questioning. I decided to change the subject again.

"Can you tell me where the doctor is now?" I asked.

"The doctor is in the main bedroom. She is treating Mr. Garifullin's wounds," Lana said.

That meant he was still alive for now. They probably would have murdered Marie there and sent an armed assassin to kill me instead of this middle-aged grandmother if he'd died. Then again, who was to say she wasn't armed or a killer? She didn't seem to have anything in her pockets or an apron bulky enough to contain a gun. She could have had a knife strapped to her thigh. It didn't seem likely, but like I said, my impressions of gangsters came from American movies.

"As soon as the doctor finishes, I will bring her up and bring you some supper," Lana said. "Mistress prefers for the guests to dine with her, and we always dress for dinner. She has foregone that formality just for tonight." If Lana meant for me to dress in fancy clothes and pretend I enjoyed men's company, I'd rather have had them shoot me now.

"You can tell your mistress she's out of her mind if she thinks I'm going to dress up like a hooker and sit at a dinner table with her," I said.

She puttered around the room a bit, picking at imaginary dirt or imperfections that I couldn't see. "We do dress for dinner," she finally said. "However, I think you will find something in the wardrobe to your tastes. If you do not, let me know, and I will find something suitable for you," Lana let out a nervous chuckle. "Since Mr. Garifullin is wounded, Colonel Kostov prefers you and the doctor to eat in your rooms. At least for tonight."

With that statement, she left, muttering reassurances that she would return with Marie and our dinner. After I heard the key turn in the lock, I went through the bathroom and into the yellow bedroom. I tried the door and found it also locked. Snooping around both rooms showed me nothing that would facilitate our escape.

I returned to my room and sat at the desk with my camera and iPad. A close examination of my equipment didn't reveal any damage, which was a plus. I could download my pictures without the internet but couldn't send them anywhere. I tried to access the internet, but none of the dozens of usernames that came up were unprotected. I scrolled through the menu on the camera. All the images were there. My offline programs worked on my iPad, so I made notes after pulling up a Word document. If nothing else, I could keep an ongoing journal about our time spent as prisoners.

I was still typing when I heard the key in the lock next door. I quickly saved what I'd written and ran through the bathroom to find the soldier who had brought me up earlier escorting Marie, Lana, and another younger woman into the yellow room. True to her word, Lana and her companion each carried a tray loaded with food.

Marie looked exhausted. Her scrubs were torn in several places and covered with blood and grime. Dark circles under her eyes told me how tired she was. She gave me a small smile, dropped on the chair beside her desk, and began untying her shoes.

"Well, he'll live," she said without looking up. "He lost a lot of blood, and I had trouble finding a suitable donor. I thought for a minute I was going to have to tap your O negative for a transfusion, Press," she said.

I raised my eyebrows at that. The only way I'd give my blood to keep him alive was if it would save Marie's life.

"Kostov finally brought in one of his soldiers who was O negative. Garifullin is getting a transfusion now. Once his levels are back up, he should heal nicely."

We both ignored the others. Lana fussed around, setting one tray on the dresser and another on the desk in front of Marie. She asked if I preferred eating in my room or with the doctor. Without waiting for me to respond, she gave some orders to the young girl, who rushed through the bathroom and returned with the desk chair from the desk in my room.

"Eat before it gets cold," Lana ordered.

Marie gave her a long, appraising look. Lana broke her gaze first. She said she would send the girl back later for the trays and shooed the other two out of the room. The lock clicked after their departure, and Marie wilted.

"I'd much rather take a long, hot soak in that tub," she said. "I haven't had a good bath since I arrived in this country."

Her smile, although it was weary, made my heart sing. I went to the bathroom and started her bath, putting in a liberal amount of bath oil beads, guaranteed aroma therapy. At least, that was what I hoped they were since the labels were all in Russian or Ukrainian. The picture of a beautiful blonde luxuriating in a sea of bubbles convinced me I was on the right track.

It caught me a little off guard when Marie appeared in the doorway completely naked. The sight took my breath away. I felt my face redden. She laughed again and put her hand on my shoulder to steady herself while she stepped into the tub. Before sliding into the bubbles, she kissed me lightly on the neck.

"Care to join me?" she whispered in my ear.

I said something suave and witty in my head, like, "My darling, I wouldn't dare take advantage."

In reality, I gasped like a dying fish and fled from the room with her giggles chasing me.

CHAPTER THIRTEEN

We talked through the door while Marie bathed and I picked at the food. Neither of us said much about our chances for rescue or escape. The room might have been bugged. I kept a respectable distance to give her a bit of privacy. As much as I wanted to be intimate with Marie, I didn't want our intimacy observed by security or anyone else who might be monitoring us.

I imagined if anyone was watching, they would be incredibly bored. Since this was my first time as a hostage, I relied a little heavily on action movies and thrillers. That our rooms would be bugged and secret cameras hidden everywhere, were assumptions on my part. It was a good guess, though. When the guards had taken her to operate on Garifullin, Marie told me she had passed a room filled with monitors and sophisticated surveillance equipment. Odds were our captors were watching.

It had been a long and exhausting day. I ate the dinner left for me while Marie lolled in the bath. She emerged wearing one of the big fluffy robes and looking a bit more relaxed. I sat with her while she ate her cold dinner. Svetlana returned to retrieve the trays and asked if we needed anything else before turning in for the night. When we both assured her we were fine, she said good night and left. She locked the door behind her. Marie said she was going to bed. She kissed me lightly and asked me to leave our connecting doors open.

It was still early, but I changed into some pajamas I found in one of the drawers. My concerns over Tatiana and Pasha, along with everyone else at the distribution center, crept out of hiding. Were they dead? Without any proof, I could pretend they'd escaped the blast and were at this very moment rounding up the cavalry to come to our rescue. I didn't think I could fall asleep not knowing their fates and berating myself all night over all the mistakes I had made that day. But a few minutes later, I dropped off. Being a hostage was exhausting.

I am an unusually light sleeper, so later that night, when I heard a key turn in the lock in the other room, I snapped immediately awake. The small alarm clock next to the bed showed a firm 2:45 a.m. I wondered why someone would try to get into Marie's room this time of night. A bed check made sense, but why would they need it if they had such excellent surveillance? My senses told me something was amiss.

The sounds coming from Marie's room suggested someone was trying to move around without making any noise, albeit unsuccessfully. I hoped Marie was also a light sleeper because the intruder didn't have a flashlight or turn on any other lights. When the door opened, no light spilled in from the hallway, either. A sense of foreboding came over me. I groped around on the top of the dresser as quietly as possible until I found a vase I'd noticed earlier.

With only the moonlight streaming through the window, I saw a man's silhouette bending over her bed. When he pulled back the covers, I heard Marie gasp in fear or surprise. The man quickly covered her mouth. I knew something was wrong. A kind of white-hot rage took over my brain.

The man's attention was focused on Marie with one hand doing something I couldn't see, while the other covered her mouth. He never saw me coming when I busted the vase over his head. He screamed like a child and went down. Marie snapped on the lamp on her nightstand. One of Kostov's soldiers lay on the floor. Bits of colored glass from the vase surrounded him, and blood gushed from the wound on his head. He groaned and made a feeble attempt to stand. I grabbed Marie's lamp, causing the light to make crazy shadows all over the room, and hit him again. This time, he stayed down.

I was breathing hard, and my brain told me to hit him again. Murderous outrage coursed through me, and I think I could have killed the man, despite how helpless he was right then. Thankfully, Marie kept calm and gently pried the lamp from my clenched fist.

"Get his door key, Press," she whispered.

She was amazing. Some guy broke into her room, with obvious intentions of rape or something like it, and her first thought was to use him to help us escape.

Someone was already coming up the stairs. The noise their boots made sounded like the whole unit was coming. I rolled the man over and started going through his shirt pockets, looking for the key to the door. I found it just as another soldier burst through the door with Kostov hot on his heels. I palmed the key as quickly as I could, hoping no one noticed.

Following Kostov and his soldiers, a couple of civilians dressed in smart-looking tuxedos, and two women dressed in those frilly party dresses crowded around the doorway. One of the women thought to snap on the overhead light, making the shadows disappear. Kostov took a minute to evaluate the scene, then started barking orders. The soldiers moved out of his way. The civilians were not so fast. Kostov shoved one of them aside and continued into the room until he stood at the edge of the puddle of blood.

"What's going on here?" Since he was looking directly at me, I answered him, letting all my outrage show.

"This man broke into Marie's room and tried to assault her." My voice shook with rage. I wasn't sure if those were the man's intentions, but why else would he sneak into her room in the middle of the night? The whole thing reeked of ill intent.

Upon hearing his commander's voice again, the semi-conscious man on the floor tried to rouse himself. I looked around for something to hit him with again. Before I could move, Kostov reached down and pulled the man to his feet.

"Is this true?" he demanded, shaking the man for good measure. The soldier was dazed and looked confused. He muttered something in Russian. Kostov's face turned a whole different shade of red. He grabbed the man by the collar and shoved him toward the doorway.

"Take him outside and shoot him," Kostov ordered. The other two soldiers rushed forward, and each one threw an arm around the man and dragged him out of the room. We could hear his blubbering and pleading fading away as they went down the hall.

In contrast to Kostov's face, Marie's had lost all its color. "Please don't kill him," she pleaded.

Kostov gave her a stern look. "What would you have me do, Doctor? Should I put him in jail to await trial? No. He will be an example. I gave orders for no one to harm you or the American journalist. Any disobedience requires swift and harsh punishment." A few minutes later, we heard the shot from outside. Marie shut her eyes but not before tears leaked out. I bit my lip so hard, I tasted blood. I was glad they'd shot him. I hated him. I hated the whole lot of them and childishly wished they were all dead. I was sick to think I probably would have killed him myself. I didn't think I was capable of murder, but there we were.

Kostov turned to the rest of the group, still crowded in the doorway. He gave one of the women an order in Ukrainian. She nodded vigorously and rushed out the door. He barked a few questions at one of the soldiers standing there. The soldier became very interested in his boots as he muttered something barely audible. Whatever he was saying caused Kostov's color to become even more inflamed.

Looking directly at me, he said, "Apparently, Nicole Sheppard, the fact that you and the doctor seem to prefer women as sexual partners rather than these fine specimens of Russian masculinity is a topic of great interest for my men. When one of them bragged he could change the doctor, and then you, his comrades decided to challenge him to, how do you Americans say it, 'put his money where his mouth is.' If he had succeeded in sexually assaulting the doctor, you would have been next."

How did he even know Marie and I preferred women? They must have been watching us both for some time. If I felt sick with disgust and rage before, my anger must have made the color of my face match his. It's hard to believe that someone thought they could come into our rooms and take what they wanted from us without our permission. Even as prisoners, I still believed we had some rights. I knew on some level, we didn't. I didn't understand the thinking of these people. Not only was I angry and sick, but I was also scared and confused, and those were the feelings I needed to hide. Kostov would exploit any weakness. It wouldn't surprise me to learn he put the soldiers up to this. After all, if rumors about him and his men were true, then rape was to be expected. I started to open my mouth to say something scathing but stopped when Marie gave her head a short shake. I bit my lip again, reinforcing the cut I'd just made.

"My apologies, Doctor." His tone was almost kind as he turned his attention to Marie. If I hadn't known better, I would think he almost cared. Marie didn't open her eyes but did manage to give him a curt nod. I put my arms around her. I could feel her trembling still. It was so different from the calm, cool Marie I had gotten to know that it scared me a little bit more.

The woman to whom Kostov had given orders came rushing back into the room carrying a crystal decanter and glass. She handed both to Kostov, who poured some amber liquid into the glass and gave it to Marie.

"Drink this, Doctor," he said almost gently. "It's brandy. It will help with the shock."

She finally opened her eyes and looked at him. This time, her expression was unreadable. She drank up and set the empty glass on the nightstand. When he offered her a second, she shook her head. He asked me if I wanted a drink, and I also turned him down. His sudden change from a monster to a concerned bystander made me trust him even less and hate him even more.

Lana and the young girl who'd helped her bring in our dinner trays came in carrying mops, buckets, towels, and other cleaning materials. Neither blinked an eye at the puddle of blood. It was probably something they'd seen before. Lana took a bucket into the bathroom and filled it with water while the girl picked up the pieces of glass and tossed them in the wastebasket.

It would have been a stroke of luck if she'd left the trash in the room because that broken glass would have made a good weapon. But once the girl removed the glass, Lana tied a knot in the bag and tossed it in the cleaning bucket. They were very efficient. In a matter of minutes, they had the room spotless again.

Kostov stepped aside to let them leave. The others backed away, closing the door behind them. Marie and I were alone in the room with him. We sat on the bed, waiting for him to say something or leave. It was a long and uncomfortable silence.

"I will post a guard outside in the hallway," he said, finally. "It will be someone I trust. You will not be bothered again." He did a quick about-face and slammed the door on his way out. I held my breath until I heard the lock click. No one asked how the soldier had been able to enter Marie's room, and no one looked for the missing key. I wondered just how many people could open these doors. I'd have to find something else to use as a weapon to protect us.

I looked around for a secure place to hide our stolen key. I was certain we were being kept under surveillance, but I didn't know how closely we were being watched. If someone had seen me take the key from the unconscious soldier, our escape efforts would have been finished before they started. Hopefully, the attack itself and the events that followed were enough of a diversion that no one had noticed me get the key.

It needed to be hidden somewhere Lana wouldn't come across it while cleaning. Marie and I expected periodic searches, so hiding it on our persons was out. When I was a kid, I would hide my valuables in the pocket of an old coat hanging in the back of my closet. No one ever looked there. I opened the wardrobe and went through everything. None of the hooker clothes had pockets. I finally stuck the key in the toe of a high heel that neither Marie nor I would ever consider wearing. A better hiding spot could wait until tomorrow. I turned back to the bed and sat next to her.

"Are you all right?" I asked.

"Yes. I think so. It all happened so quickly. I was asleep, and then you were in my room bashing in the head of a man trying to assault me." She gave me one of her special smiles. "You're my hero."

Her lips brushed mine. Her body shifted, those lips pressed in, and the kiss intensified. Every molecule in my body stood up and paid attention, quickly meeting her intensity level. She pushed me back on the bed and spread herself over me. God, I wanted her. What stopped me was the thought that she just survived an attempted rape. Sex, even consensual sex, was a bad idea.

By some miraculous feat of strength, I pushed her away. Not entirely, but far enough that we could both take a breath. She stared into my eyes, and I saw a million thoughts march across her expression. Then, she smiled again, kissed me on the tip of my nose, and rolled off me.

"You're right," she said. "This is neither the time nor place for such things." She rolled on her side and propped her head up with her right hand. Her left hand lay across my stomach, making little circles. Each rotation left a blazing trail of desire behind.

"I want to," I said. "More than anything, but not here and not now. When we're somewhere safe. Somewhere we can be alone."

She nodded. "I want you to promise me something, though."

"Anything." If she asked for the moon, I'd find a way to be at NASA tomorrow.

"If it comes down to it and we know they will kill us before they let us go, promise me we will make love before that happens."

It didn't seem like an unreasonable request. If we were going to die, I would make love to her exactly like it was our last day on Earth. I agreed and tried to get up and return to my room. The arm across my stomach tightened.

"Stay here with me. Please?"

There was a slight trace of fear in her eyes. I was relieved because I didn't want to be alone, either. Not trusting myself to speak, I nodded. Marie smiled happily and pulled the blankets up to cover us both. She wiggled around until she snuggled comfortably under my arm.

Speaking quietly, so if anyone listened, they wouldn't make out what I said, I quietly suggested we watch for the next couple of days to see if an opportunity arose to use the key. We were going to need some help. Just having a key to our door wouldn't do us any good if guards stopped us in the hallway. It seemed evident Lana wouldn't be willing to take the risk to help us escape.

Tomorrow, we could make mental lists of people willing to help us. We could make a better plan once we found some suitable allies. Hopefully, we could do all this before they killed us. I was still talking when I noticed Marie was quiet.

Her breathing evened out. Every time she exhaled, the breath tickled my neck, expelling the visions of escaping dancing in my head, replacing them with dreams of making love to her. I didn't think I would be able to sleep thinking about it. Eventually, I fell asleep with her in my arms.

CHAPTER FOURTEEN

Lana woke us practically at the crack of dawn. If seeing us in bed together surprised her, she didn't let it show. This whole place was a conundrum. They balked at two women sleeping together but thought nothing of selling their bodies. Surely, there was a demand for same-sex prostitutes in Russia and Ukraine. Perhaps it wasn't as out in the open as the need of males for female companionship, but they couldn't deny it existed.

Lana's presence did cause me to wonder how difficult it was going to be to find allies among the staff and the soldiers. The language barrier could work in our favor, but the most likely scenario was that we would end up with no one willing to help us who spoke English or French. Marie did speak some Ukrainian and some Russian. I made a mental note to discuss it with her later to get her thoughts on approaching potential allies.

211

A guard waited in the hallway to escort Marie to Garifullin's room to check his condition. Another guard was to accompany me to breakfast. Marie gave me a deep, passionate kiss before following Lana out the door. I guess we were going to show them we were lesbians. The kiss reeked of defiance, and I was all for it if it meant kissing Marie. Lana's lips pursed in disapproval. I made a mental note to myself to do everything I could to flaunt my sexuality during my stay here.

Grabbing my camera and iPad, I followed them out. When we reached the second-floor landing, a soldier indicated I should follow him while Lana and Marie turned down the hallway toward what I assumed was Gurifullin's room. Downstairs, Kostov and a few others were seated around the breakfast table. I'd dressed in some jeans I found in the dresser and a pink T-shirt. I wasn't sure what the witty comment printed across the front of the shirt said, but Kostov smirked when he saw it.

"Nice choice of attire," he said.

I shrugged and pulled out a chair across from him. Yet another servant rushed to fill my coffee cup next to my plate. One sip of the strong, bitter brew had me reaching for the sugar bowl and the milk pitcher in the middle of the table. Kostov laughed and said something to the others, getting a laugh out of everyone but me. To hell with him. To hell with all of them. When I had the brew the way I wanted, I enjoyed it.

For being in a country at war with shortages everywhere, there was a lot of food on the table. Fresh milk and pitchers of orange juice sat at each end. Pyramids of biscuits, bacon, sausage, ham, pancakes, and waffles lined up on both sides of the table. There was also toast, croissants, and an assortment of other pastries. The coffee was what Americans called the bottomless cup. No sooner had I taken a sip than the servant was at my side, ensuring the cup stayed full. There were plates of scrambled eggs, but the servant pouring coffee assured me that if I preferred my eggs cooked another way, she would get the cook on it. I declined as Kostov translated.

All of this was meant to feed the five people around the table, unless other people were waiting in the wings for their turn at breakfast. I could only assume that a small army would be partaking in this bounty, and we were only the first shift. I'd been to all-you-can-eat buffets that served two or three hundred people with less food than this. I got pictures of each dish and a couple of setup shots. If nothing else, I could show the decadence these thugs and mercenaries wallowed in daily.

Kostov noticed. I wasn't trying to hide it. He didn't say anything, and he didn't try to stop me. I wondered what his endgame was. What was he getting out of this symbiotic relationship with a Ukrainian gangster?

When I finished breakfast, Kostov rose and ordered me to follow him. I tried to memorize the rooms and the doors. I wanted to determine what doors led to the outside and which would take us to other rooms. I pulled out my notepad and tried to draw a crude map. I needed some code in case Kostov confiscated my notes. I wrote down what I could think of in Pig Latin. It was juvenile, yes, but all I could think of at the moment.

We were in a large foyer, more like a giant hotel lobby than the entrance to a house. I tried again to remember what the survival manual had said about being kidnapped and taking in your surroundings. My knowledge was severely lacking. The downstairs was sparsely furnished with a small sofa and a few chairs set off in a corner and out of the way. A baby grand piano stood open and inviting.

On the other side of the piano was an ornately decorated set of French doors. They led to an outside patio that looked like a place where people hung out and barbecued or the Ukrainian equivalent. A neatly trimmed hedge surrounded the deck, and on the other side was a small flower garden and an enormous yard. It seemed to be roughly the size of a football field. The yard was our destination. Kostov's squad of Wolf Packers was doing practice drills. I hated calling them mercenaries, but did they deserve to be called soldiers? I didn't think so.

"My men have discipline," Kostov said. "You Americans have labeled us as brutes for hire. You say we murder, rape, and steal without conscience. I will show you my men are loyal patriots fighting for their country."

"From what I've seen, you and your men are murderers, rapists, and thieves. Last night only cemented that perception."

His lips tightened, and his right hand hovered around his holster. I wasn't in Austin, Texas, where an armed man might take offense at my words, but he usually wouldn't shoot me. Most Texans who openly carried weapons rarely used them. Kostov would. When would I learn to keep my opinions to myself?

"Last night was an isolated incident," he said through gritted teeth. "I can show you where we buried the man if you like."

"I'll take your word for it," I said. "For now."

He gave me a curt nod and ordered the unit to stop. I had to admit that their response was instantaneous. As one, they stood still, almost as if they were playing freeze tag. Kostov took them through several elaborate drills while I snapped dozens of photos. He pulled two men who spoke English out of formation. With a large amount of dry cynicism, he remarked he didn't believe I would trust him to translate. I didn't tell him I didn't trust him not to have already directed his people on what to say, even the ones who did speak English.

One of the two stood solid as a brick. He was older. I would guess about thirty-five. His face wore a permanent scowl. A jagged scar started behind his ear and ended at the corner of his mouth. I started with easy questions like where they were from. The younger man looked like he was barely old enough to shave. With a bit of encouragement, he told me about his family and his girlfriend. The older guy growled his answers. He didn't intimidate me. I'd interviewed Republicans.

Once I determined they were comfortable with me, at least the younger one seemed to be, I started with the more challenging questions. I asked the young soldier about the rumors that Russians had to go without essentials like food, clothing, and bedding. His eyes darted nervously between me and Kostov before he answered. They had everything they needed, he assured me. Kostov stepped up and told me the only shortage his troops experienced was a shortage of enemy soldiers to fight.

"Not many Ukrainian soldiers in this neighborhood," I said sarcastically. The young man chuckled nervously. The older one growled at me again.

When I asked him how many women he'd raped, Kostov stepped in again, barking at them in Russian. The older one gave me a menacing glare. The younger one looked terrified. They each saluted Kostov and rushed back to their practice drills. Kostov grabbed me by the arms and jerked me around until I faced him.

"Let me tell you something, Nicole Sheppard," he said, spraying spittle in my face. "Rape is a tool. It is a weapon. When the peasants hear my men will rape their wives and daughters, and yes, even their sons, before they murder them, they quake in their shoes with fear. They hear the Wolf Pack is coming, and they run and hide. When they do that, we do not have to fight them.

"That is why I had that soldier shot. He disobeyed my orders. My men do not rape women for any other reason. If they desire sex, they can have any of Garifullin's women."

"That is possibly the most horrifying thing I have ever heard," I said quietly, leaning away from him as far as his grip allowed.

Kostov muttered something about being tired of babysitting me and grabbed a platoon member by the arm. Kostov yelled at him for several minutes, pointing at me and gesturing wildly. I could only assume he ordered the soldier to take charge of me.

"This is Corporal Lev Bolshevik," Kostov said. "He speaks passable English. He will show you around the grounds and make the staff available for an interview. He will also translate. I want to hear nothing else about rape."

Without another word, Kostov turned and marched away from us. Lev was older than the soldier I'd interviewed before but younger than the growler. I estimated his age to be around twenty-five. He was long and skinny. With his dark hair and almost black eyes, he reminded me of Abe Lincoln. All he needed was a beard and a top hat to add another foot to his already more than six feet.

"Well, Lev, got any ideas on how to bust out of this joint?" I asked.

He took the question quite seriously and told me in English, with a very thick accent, that his orders did not allow me to leave the grounds or the common area. I shrugged and told him I'd like to walk around the estate and take some pictures.

"That is acceptable," he said.

We started walking around the house. I knew the estate was huge, but I hadn't expected the massiveness of everything. There was a garage that housed three vehicles. A Mercedes SUV, a BMW sedan, and a big ol' honking Ford truck, just like an insane number of Texans drove. Outside the garage were three black SUVs. There was also a green military Jeep and a Suzuki motorcycle. I got shots of them with license plates prominently displayed.

Feeling quite proud of myself, I took more pictures. This time, I made sure to include the grounds and the doors, and I even got a shot of a security panel. It controlled the estate's entire alarm system. Criminals were notoriously paranoid about someone else stealing their stolen goods, so it made sense that Garifullin would have an elaborate alarm system. Maybe having a picture of the panel wouldn't help me decipher the alarm code, but it couldn't hurt.

There were other buildings on the grounds as well. A few were prefabricated and served as barracks. There were also a couple of guest houses, a boathouse, and an Olympic-sized pool. Several beauties lounged around the pool in bikinis. One or two were even sans tops, their bare breasts standing loud and proud. A group of armed men stood at strategic corners of the area. Most of them gave the impression they were trying very hard not to ogle. My camera caught them all in the act.

Five women were in a cluster at the shallow end of the pool. A couple of them trailed their feet in the water. It wasn't that hot, but it was warm for early autumn. All five women looked up when I approached. I asked Lev to ask them if I could take some photos. Lev turned about a dozen shades of red and averted his eyes as he asked. Their reaction was akin to what I would expect if I were photographing models for this month's *Vogue*.

"You make me famous?" one of them asked. She was older than I expected, at least in her twenties. Since my experience so far was based on Lidiya, I suppose I'd expected most, if not all Garifullin's ladies, to be in their teens. These girls didn't have the same haunted look in their eyes that Lidiya had. Maybe it was because their benefactor hadn't fathered children with their sisters or threatened their lives and the lives of their loved ones. As far as I could determine, this flock of giggling girls was there because they'd been promised something in exchange for their cooperation.

"Sure," I said. "Why not?" Before we even started, a servant was by my side asking me what I would like to drink. I asked her for a Diet Coke, not expecting much. After all, this was a war zone, and such luxuries were hard to come by. Much to my surprise, she nodded and rushed off. A few minutes later, she returned with an ice-cold Diet Coke, the condensation streaming down the sides of the can like a waterfall. More evidence of this group's excess. The servant also had a large glass of ice cubes. I asked her if there was some drink she could not get for me. She looked puzzled and shook her head.

"Maybe Starbucks," she said.

I made a note of that in my notebook. I took a deep drink and relished the icy burning sensation. This whole situation was absurd. I didn't know if I should laugh or cry. Either way, I felt a little bit hysterical. I'd been kidnapped by the Ukrainian version of the Richie Rich.

The rest of the morning, I took pictures of near-naked women adopting what they thought were modeling poses. As lunchtime approached, more joined us. One brought a current Russian fashion magazine. When they showed me the pictures and said they wanted similar poses, I obliged. Who was I to dash their dreams of stardom? Pretty girls looking to become models, actresses, or whatever while working for a gangster who pimped them out. It would make a great story, even if one told many times.

They gladly answered my questions about how many men they had sex with and even relished telling me about the most peculiar thing a man had asked them to do. They also talked about how Garifullin cared for them. One said he could be harsh sometimes, but it was for their own good. I could only shake my head at the extent these women had been brainwashed. It was typical of abused women.

They were just as curious about me as I was about them. Word had gotten around that Marie and I were in the same bed this morning. They also asked many questions about what having sex with a woman was like. I tried to answer their questions as honestly as they had responded to mine. Oddly enough, I found myself at a loss for words when confronted with some of their perceptions of lesbian life. Their ideas of two women together must have come from the same streaming services where I'd found my perceptions of kidnapping and gangsters.

Lev stood off to the side, his back turned to the pool. After listening to their questions, he beckoned me over. Many of the women spoke passable English, so I didn't need his services. I could tell their near-nakedness made him uncomfortable. I'd told him he was dismissed, but he hovered on the edge of the pool, casting furtive glances our way.

"I do not think you should talk to them about your sexual deviants," he whispered fiercely.

"My deviants?" I stared back at him incredulously. He worked for a man who used rape to produce fear and another who sold teenagers for sex. And he had the nerve to call me deviant. I turned away from him, laughing in genuine amusement. "That's rich."

My hatred and disgust for the men in charge of this operation grew with each story the women told me. As escorts, they seemed naive to me. In my mind, having sex with men for money because their boss ordered them to was outrageous, but it was a typical day for them. I consider myself an open-minded liberal. There was nothing wrong with prostitution if it was between two consenting adults, but when children were involved, it was not okay. Most of them were in their early twenties. From their conversation, I gleaned they had been doing this for years. Some of them must have started when they were barely in their teens. I noticed the older women were almost all maids, cooks, or some other kind of servant. It was a hell of a retirement plan. When you got too old to lie on your back, they put you to work in the kitchen.

At a little after noon, Lana showed up, followed by a line of servants carrying trays of lunch meat, loaves of bread, cheese, and other delicacies. Three soldiers trailed behind her, carrying small foldout tables. They set up the tables while Lana waited. They set out food, plates, flatware, and glasses. Then Lana arranged everything so that it was aesthetically pleasing. A couple more servants brought out pitchers of lemonade, what I suspected was the Ukrainian version of iced tea, and some other drinks I didn't recognize. When everything was in place, Lana officially announced lunch. All I'd seen these people do was eat and lie around the pool. I wondered where they conducted the actual dirty business. I suspected they were showing me the touristy side of their life. Plus, their pimp, Garifullin, was incapacitated. I decided I didn't want to know where and when they had sex. It was repugnant to me. Maybe I wasn't so different from Lev after all. We were both judgmental jerks.

When the lunch spread was all laid out, all but two of the servants left the pool area. In English, Lana ordered these two to make sure I was taken care of. The women by the pool wrapped towels around their waists or pulled on elegant robes. They dragged me over to the table, carefully explaining each dish and asking me to try it. Each one

221

seemed to have a favorite, and it seemed important to them for me to approve.

If I liked their favorite food, I was a kindred spirit or something. If I approved of what they fed me, I would make good on my promise to make them all superstars. I allowed them to put a little bit of everything on my plate. While we were filling up on deli slices, one or two of them talked about going to America and trying their luck as actresses or models in New York or LA. When I heard that, every single episode of *Law and Order: Special Victims Unit* flashed through my head with pictures of dirty, abused women chained in even dirtier abandoned buildings, until someone unfortunate stumbled across their bodies and called Detective Olivia Benson. Without ever laying eyes on the man, I knew Garifullin would never let any one of them leave freely.

Marie finally emerged from the house. My lunch companions must have noticed me noticing her because they started to giggle and poke each other conspiratorially. Marie sat beside me, picked up my drink, and downed the rest in one gulp. The casualness of her taking my drink was not lost on the other women. The giggling, whispering, and poking stepped up a notch.

After checking Garifullin's injuries, Marie had spent the rest of her morning conducting an impromptu health clinic for the soldiers. She did this at Kostov's request. I would have found a way to poison them all, I stated in a low voice, hoping the others wouldn't hear. Marie laughed at my viciousness. This group had more cases of STDs than she'd thought she would ever see in her life, she told me in a lowered voice. The thought made my skin itch, and I wanted to scoot as far away from my afternoon companions as I could. Did they even know they were unclean?

Marie said she told Lana to order some good, strong antibiotics and ensure all the women and the men took them for at least a week. She told Kostov to tell his men to learn to use condoms. I was sure he took that well. I could just picture him pulling out his revolver and holding out a pack of Trojans to Lev. The smallest size available, of course.

"Put it on or I will shoot you," Kostov would say. I couldn't hold back my giggles.

Marie's mini-clinic treated a few minor cuts, bruises, and burns throughout the rest of the staff and soldiers. A couple of Kostov's men suffered broken bones and sprains. Many of them were reluctant to seek her attention. Any sign of weakness made them vulnerable. Being vulnerable made them targets. They carried on even though they were causing permanent injury to something that a couple of days of rest could fix. Only when Kostov insisted, had they entered the office where she'd set up shop.

"It's almost like they were ashamed of being sick or injured," she said. "Especially the men with STDs. At least two begged me not to tell Kostov or Garifullin."

It was curious that they would not want Kostov or Garifullin to know. Kostov had given me the impression it was encouraged. Maybe they didn't call it rape, but according to Marie, Kostov's mercenaries frequently partook in the women's services. His very words were that sex was available if the men wanted it. It wasn't the sex he objected to, it was the spread of STDs, Marie told me. It made me wonder if the soldiers had brought the diseases in and passed them along to the girls, or had the girls picked them up from somewhere, and in turn infected the soldiers? I guess it didn't matter. All that could be done now was to treat everyone infected and hope they learned their lesson.

I gave Marie a brief rundown of what Kostov had told me earlier about his men and their use of rape as a weapon; she looked as horrified as I had been. "That's appalling," she said. She picked another piece of meat off my plate and popped it in her mouth. Appalling or not, she still had to eat.

I couldn't do anything about her disgust at Kostov and his attitude; after all, it mirrored my own. Instead, I handed her my plate and returned to the table for another. Lev stood at the end of the table. He glared at me as I walked over to get more food.

"You should not treat a woman like she is a man," he whispered harshly in my ear. Again with the homophobia. "In Russia, if you declared your attraction to another woman, you would be jailed, tortured, or even executed. In my country, women do not seek out the affections of other women."

I whirled around so fast that I almost knocked him down. "I'm treating her like she's a human being," I said. "Something you and your friends could learn. It is called common decency. And if you think lesbians don't live in Russia, maybe you'd better ask your sister." It was a childish insult, but all I could think of at the moment.

I turned my back on him and returned to take my place next to Marie. The women were grilling her about France, Paris, and Frenchmen. Their heads were full of love, romance, flowers, and other sweet things. They had all seen too much TV and read too many fashion magazines.

One of the women asked Marie if she was in love with me. Marie glanced at me and smiled. "We'll see," she said.

That caused the women to go off in another fit of giggles. The one sitting closest to me jokingly poked me in the ribs and told me I had better try harder. I was sure I was blushing now At least they were open-minded enough not to think that the penalty for falling for another woman was worthy of death. Their society might have condemned homosexuality, but I'd be willing to bet that the subject came up around here more often than anyone admitted.

"What made you want to become a model?" I asked Eva, the girl sitting closest to me, as she gushed about how she longed to go to Paris and dazzle the runways there. A glossy fashion magazine lay open on the table next to her. She picked it up and flipped to a two-page spread featuring the latest supermodel.

"She is so beautiful," Eva said. "Everyone loves her. She goes all over the world. She wears beautiful clothes, and everyone wants her."

"Don't you have that here?" I asked, feigning innocence.

For a second, her features darkened. The other ladies were all watching her to see how she would respond. "Of course," she said brightly. "We don't get to travel so much, but Mister and Mistress make sure we have the finest clothes and meet all the important people."

"Have you ever told them you want to go to Paris?" I asked. I knew I was tiptoeing through a verbal minefield, but I was genuinely baffled by how these women could think this kind of life was a stepping stone to a glamorous career. It made me wonder if they even knew what had happened to Lidiya and her sister.

"Mistress promised us that she will help us pursue our careers when we are ready," Eva said. The other girls nodded. Their mistress, I assumed, was Mrs. Garifullin, who seemed to oversee their activities.

"She told us only this morning that you are going to help us by taking many pictures we can put in magazines and advertisements," one of the other girls spoke up. So that was what they had in mind when they decided to blackmail me into doing their bidding.

I wanted to ask about Lidiya but decided it wasn't a wise idea while things were going so well. If I kept the truth in front of me, I could buy some time to figure out a way for Marie and me to escape. Until then, I would pretend and go along with their fantasies of a better life.

Garifullin used their labor to pay for his private army and elaborate lifestyle. It was probable they did have a better life working for Garifullin than if they were on their own. If they weren't working for the gangster, they would likely face starvation and possibly death. At least here they were well fed, and it gave them some illusions of glamour. Some might experience the high lifestyle with parties, expensive clothes, and gifts from grateful men, but the endless parade of sexual partners would eventually wear them down. They didn't even get to keep the money they earned. Garifullin provided everything they needed, they assured me. The worst revelation was that they didn't believe anything was wrong with how they lived if it helped them achieve their dreams.

I'd seen documentaries and read articles about sex workers in Ukraine back when I studied everything I could get my hands on about this country. The stigma attached to the profession in America didn't exist here. Maybe I was the one who needed to update my point of view. It wasn't the sex for money I objected to. It was what often came with it. It was the STDs, unwanted pregnancies, and physical abuse that often accompanied the trade. It might not be evident here in the open, but knowing what happened in the shadows could not be overlooked.

I moved to a new line of questioning. Since the war began, had the men who chose them as escorts, I used the word without sarcasm, changed in their social standing? Again, the honesty of their answers surprised me. The war had changed things for them. Instead of wealthy Ukrainian men, they found themselves more often paired with Russian middlemen and soldiers. They disliked Kostov and his men. This was relayed to me in exaggerated whispers. They wanted Lev and the others to overhear but wanted to pretend they didn't.

When they were introduced to Russian businessmen and Russian political leaders, the women found themselves having to rely on what they called their considerable acting skills to convince the men they found them desirable.

"Russians are cheap and coarse," one of them whispered in my ear while casting furtive glances in Lev's direction.

A couple of the women expressed their distaste at being mauled by someone they described as more of a gorilla than a man. She pulled out her lips and made noises like a monkey. We all laughed at that while Lev's ears turned an even brighter shade of red, and he squeezed his hand into a fist while the women's giggles taunted him.

A few minutes later, Lana appeared with a few staff members behind her to remove the remains of lunch. The housekeeper told the girls it was time for them to go inside and see to their duties. When I asked what duties they were assigned, Eva grinned back at me as Lana herded them all toward one of the outbuildings. I expected her to tell me they had to make their beds or something similar.

"We have to make ourselves beautiful," she said. She mimed shaving her legs and plucking her eyebrows. I'd like to get some pictures of that, I thought. "We are entertaining tonight."

Marie and I were finally alone, except for Lev and a couple of house staff who were cleaning the area around the pool. Marie moved closer to me to tell me what she'd learned while doing her impromptu clinic.

Not only did Garifullin have a stable of women, but he also had entire outbuildings filled with guns and all types of weapons, Marie told me. He had his own private army in addition to the Wolf Pack. His soldiers distributed drugs and weapons. She'd overheard Garifullin and Kostov talking about it. When she'd given the order for antibiotics, she'd discovered they had an abundant supply of medications. Lana had asked her to name the drug, and not ten minutes later, she'd returned with three bottles of the stuff. Marie and her colleagues struggled to find enough drugs, bandages, and antiseptic to prevent infection for wounded Ukrainians while this guy hid rooms of it. He had enough stock to open a pharmacy as far as Marie could tell.

Marie had also learned one of the outbuildings on the estate had a regular assembly line of heroin and another of cocaine. There was also a full-scale meth lab. She'd treated a burn on one young man's hand, and another had a burn on his face. They spoke in Ukrainian, not knowing she understood much of the language. An accident in the meth lab had burned them both.

I wondered if there was any way we could take Garifullin down and confiscate his booty. I wrote myself a note to try to find out if the Ukrainian government got to keep his profits if Garifullin ever saw the inside of prison. Back in Texas, anything a drug dealer possessed automatically went to the police department that arrested him. That included weapons, cars, and money. I doubted the Ukrainian government had similar laws, but it wouldn't hurt to find out once we escaped.

That is, if we escaped before they murdered us. Maybe we could steal a couple of guns and shoot our way out. That didn't seem likely. I'd seen the Wolf Pack on the shooting range this morning. None were lousy shots. In the movies, the good guys only escape because of the incompetence of the bad guys. I needed to get my head back in reality if we were going to get out of here. Fantasy-TV-fueled escapes wouldn't do anything but probably get us killed.

Lana came back outside after shooing the women inside to oversee the cleanup of the remains of lunch. I asked her what happened to all the leftover food. People in the city were fighting over scraps, and here, they threw out more than a family of four could consume in a week. Lana pulled herself up to her full height of five-foot-four.

"We are aware there are shortages," she said. "But we feed many people every day. The ladies, the soldiers, the servants, no one goes hungry here."

Lana told Marie and me she would escort us inside now. Mrs. Garifullin was having a big dinner party tonight. The girls who had just left would all have a nap and then spend several hours getting ready. Mrs. Garifullin expected our attendance at this dinner party. She had insisted we be there.

"I am ready to assist you with preparations for this evening," Lana said stiffly. A mental image of Lana standing by while I shaved my legs and Marie plucked her eyebrows popped into my head. This time, I didn't withhold my snort of laughter.

Why would Garifullin want Marie and me to come to his dinner party? We were prisoners, for God's sake, not guests. He was nuts if he thought we would wear fancy dresses and high heels. I reminded Lana that I had told her as much last night.

"Is he even well enough to host a dinner party?" I asked Marie. Yesterday, he was at death's door, needing a transfusion. Today, he was throwing parties? God forbid his wife let anything as trivial as her husband being stabbed interrupt her plans. Marie elbowed me sharply in the ribs. I quit complaining.

"He believes he is well enough to host," Marie said. "Mrs. Garifullin wants you to take pictures."

"The Madame often has guests in the evenings," Lana said. "If Mister is not able to come, Col. Kostov will fill in as host."

I bet Kostov loved that. The gangster's wife, desperate for legitimacy, wanted pictures for the society pages. A few glamor shots of a local gangster throwing a party might not go over in Kyiv or anywhere else in Ukraine, but if the Russians got a good look at the party girls, and the elaborate food and drink, it could make a difference in the Russian attitude about the whole invasion.

I had to wonder what the society pages in a major Russian newspaper were like. Not that they called them society pages anymore. At least, not in the United States. They were features now. Maybe the Russian news agencies hadn't evolved to features yet.

No matter what they called it, Mrs. Garifullin wanted publicity. It was a gathering of the criminal elite, and only I had the scoop. It would make a good feature story. I'd be a cinch for the Pulitzer if my captors let me live long enough to send my news agency another story.

That thought led me to wonder if Pamela had received the news of my abduction and if she'd called out the cavalry yet. How hard could it be to track us down? An entire warehouse full of people had seen us taken, and they knew who had taken us. Then, I remembered Kostov had his men firebomb the distribution center. My thoughts turned from curious to brooding in a matter of seconds. For all I knew, Tatiana, Pasha, and all the other people there looking for food, shelter, or medical assistance were dead. Pamela might not even be aware I was missing.

With that depressing thought, I let Lana escort us back to our rooms. Lev sort of clumsily tried to follow until I brutally dismissed him. He slunk off like a whipped dog. I didn't care. His remark about treating Marie like a man still burned. His attitude crossed him off my possible ally list. On the other hand, I could have one or more of the women expose their breasts in front of him, and we could slip out while he pretended not to look.

What made him so different from the rest of his troops? The other men had no problem at all taking advantage of the women available to them. Lev seemed to be the exception to the rule. Maybe he was raised by insanely religious parents. Either that or he had a massive inferiority complex. Kostov had promised Marie he would assign one of his men to watch us who could be trusted not to attempt another rape. I wasn't sure if that reassured me or not, given Lev's obvious dislike of any display of sexuality. Hell, he could even be a latent homosexual himself. "Methinks the laddie doth protest too much," I muttered.

Back upstairs, Lana practically ordered me to take a bath. She even filled the tub and poured all kinds of concoctions in. One was suitable for the skin, she said. Another cleared the sinuses. A third boasted a scent guaranteed to calm the nerves. Satisfied with the bath's rejuvenating powers, Lana ordered me to get in. She would lay out clothes for Marie and me to wear tonight. That would be as far as I would allow her ministrations.

"Nothing strapless, no low-cut blouses showing cleavage, no short skirts, in fact, no skirts, and most definitely, no heels," I said. When Lana turned to leave, she found Marie standing in the bathroom doorway.

"What she said," Marie informed her.

Lana nodded curtly, glaring at me. She seemed more willing to take Marie's demands than mine. The servant told Marie that she should bathe after me. Lana promised to choose something pleasing to both us and the mistress of the house.

Marie started to unbutton her shirt, causing my heart to dance the tango. I thought, perhaps even hoped, she would strip and crawl into the tub with me. There didn't seem to be any cameras in here. If there were, they were well hidden. There could still be microphones to pick up the audio, but I found I didn't care. My heart leaped like a dolphin trying to ring the bell at Sea World. Marie pulled off the shirt and tossed it in the general direction of the hamper. What the hell was wrong with me? One morning in the company of women who made a business out of sex, I was ready to throw caution to the wind and make love to Marie like a horny teenager.

"I'll just get out of these clothes," Marie said. She wasn't wearing her scrubs. I noticed her jeans and shirt had the bloodstains I'd come to associate with her wardrobe. It struck me that I must have been captivated not to notice that almost every time I saw her, some bodily fluids stained her clothes. I must be starry-eyed to overlook those details.

Lana shook her head at us as she gathered our dirty clothes. I tried not to laugh. There was no point in offending the woman's sensitive feelings any further. I tossed some of the foamy bubbles in Marie's direction. Lana muttered something about adults behaving like children and left the bathroom in a huff.

"Want to join me?" I asked Marie again.

She approached me with a wicked gleam in her eye. All she wore was underwear. I found it impossible to look away. She placed the palm of her hand on top of my head and shoved me under the water. I came up sputtering and blowing out soap bubbles. Her laughter trailed off as she sashayed out of the room.

Life with her would be fun, I thought. Then I realized that thought caught me off guard. If I was honest with myself, I was in love with her. Good for me. At the same time, the realization terrified me because of the situation we found ourselves in. This could be one of the shortest love affairs in history if we didn't get out of this alive.

So far, our captors had not made any serious attempts to harm us. If I disregarded the couple of times Kostov had slapped me, and of course, the attempted rape and the almost hourly death threats, I could lose sight of the fact that a four-star prison was still a prison. As an emissary of this criminal empire, Kostov had threatened me every time we'd met. I couldn't afford to become complacent about that. Kostov did not make idle threats. Admitting my feelings for Marie were a coping mechanism. If we had feelings, we were still alive.

I finished bathing and rinsed off. Lana must have been standing right outside the bathroom door. The second I pulled the plug, she was there, shooing me out of her way to give the tub a quick rinse and prepare it for Marie.

The clothes Lana had picked for me lay across the bed in what I referred to as the blue room. It was a nice pair of white slacks, a matching blouse, and a bright red cardigan. The outfit was more for a business professional than a hooker. For that, I was grateful.

It was also surprisingly comfortable. I expected to feel like I had donned a suit of armor for the evening. It was a perfect fit, and it was flattering. I dressed and added the complimentary accessories Lana also provided. The diamonds and gems were genuine. I wondered how often Garifullin's guests stole from him. Or did he give it away as a bribe or a reward?

"Wow!" I whirled around at hearing Marie's exclamation of admiration. "You look fantastic."

She should talk. The green dress she wore accented her color and eyes. It clung to her frame, but instead of pointing out any flaws, it suited her body to perfection. My brain struggled for something witty to say. I wrapped my arms around her and kissed her, hoping everything I felt translated into that kiss.

"You're not so bad yourself," I finally said. I mentally kicked myself for not saying something that more accurately expressed the raging emotions in my heart and mind.

When we separated, we both sucked in a breath of air. All the oxygen seemed to be gone from the room. I could barely unwrap myself from her. So much for caution. If we had been in another place or time, I would have continued to kiss and caress her until she'd begged me to make love to her. Unfortunately, the sound of the key in the door caused both of us to let go and take a step back.

When Lana reentered the room, she gave us a disapproving look, as if she had caught us in the act instead of a harmless embrace. Her lips pursed, she announced that dinner was almost ready, and the mistress requested our presence downstairs for pre-dinner drinks. She instructed me to bring my camera, as Mrs. Garifullin wanted pictures of their distinguished guests. I thought about refusing to be a puppet, but it occurred to me that it might be good to have documentation of the people who did business with the mobster. Besides, I've never been good at passive resistance.

Lana escorted us downstairs to a room off the main dining room. There were twelve others present. Garifullin was there, a little pale and sitting in a wingback chair. A frown crossed Marie's face as she observed him. It was a testament to her values as a doctor, making her want to do everything she could to save him, despite his disobeying her orders to rest, and despite the fact he had kidnapped and threatened to kill us. Kostov was present with four other men who seemed to be too old and too well dressed to be soldiers.

For each male guest, there was a female counterpart. Kostov ignored the woman standing next to him. I wondered what transgression the poor girl had committed to be assigned his escort for the evening. I recognized two of the women from our photo session by the pool. The other two were new faces.

All four women were considerably younger than the men, at least half their age. Sonja Garifullin was in her early forties, handsome but not comparable in looks to the younger women. She was thin, almost to the point of being anorexic. She was also elegantly dressed without the sultry component of the younger women's wardrobes. Her wardrobe and stature recalled Cruella de Vil, the villain in *101 Dalmatians*. I had to bite my tongue to keep the song from that Disney movie out of my head.

When Marie and I entered the room, she rushed to us and introduced herself. Sonja apologized for not being there to greet us when we arrived. A million questions went through my mind to ask her, but it wasn't the time or place. Was her politeness all for show?

Pulling us farther into the room, she took us to each of the men and introduced us. She gave them the impression that Marie and I were guests, not prisoners. She pretended the people she introduced us to were legitimate friends and business associates, not criminals. Sonja made it sound like I was a world-class photographer asked to photograph their events for the society pages. She dropped the name of a couple of prominent Russian papers and websites. The women she'd picked for this event, all clinging to a male, were omitted from introductions. Pretending to be a guest challenged my limited acting skills. Falling back on my scant knowledge of Ukrainian, I nodded a lot and pretended to smile.

Another of the many servants announced dinner was ready. Geez, just how many people lived and worked here, for Christ's sake? Sonja led the procession from the parlor to the dining room. Each place setting held elegant matching China with a salad plate stacked on top of a dinner plate. There were three forks, a cloth napkin encased in a jade napkin ring on the left, a butter knife, and some knives I didn't recognize. I'd missed that episode of Martha Stewart. Two wine glasses and a smaller glass were on the right above the knives and spoons, finishing off the place settings.

Sonja took each man and positioned them in front of a seat. She placed her husband at the head of the table and took her place at the foot. Markar Garifullin was shorter and rounder than I expected him to be. He appeared in his early to mid-fifties, but it wasn't easy to tell. Instead of letting his hair turn gray, it was dyed jet-black. His matching mustache made him look like he had a small, dead animal on his upper lip. His regular coloring wouldn't have been as pale as it was tonight if he hadn't lost so much blood yesterday. I had imagined him as a ruddy-faced officious bastard. All I got wrong was the ruddy part, and that was mainly due to his recent blood loss.

Throughout dinner, I observed him trying too hard to impress his guests. The lavish meal, the expensive place settings, and even the beautiful women were meant to scream Garifullin's success. In other circumstances, I might have had some pity for him. Considering his actions over the past few days, I only felt contempt.

237

Marie was placed on Garifullin's left while I was beside Sonja at the foot of the table. Kostov sat across from me, still ignoring the young woman beside him. At our end of the table, Sonja tried to keep the conversation going. I limited her efforts to engage me by pretending I didn't understand her English. I was attempting to eavesdrop on the others. Since the rest of the party spoke in Russian or Ukrainian, my attempts were fruitless.

Sonja tried interacting with the Wolf Pack commander, but Kostov only grunted in response to her questions. She still gave the impression of a gracious hostess. After a while, I gave up trying to catch Marie's eye and answered Sonja's questions about Texas. No, we were not all cowboys, and we were not oil-rich billionaires.

The luxury of the dinner seemed obscene to me because a few days ago, we were talking to people lined up at an abandoned warehouse to get a bag of potatoes. It wouldn't have surprised me if the topic of peasants came up, and Sonja shouted, "Let them eat cake."

I was exhausted with this game of pretend and wanted nothing more than to get some sleep. Since most foreign countries didn't start dinner until after nine p.m., it was almost midnight when the final course was served. The pomp and ceremony seemed to go on forever. There was no hope of being excused. We were not guests, we were prisoners, and if we wanted to stay alive, we had to do our captor's bidding.

Finally, the dessert came. It was *stolichny* cake. It had tons of powdered sugar and seemed an odd choice since it was less extravagant than the rest of the dinner. I expected some outrageous dessert that took tons of preparation, like those ice cream sundaes made with edible gold flakes in New York City. As it was, the cake was too sweet for my taste. I took a few bites, but that was all. I never ate food this rich, not even at home.

Sonja did enjoy showing off by telling me the name and origin of each dish. Considering the famine in the rest of the country, her bragging disgusted me. When the male guests claimed they could eat no more, Sonja invited us to return to the parlor where glasses of digestifs awaited. By that, she meant a type of drink designed to aid digestion. I could certainly use one myself, or a package of Rolaids, but I doubt I was included in that invitation. Afterward, Sonja said she hoped the guests would be so kind as to allow me to photograph them.

Once everyone was in the parlor, Sonja directed one of the men to an antique settee, where she posed each man in a position designed to make him the dominant figure in any portrait. It was subtle, but any trained photographer would pick up on it. That answered my question about who had decorated this monstrosity of a house.

Because they were all middle-aged men, I assumed most of them were married. Why would they want photos of themselves with beautiful young girls? Unless it was one of those male ego things. They could display the photos in an unspoken boast. "See how strong and virial I am to attract such a beautiful young woman." It wasn't unheard of. Maybe Garifullin wanted pictures of them with his women for blackmail purposes.

While I took pictures, Sonja circulated around the room, getting the men in and out of the poses she wanted with frightening efficiency. Everyone but Sonja and Kostov drank copious amounts of alcohol. I wondered if this would be a good time for Marie and me to make a break for it. That was until I noticed Kostov watching every move I made. When the evening started to wind down, Sonja dismissed the girls by announcing the men would retire to another room to discuss business matters. Markar Garifullin had escaped the room some time ago.

"Give me the SIM card from your camera," Kostov said, approaching me.

"What? No way!" I took a few steps back. My response was louder than he was comfortable with.

He grabbed me by the elbow and led me out of the room. "I am not asking, Nicole Sheppard. One of my men will download the pictures into our computer."

"That's not the point," I said. "If a photo has my name on it, I want to ensure it is the best version possible. Sometimes certain photos need to be tweaked a bit."

"I will look at your pictures," he said. "If any need to be 'tweaked,' I will let you proceed. Under my observation."

"I'm sure," I said, heavy on the sarcasm. Kostov knew I planned to download the pictures even if I couldn't send them anywhere. He probably also knew that in the back of my mind, I calculated that having photos of Garifullin's guests would be a prize if we were rescued or escaped. I opened my camera with much bad grace and removed the SIM card.

"You have no hope of ever leaving this place, Ms. Sheppard," he said quietly. He wasn't stupid. He knew I planned to use the photos for my own gain. "We're only keeping you alive until the Garifullins tire of playing the big shot. You should remember that."

My heart sank at his words. I shook off the feeling, determined not to let him see any fear. "And here I thought we were becoming buddies," I said.

"Make no mistake. We are not 'buddies.'" He pocketed the SIM card, told me not to move, and returned to the parlor. A few minutes later, he returned to the foyer with Marie in tow. He escorted us back upstairs to our rooms. When he shut the door and locked us in, she took me by the elbow and sat me on the bed.

"What's wrong?" she asked. She took a step back and searched my face for clues.

"He threatened us," I said. Technically, he'd threatened me. He'd never directly said he would kill Marie, but it didn't seem unrealistic to think he would order my execution and let her go.

She sat beside me, pulled me down on the bed, and stroked my hair. A fine mist of sweat covered my body, and a not entirely unpleasant ache took over my entire torso. She had a way of making me feel brave.

"I don't care if they are watching or listening," Marie said, her voice husky. "Make love to me, Press."

I reached behind her and found the zipper to her dress and pulled it down while she reached over me and switched off the light. After a few minutes, I forgot about Kostov and everyone else.

CHAPTER FIFTEEN

The following day, Lev pounded on our door as soon as the sun peeked over the horizon. I untangled myself from Marie's embrace. She murmured something sleepily and turned over, pulling the covers with her. I yelled at Lev to give me a minute to dress.

He led me downstairs to the office Kostov had commandeered. A new laptop sat in the middle of the desk. My SIM card lay next to it. My orders were to do whatever I wanted with the photos and then delete everything on the SIM card. Lev would ensure it was blank before I could put it back in my camera. The images would stay on the computer until Kostov looked them over. He would print them out and give them to Sonja if everything met with his approval.

The first thing I did was Photoshop Kostov's head on the body of a jackass. Then I made it his wallpaper. It was

242

probably a bad idea, antagonizing him like this, but I hated him so much that I found myself looking for ways to get under his skin. Maybe some small part of my brain refused to believe he would murder me. Besides, I was sure the survival manual did say something about doing whatever we could to throw our captors off guard. At least, I hoped it did anyway.

For the next hour or so, I lost myself in editing. Creating photographs that stood out brought me a lot of satisfaction. I was able to forget the real reason for the photos and lose myself in the creative process. That was until Marie came to find me. When she saw the laptop with Kostov's head on top of a jackass, she bit her lip and frowned.

"Press, you have got to stop picking away at him," she said. Before I could respond, Lev answered a knock on the door. Kostov himself came in and stood behind me.

When he noticed the altered wallpaper on the laptop, he bent over and put his mouth practically on top of my ear. "You think you are funny, Nicole Sheppard. We'll see if you can laugh at a bullet in your brain."

He straightened and ordered me to print out the pictures. Per his instructions, I hit print. Lev removed the photos from the printer. When he had a small stack of them, he took them to the door and handed them off to someone on the other side.

Kostov stood by while I deleted everything on my SIM card and returned it to my camera. I didn't know how much he knew about computers, but it seemed like he didn't realize I had set up a hidden folder where I could keep everything. Somehow, I would find a way to copy it, print it, or even email it to Pamela.

Kostov said Sonja wanted me to join her for a late breakfast. Marie would check in on Markar Garifullin, and then Kostov wanted her to continue triage on his men. An image of her grabbing Kostov himself by the balls and telling him to cough came to mind. I hoped she made it hurt.

I'd already had a couple of cups of coffee, but I was getting hungry. I turned off the laptop and followed Lev out the French doors and to the garden, where Sonja sat at a small round table. She wore a white pantsuit that probably cost more than my entire wardrobe and a large sun hat. The table had a variety of juices and pastries. She had my photos of the women from yesterday fanned out in front of her.

When Lev and I entered the garden, Sonja stood and beckoned me to sit opposite her. She ignored Lev. Ever the gracious hostess, she poured me a cup of coffee and pushed the tray of pastries closer to me.

"I wanted to thank you for taking such wonderful photographs of our girls," she said. "I was wondering if you would consider putting them together in something of a magazine. What do you Americans call it? Oh yes, a brochure or catalog."

Once, in college, I'd come across a catalog in the university newsroom. The glossy front cover showed several pictures of beautiful women. It had horrified me because it was a catalog for Russian women offered as mail-order brides. Instead of seeds, you could send in a check and have a beautiful Russian woman delivered to your door. That was an oversimplification, but didn't it amount to the same thing? When I asked Sonja if that was her intention, she vehemently denied it.

"Oh no," she cried. "Markar would never hear of it. And our girls would never want to leave us. I thought it would be nice to give to our business associates who sometimes require female companionship when they visit. I would be happy to pay you."

Although I believed it was a futile effort, I decided that while I would go along with their attempt to legitimize them, I would remind them at every turn that I knew the truth of our presence here.

"I'd be happy to do it for you," I said. "As soon as I'm done, you will arrange transportation back to the hotel in Kyiv for myself and Doctor Dubois."

All her efforts to pretend we were guests faded from her expression. "It was my understanding Markar brought you here to take pictures and write stories about his business," she said. "Colonel Kostov also brought the doctor because that foolish girl stabbed my dear husband."

"Probably because he threatened to murder her and her parents if she didn't bring back his child that he fathered with one of the women you pass out to men like after-dinner breath mints."

It took her a minute to regain her composure after my accusations. "None of our employees are forced to do anything," Sonja said haughtily. "When they work for us, they receive the best of everything. They eat well, have the best clothes, and receive wages much higher than the local factory pays. They lack for nothing."

I decided to cut my losses. It was worth a shot, even if it missed. Before I could say anything else, Sonja scooped up the photos and slid them out of sight in a manila folder. The same way she had swept away our conversation from a few minutes ago.

"I'll make you your 'brochure,'" I said, emphasizing the word brochure. "But just know that the only reason I'm doing it is because I don't have a choice."

"Fine! As long as you do it," Sonja said. She cleared her throat and set her facial expression to neutral. "There is one other thing I would like to discuss with you since you brought it up. I wanted to talk to you about Akim."

Hopefully, my expression matched hers. "I don't know where he is," I said.

"Perhaps not." Her tone indicated she didn't believe me. "But I find it hard to believe you and the doctor, for that matter, would hand him over to strangers without a way of reconnecting with him. I have read your stories from your news agency. Those stories tell me you are lying."

It was not a good idea to call me a liar if she wanted to get something from me, but she did it with such finesse, that it was almost subtle. I shrugged it off. "Why do you want to raise a child that is not yours? Somehow, you don't seem like the maternal type to me."

"It is different for men. They need proof of their masculinity," she said. "That is one reason our girls are so successful: we train them to stroke the male ego. Markar has always wanted an heir. I let him have this, and it gives me, how do you call it, leverage?"

The thought of this woman raising Akim made me want to punch her. If I could do it without Kostov or one of his men shooting me, I would. Once again, I denied any knowledge of the kid's whereabouts. Sonja stood and tucked the folder of photographs under her arm.

"You really should reconsider telling us what you know," she said. "It is a matter of your personal safety." I recognized the statement for what it was: a not-thinly veiled threat. No doubt she was thinking what a coup it would be if she could get the information that no one else could pry out of me. I shook my head as she turned and left.

The colonel was waiting for me in the office. Upon entering, I noticed the laptop open to the wallpaper photo of his head on a jackass. Maybe I didn't get a shot of his good side. Either he would shoot me for it or tell me to get rid of it. Since I would probably die today anyway, I was glad I'd done it. If that made me petty, then so be it.

"Amusing picture," he said after staring at me for a long minute. "You do have talent, Nicole Sheppard." Then, he made a big deal of highlighting the picture and hitting the delete button. He took another minute to stare at the computer screen as if he wanted to make sure it was gone.

"Mrs. Garifullin said she tried to hire you for a project. You told her your price would be your freedom, yours and the doctor's."

"I gave it a shot," I said with a shrug. Even though I hadn't procured our release, I had to keep up appearances. Wouldn't he expect us to try any means to escape? I thought that was one of a soldier's creeds.

"Yes. Sonja was most distressed that you believed you were a prisoner here. You are. However, Mrs. Garifullin was blissfully unaware of that fact until you sought to inform her. She honestly believed her buffoon of a husband hired you. You may have noticed, but as far as her husband is concerned, she put blinders on to his activities a long time ago."

"I noticed," I said. "Don't kid yourself. That she-devil is aware of everything under her roof. She is sensible enough to know how to pick her battles."

Kostov looked up at me. I suspected he was searching for a hint of sarcasm. The suggestion was there. He just chose to ignore it.

"I have convinced her that your reluctance to cooperate in finding Akim resulted from your strange American values. Life is different here. This is something you need to accept. With Mr. Garifullin still recovering, his wife has become more dependent upon me to make decisions." Kostov frowned, and it seemed like he was talking to himself more than he was to me. If he thought I would commiserate with him, he was incredibly wrong. He shook off whatever monkey was on his back and gave me a look. "You will do as I say. Since she convinced herself to believe her husband hired you, you will pretend that is the case and do the magazine she wants. And when she pays you, you will gladly accept the money. When you finish, and Mr. Garifullin is well, you will tell us where to find his son. If you like, I will distribute the money to the poor after you and the doctor die."

So, he still planned on killing us. Maybe I should have refused and let him shoot me then. I also wanted to tell him that even though I knew how to assemble a catalog, it wasn't one of my primary talents. If I produced something shoddy, he'd shoot me anyway. Hell, if I created something great, he'd shoot me.

"Why should I do the brochure and take the money if you'll kill me anyway?" I asked.

He stepped around the desk until he stood toe to toe with me. "Because there is a slight chance that, if you do as I say, I will let the doctor live," he said between clenched teeth.

It all made sense now. Maybe part of the reason Garifullin kidnapped us was to make me pay for hurting his business and withholding information on his son. I had humiliated him, so he had to pay me back in humiliation. He would make me a party to selling his whores, literally at gunpoint. Neither Garifullin nor Kostov had any qualms about using Marie as the carrot tied to their stick.

"I'll do her damn brochure," I said, slinging the words at him. "I already told her I would."

"Good," he spat. He stepped back and walked out of the room.

CHAPTER SIXTEEN

Ten days came and went without an opportunity for us to make our escape. We discussed plans, using furtive whispers and crude drawings on napkins that we tore to pieces and flushed down the toilet. The weather was beginning to turn cooler, and neither of us had a coat or even a jacket other than our flak jackets. They were designed to keep out bullets, not freezing temperatures. The cold in this part of the world was harsh and unforgiving. While Marie and I discussed ways to work around this, she put a halt to it after several fruitless ideas.

"Let's concentrate on getting out of here alive," she said. "We can worry about freezing to death afterward."

Some days, I helped Marie in her makeshift clinic. Kostov's troops seemed to break, sprain, or pull something every other day. Marie was not allowed to dispense any medication. Her orders were that if one of the many people vying for her care needed any drug, even aspirin, she would submit a request to Kostov. Kostov would either send someone or come himself to administer the dose. I assumed he was afraid Marie would either poison his men or overdose them, allowing us to escape.

In those ten days, I had either interviewed or taken a picture of almost every person on the property. Most of what I got from my interviewees was a jumble of praise heaped on Garifullin. He was a humanitarian. He was a great employer who took care of his employees. He was a loving husband, this from Sonja. Her only regret was that she had never been able to give him children. She even said it with a straight face.

During that time, men in suits came and went. Mercenaries with the Wolf Pack ran drills on the property. Sometimes, Kostov took them out on maneuvers. Even if I forgot the underlying threat of Kostov ending our lives at any second, it was still frustrating. Trucks and vans came and went in the middle of the night. Armed guards stood next to the vehicles. They were hypervigilant. I documented it all while Marie slept. I didn't see any way to use any of this to our advantage, but I had a feeling that could change at any time.

Every night, Kostov retrieved my SIM card and downloaded the photos I'd taken onto the laptop he kept locked in a safe downstairs in Garifullin's office. He disabled the Wi-Fi on all the computers he thought I might gain access to. He didn't want to risk me guessing a password. He let me use the computer to enhance the pictures or write copy to accompany some of the photos. By writing copy, I mean Kostov gave me something he or Sonja wrote and wanted me to type it up. The document repeated accolades for Garifullin and his "humanitarian" works. Every journalistic bone in my body rebelled at doing this. Sonja assured me copies of the catalog were not for public distribution but reserved for an elite few.

I had to wonder what was taking our rescue so long. It wasn't like Garifullin had a secret lair or anything. This mansion and acres and acres of land had to be highly visible. The only reason I could think of for the delay was that storming the place would be difficult. Either that, or neither Marie or I were important enough to risk a rescue operation. A third possibility was the outside world thought we were dead. This last thought disturbed me more than the first two together.

In my version of our rescue, the Navy Seals, led by Brad Pitt, parachuted onto the grounds, blew the doors open, and escorted Marie and me to a waiting helicopter. My mind ran through a million scenarios daily about how and when help would arrive. I imagined Kostov killed by his men for being such a coldhearted bastard and Garifullin arrested on drug and sex trafficking charges.

While we looked for ways to escape or waited to be rescued, our imprisonment was getting boring. Marie would see patients in the morning while I worked on the brochure. We spent our afternoons hanging out around the pool with the ever-changing beauties.

The question of Akim's location moved to the back burner for now. Either Kostov didn't care if we gave up the kid, or it amused him to imagine me planning to escape. He knew I was trying to get a sort of blueprint of the house. He took a morbid delight in telling me at least once a day that escape was impossible, and that he would kill me as soon as my usefulness ended. It began to wear on my nerves.

Marie and I developed the habit of sleeping in the same bed. Sometimes we quietly made love. She was a demanding lover but had no problems reciprocating anything she asked me to do. After, she would drift off to sleep. I lay awake long after she fell asleep, contemplating our escape and fantasizing about our life together while I watched her.

As our eleventh day of captivity began, I caught a break. Even with Kostov's interference, I had assembled a workable map of the house and grounds. At least the part I traversed. There were acres of land and a lot of outbuildings where I was denied access. Overcoming or escaping the guards remained our most significant problem. I hadn't found a hole in their security.

Lev was my guard for most days. It came to my attention that he was easily distracted. Even when the women were not around, he appeared preoccupied and paid little attention to me and my actions. The boy seemed to have some severe attention deficit.

I was downloading some photos from my confiscated SIM card. Kostov let me add my notes to an offline program. Any stories he allowed me to write, he kept stored here. While I waited for the images to load, my eyes wandered around the room, searching for something Marie and I could use to possibly escape.

I noticed the top drawer of the desk was open. It was only a crack and seemed slightly askew, as if someone had slammed it shut and didn't bother to check that it had closed all the way. After verifying Lev was not paying any attention, I tugged at the drawer. It did seem to be stuck. Lev was concentrating intensely on something other than me, so I jiggled the drawer a little and gave it another tug. It clattered open, not loudly, but enough to make Lev look around to see where the noise came from. My attention was on the computer screen, so after a few seconds, Lev went back to contemplating the universe of his thumbnail.

As soon as he stopped paying attention, I slid the drawer open farther. It was a typical junk drawer filled with pencil stubs, broken pens, paperclips, rubber bands, and other assorted bits and pieces. I didn't want to shift around too much for fear of making noise. One gleaming object caught my eye. A brand new flash drive was inviting me to steal it. I snatched it up and jammed it into the computer before Lev noticed.

The blank drive was a blessing. It would have been even more so if it contained all Garifullin's dirty dealings, but I'd take what I could get. I started downloading all my pictures and notes from the secret folder onto the hard drive. While waiting for the data to transfer, I searched through the hard drive and added anything I thought might be incriminating. If and when we got out of here, I wanted evidence to take this empire down.

The download crept along at a snail's pace. I watched it slowly inch toward completion. When it was ninety-nine percent, Kostov appeared in the doorway, demanding my progress. I cleared my suddenly dry throat and told him it would be a few more minutes. Hopefully, he wouldn't notice the extra drive sticking out of the side of the laptop.

Since he always looked suspiciously at me, I clutched my silence like it was a wallet at a thieves' convention. Kostov broke eye contact first and said something to Lev in Russian.

He turned to me and ordered me to find Sonja when I finished. Unable to speak, I nodded.

"Do not upset her," Kostov said. The threat was implied. I almost bit my tongue in half to keep from responding. Sonja seemed to be coping quite well, despite my attempts to call her empire what it was.

The download finished, and as soon as Kostov turned his back, I ripped the drive out of the computer and slipped it into my pocket with one swift move. I would hide it, along with the key to Marie's door when I returned to my room. Since acquiring the key, I'd changed its hiding place to a secret pocket in my messenger bag. Guards had searched my bag immediately after our capture. I sincerely hoped my captors saw no need to search it again. I left it hanging in the wardrobe. No one noticed I obsessively checked it every night before bed.

I stood so Lev could take me to Sonja. She sat at the same table in the garden, wearing similar clothes as at our first meeting almost two weeks ago. I'd seen her in the interim, but she avoided direct contact. After that one dinner party, Marie and I ate in our room or dined with some of the women. I sat down across from Sonja and helped myself to a drink and pastries.

"This is my favorite spot on the entire grounds," Sonja said. She seemed wistful and gazed out over the garden hedge. I wondered if she regretted her life here or if the war caused her dissatisfaction when she couldn't get her name in the Russian society pages.

I started asking her questions. How often did their power go out? She said they had two generators, so they could restore power within a few minutes when it did go out. Her husband had acquired the generators some months ago from a Russian business partner. I asked her how they could obtain such lavish food and abundant quantities. I didn't tack on, "when the rest of the country is practically starving."

"It is so difficult to get supplies these days," she said with a huge sigh. "We are most fortunate. I only have to tell Colonel Kostov what I desire, he contacts his superiors, and they send a shipment every few days."

I ignored the delicacies she pushed my way again. I'd lost my appetite. Sonja had no such qualms and helped herself. "Of course, there are some things even the colonel cannot provide." She heaved another sigh. "Sometimes, I think everything would be so much easier if Ukrainians would only do what is expected of them, and surrendered to Mother Russia."

I choked on the coffee I was attempting to swallow. It went down the wrong pipe, and a coughing fit made me spit what was in my mouth all over the table.

Sonja pretended I hadn't just blown hot coffee all over her immaculate blouse. "Oh dear," she said. "Are you all right?" Her expression couldn't have been any more innocent. I wasn't about to get into a debate with this woman over the intentions of the Russian government, that much was certain. After I got myself under control, I wadded up some napkins and mopped up the coffee from the table. I didn't touch her blouse.

Changing the subject, I turned to questions about the women, asking what they did when they weren't working. As far as I could tell, they spent their days hanging around the pool, working on their tans. Sonja said the girls mostly worked at night, so their days were free to pursue other interests. She insinuated that they went to school or pursued careers in the performing arts. I could not tell if she believed that or was blind. I reminded her I needed the information for the catalog. Fat chance any of them studied ballet or sculpture in their spare time.

I asked her if all the girls lived here on the grounds. Sonja said most of them did. Several of the outbuildings on the estate were dormitories where the girls stayed. A few, who had been with the family for many years, kept apartments in the city so Garifullin's clients did not have to leave the city when they wanted companionship.

When I asked her how those women fared inside the city, given current conditions, she dismissed the question, saying, "Markar worries about all of that."

I asked her a few more questions about any other shortages they might be experiencing. She lamented, again, the inability to go shopping. Markar usually took her to Moscow at least once or twice a year. She gushed about the boutiques and shops where she could get a private show of all the latest clothing designs from Paris and other places. On one memorable occasion, before all of this unpleasantness started, he'd taken her to Paris and let her shop to her heart's content. She looked forward to doing that again when the locals came to their senses and allowed Russia to annex the country.

Sonja pretended she was a handsome face with a head for nothing but making other things look pretty. I knew there was a cold, calculating mind behind the façade, with an even harder heart. Politics bored her. Poverty was the byproduct of lazy people who did not want to work and sponged off hardworking citizens like her husband.

After an hour passed, she glanced at her watch and said she must end our conversation, although she'd enjoyed speaking with me. She was off to have a massage. Her masseuse, Henri, would be positively livid if she was late. She invited me to stay and have some more coffee and pastries. Otherwise, the staff threw them away, which seemed to be the worst atrocity, and belied her previous remarks about her staff getting the leftovers. Hopefully, her staff pocketed the remains and doled them out to people who couldn't make it to the manor for meals.

I waited until she disappeared inside the house, pocketed a couple of honey buns myself, and went in search of Marie. I found her in the parlor treating some cuts and scratches on a kid about eight years old.

"This is Lana's grandson, Seigeri," she said. There was a resemblance between the kid and the servant. Lana stood by, watching Marie as she ministered to the boy. Giant tears rolled down her face.

"The Russians bombed their street," Marie said. "Seigeri's mother and sister were killed. He hid under the bed. It protected him from most of the shelling."

I glanced at Lana. "I'm sorry for your loss." I tried to sound sincere, but so much death and destruction around a household oblivious to it, forced me to dig deep to find any sympathy.

"I begged the master to allow them to come and stay here, but he says there isn't room," Lana cried.

The door opened, and Sonja came in wearing a silk kimono with her hair pinned up. Her massage had ended, I guessed. She looked at the scene before her and sneered at her servant. She spoke in English. "What is that urchin doing here?" she asked. She directed her question to Lana. "I have told you before, I do not want your ruffians underfoot."

That caused Lana to sob harder. She explained about the bombing. The boy had just lost his mother. He needed to be with his grandparents. Sonja ignored Lana's pleadings and ordered her to take the boy away when Marie finished treating him. She spun around and left the room, slamming the door behind her. Lana stared after her. She dried her tears and set a determined look on her face.

Marie finished bandaging the last cut. Then, like a magician pulling a rabbit out of his hat, Marie produced a chocolate bar from some inner pocket. Sergeri's face lit up when he saw it. He grabbed the candy, thanked Marie, and tried to make a quick getaway.

Lana caught him and told him to wait in the hallway for her. She gathered the trash from the boy's bandages and stepped as close as possible to us. "There is a tunnel under the property," she said quietly. "They use it to smuggle girls in and out when they don't want too many people seeing them. The end of the tunnel comes out by the garage. There is a gate near the far end of the garage. You can use it to get to the road. The main road is about one-quarter of a kilometer." She looked furtively around the room. Fear rolled off her like a cold sweat. Access to the tunnel was through the kitchen. There were flashlights, water, and other necessities just inside the entrance.

"Find Akim and take him as far away from that woman as possible," Lana whispered. "Leave tonight. I am taking Seigeri and the rest of my family to Poland. I can only hope God forgives me for waiting this long."

We heard her sob again before she reached the door. Whether she was crying because she'd just betrayed her boss or because she just lost her daughter and granddaughter was unclear. Either way, I appreciated the help.

We still had to plan how to get past the guards in the hallway, get into the tunnel, and escape, but this information was a game changer. For the first time, I was hopeful we might get out of this alive.

"Where did you get a candy bar?" I asked Marie finally. There didn't seem to be anything else to say.

She grinned at me. "I swiped them from a table in the foyer," she said. "You never know during wartime when you will have to bribe some local beauty with chocolate."

"Better grab a few more of them," I suggested. "We might get hungry."

Now we had work to do.

CHAPTER SEVENTEEN

I was antsy for the rest of the day. I'd hoped to get a chance to pull Marie outside so we could talk without the risk of being overheard. I'm sure they had surveillance outside, but covering up voices in the open was easier. Lana foiled that plan when she returned and told Marie that Mr. Garifullin had asked for her.

"He seems to be in much pain," she said.

"He's probably not drugged enough," Marie whispered under her breath. "He won't allow me to administer any painkillers, but I think he either gets his wife, Lana, or one of the other girls to do it. Most of the time when I see him, he is in a morphine haze."

"Maybe you could see about lacing his food or something," I suggested. Having him out of the way would help our escape. Kostov on our tail was scary enough.

Garifullin was scared, Marie told me. Certain people were coming tonight to "confer" with him, and he was determined to appear the picture of health. The men coming were even more cutthroat than he was, and he was afraid they would take drastic measures if he showed any sign of weakness. She had learned all this information by casually eavesdropping on the monster. My appreciation for her skulking abilities had grown significantly over the past couple of weeks.

"You'd make an excellent spy," I said.

Since that first night, Garifullin had taken to his bed and relayed orders through Kostov and Lana. Sonja, without the support of her husband, had also begun to rely on the Russian mercenary for the day-to-day business of operating a large household. A growing sense of tension between Kostov and Sonja had increased almost hourly.

The big Russian marched around the estate barking orders, and God help any of his poor, hapless soldiers who hesitated. Sonja seemed to follow him around, chatting incessantly. It wasn't worth the effort to try to eavesdrop on them. Sonja's shrill nasal whine practically echoed off the walls of the estate. The other sound I kept hearing seemed to be Kostov grinding his teeth. Despite my intense hatred of them both, I cheered Sonja on. The more unbalanced Kostov was, the better.

While Marie went off to make sure the man of the house wasn't dying, I wandered back out by the pool. I'd done a mockup of the catalog Sonja wanted. The women were gushing over it. I had to say, I'd outdone myself. I'd given each of them the intelligence of a genius and the beauty of a goddess. I'd made them sound like they were all Wonder

Woman and that all they wanted to do was make a man's life better. There was no mention of any sexual activity, but it was implied in most, if not all of the short bios. The women flocked around me, telling me how wonderful I was and how I'd made good on my promise to make them stars. I hated myself, and depression started sinking in.

Sonja was extraordinarily pleased with it. She gave me a massive wad of Russian currency to prove it. The ruble was worth twelve cents compared to the US dollar. It was worth slightly more with the Ukrainian hryvnia. If we left here, I'd give the money to Tatiana or Pasha. If they were still alive. Maybe they could put it to good use. Holding it in my hand made me want to puke when I thought of how Kostov had forced me to earn it. I wouldn't say he'd pushed me into prostitution, but he did force me to sanction it.

The problem I had with it was that for every one of these ladies who swore their lives were perfect, there was a Lidiya out there who hated it. People like Garifullin exploited women. I hated them all. I hated Garifullin, Sonja, Kostov, and his whole band of merry rapists. My hatred ran so deep, I wouldn't have been surprised if it choked me.

All I'd done was give their pimps a way to exploit them even more. My name was not on the brochure. I could only imagine it coming back to haunt me in the future. I'd be stepping up to the podium to accept my Pulitzer, and Lev would come running down the venue aisle, waving it in one hand and shouting in Russian that I was a lesbian responsible for publishing pornography. Both those things were considered abominations in Lev's part of the world. Funny how rape and prostitution were okay, but printing pictures of nearly naked women or women loving women was not.

When I complained about this to Marie, she held me tighter and murmured reassurances in French. She'd already taught me a few words, but I could see a complete course in my future. If that disgusting catalog ever popped up, she promised me she would swear I'd done it under threat of death. I decided as soon as I got back to Texas, I'd show it to Pamela. Hell, I'd even put the whole sordid story in the book I was planning to write about this ordeal. Maybe I'd even print some pictures of the girls. Publishers seemed to like that kind of shit.

I took the money Sonja gave me and stuffed it in my bag. The key to the room and the flash drive with all the evidence on it was in the secret pocket. I didn't need to hide the money. They knew I had it. It might come in handy when we made our escape.

Lana brought us our supper on a tray. She was alone tonight. When one of Kostov's guards let her in, she shooed him back out the door and locked it behind her. Her eyes darted around the room and came to rest on the light fixture. That was where they hid the surveillance camera, I assumed.

Lana placed her body firmly in front of the desk where she laid out our food. Marie stood on one side of her, and I was on the other, blocking any chance of anyone seeing what she showed us.

She drew a crude map on the back of a napkin, including dots to represent where the guards usually did sentry duty. There were four spots between us and the door leading to the tunnel. Since the people around here didn't have dinner until nine p.m. or later, their bedtime was usually after midnight. Our best bet for escape would be about three or four in the morning. That was when one, sometimes two, of the guards would sneak into the kitchen for a snack.

The cook had a soft spot for young soldiers, Lana told us. Her son was in the Ukrainian army at the beginning of the conflict. He'd died early on, leaving her without anyone to mother. She poured her affections out on any enlisted man, even the evil ones from the Wolf Pack. Every morning in the hours before dawn, they snuck into the kitchen for a treat. Lana told us all this, warning us to wait until the guards left the kitchen. The cook, who was sympathetic, would show us how to find the entrance to the tunnel.

Lana said she would return to pick up our supper dishes, but after that, we would not see her again. She had her escape plan. One did not just turn in a two-week notice when working for the Garifullins. Especially when the employee knew where the bodies were buried. She encouraged us to eat and get some rest. It was going to be a long night.

"Goodbye," Lana said, "and good luck."

I was too nervous to eat much. Marie had no qualms about scarfing down her dinner. I noticed her subtly stick some bread in one pocket and some cheese in another. I followed her example and stashed away a few morsels myself.

Instead of Lana, however, the younger maid knocked on the door to pick up the dinner tray. The young lady spoke no English, so Marie thanked her in Ukrainian. The girl nodded and furtively slipped Marie another note.

The note was from Lana and said Sonja was going away for the night. She wanted to visit her sister in Bila Tserkva, just southwest of Kyiv. The fighting there had died down, and Sonja was concerned about her family. Colonel Kostov and two of his men would escort her to ensure her safety. That was a break we hadn't counted on. With Kostov and some of his men gone, our chances of getting out rose drastically. When he wasn't around, the men slacked off quite a bit.

Marie and I performed our usual nightly routine for the camera. Lana had stashed some dark clothes under the bed when she cleaned our room. There were even a couple of leather jackets to ward off the cold. If this mission was successful, we'd have her to thank for it. I slipped between the sheets after Marie, and we moved into the positions we'd become comfortable with, me on my back and her with her head on my shoulder.

She told me in a low voice how much she looked forward to showing me France. The immediate future concerned me the most. My priority would be contacting Pamela. I wondered how she would react when I told her I was going to France. We had correspondents there, but they were French citizens.

Maybe Titan would make an exception to compensate me for being kidnapped. I couldn't imagine leaving my career to follow Marie around, but the beauty of it was if she planned on continuing to work for Doctor Without Borders, I could stay with Reporters Without Borders. It would break my heart to leave Titan because I loved my Titan Global family. But I'd go freelance if it meant being with Marie. I think I loved her more.

We lay there in the dark for a long while. Marie slipped her hand under the T-shirt I wore to bed and began caressing my stomach. "Make love to me, Press," she whispered. She ran a row of kisses down the side of my neck. "Make love to me like it is our last night on Earth."

Any objections I might have had at that point melted away under the fervor of her embrace. I pulled the shirt over her head and drew her closer so I could kiss and caress her beautiful breasts. She gasped and wiggled out of the pajama bottoms. I took my time, making sure I had her so aroused that she begged me to penetrate her and get it over with.

I've often been told I was an excellent lover. I took my training from movies from the 1970s. In one case, the woman speaking to her friend says, "If you knew it was going to be the last time, you would have enjoyed it more." My motto was to make sure my lovers never had that regret. I enjoyed making love to Marie DuBois more than I had ever enjoyed sex with anyone.

I kissed every square inch of skin my lips could reach. While I did that, I made sure my hands were not idle. I used to think multiple orgasms were a myth, but that night they were very real as Marie buried her face in a pillow to muffle her screams of ecstasy. Wouldn't that be embarrassing if the guards posted outside heard her muffled screams and rushed in to her rescue?

She was adept in her reciprocation when it was my turn. When it was over, I don't think I had ever been so thoroughly made love to in my entire life. We lay tangled together, naked and exhausted, as the sounds of the mansion wound down outside our door. I didn't whisper words of love. Neither did she. There would be plenty of time for that later when we were out of there and somewhere safe.

I didn't think either of us would be able to sleep, but soon I heard the familiar sound of Marie's breathing. She didn't precisely snore, but occasionally, she would put out the tiniest snort. It was a beautiful sound. I could lie there all night and listen to it. At least, I thought I could. It wasn't much longer when I nodded off as well.

Marie had set an alarm on her watch to wake us at two a.m. It was on vibrate, but it wasn't necessary. A few minutes after one, we were startled awake by explosions, gunfire, running boots, and shouting.

"Get dressed, Press," Marie whispered. "And keep your head down."

"What's going on?" I asked.

"The estate is under attack," she said, pulling on a pair of black pants.

"Who is attacking us?" I asked. "Is it the Russians or the Ukrainians?"

"I don't know," Marie said. "Hurry! If it is the Russians, we can't let them catch us."

That got my attention. We'd all heard rumors of the inhumane conditions of Russian prisons. Fear motivated me as I rushed to don my black pants, shirt, and shoes. I ran into the other room and grabbed my bag and camera. For a minute I couldn't afford to waste, I wondered if I should put on my flak jacket. Then I decided there wasn't time, so I left it lying on the bed next to my helmet. I was so nervous, I dropped the key to the door twice. Marie took it from me while I was still hopping around, trying to get my shoes tied. She unlocked the door and opened it just enough to peek into the hallway.

"Okay, it's clear. Come on," she said.

I threw the bag strap around my neck to free my hands. Another explosion shook the house. Members of the Wolf

Pack rushed around the foyer, vainly trying to form some kind of defense. I suspected they were useless without Kostov whipping them into shape. Further hindering their progress were the women and servants screaming in panic and trying to get somewhere safe. The entire house was in chaos. People seemed to be running in all directions, not knowing where to go.

I cringed as a missile shattered the front door of the mansion. Several of the women who were trying to get out that way were peppered with flying wood, metal, and other debris. Screams of pain and fear drowned out the cries of the soldiers trying to bring some semblance of order to the melee.

Marie hesitated. Everything that made her who she was told her to stop and help those who were injured. She wouldn't be Marie Dubois if she wasn't torn between stopping to help and escaping. My fingers tightened around hers. Every fiber of my being was telling me to run the other way. Even my desire to take some pictures was overpowered by my fear of getting recaptured. Drawing a deep, resolution-filled breath, I knew if Marie decided to stop and help, I would support her.

Shaking off her hesitation, Marie took off again in the opposite direction. When we got to the last tier of the staircase, Lev was standing there shouting orders. Everyone seemed to be ignoring him and continued running. When he saw Marie and I standing there, he glared at us both and climbed the steps until he was in front of us. He reached for me first as if he didn't even see Marie moving toward him. She let go of my hand and took two steps until she was right in front of him and kneed him right between the legs. He dropped to his knees and collapsed over on his side, holding his injured balls and moaning loudly.

"Nice move, Doc," I said.

She grinned back at me and stopped for just a second to give me a quick kiss. "You're mine now, Press," she said, her brown eyes alight with a gleam. "I'll take out anyone who tries to take you away from me."

Marie grabbed my hand again and pulled me away from where Lev lay, cursing her in Russian. You didn't have to be fluent in the language to get the gist of the names he was calling us. It didn't matter. My heart pounding wasn't because we were in the middle of a firefight and could die any second. It was because she'd said I was hers.

Garifullin came rushing out of his bedroom wearing a pair of red silk pajamas, a kimono with a dragon emblazoned across the back, and a pair of slippers. He was yelling for Kostov. In his right hand, he brandished a pistol. It seemed he'd forgotten that his Russian lap dog had taken his wife to visit her sister. He and Marie stopped at the same instant. All his focus was on her. There was a crazed look in his eyes, and he yelled something at her in Ukrainian before he switched to English.

"I will have your heart cut out of you and feed it to my dogs," he said, his accent heavy and thick. I wondered if he'd been drinking before the attack or if it was painkillers making him look so deranged. He stepped onto the stairs, his eyes blazing with hatred. He waved the gun back and forth between us. It was almost hypnotizing.

"I think I will kill you both myself. Then, I will have Kostov and his men tear this country apart until they find my son."

Marie spat a French curse back at him. He raised the gun and aimed at her.

"No!" I screamed. If I threw myself in front of her, she could get away. Without thinking, I rushed him, hitting him on his left side. It was a tackle that would have made the Dallas Cowboys proud. We both tumbled down the stairs.

Garifullin rolled into the curve of the staircase and stopped there. While he struggled to raise himself, or at least get the gun pointed at us again, I landed on top of him, knocking the wind out of both of us. I recovered first, grabbed the pistol, and hit him in the face. Once, twice, I cold-cocked him. I would have kept hitting him if Marie hadn't grabbed my arm as I drew back for a third strike.

She pulled me off him. "Come on, Press. We're getting out of here." Marie jumped over his now unconscious body, and we ran down the stairs. There wasn't any need to keep quiet now. There was so much noise and confusion that no one else bothered to try and stop us. Marie held tightly to my hand and dragged me toward the kitchen where the entrance to the tunnel was supposed to be.

When we reached the kitchen, the cook whirled around to confront us with a massive knife in one hand and a meat cleaver in the other. When she saw it was Marie and me, she jerked her head toward the pantry. "You two go there," she said in broken English.

I'd not been in the kitchen before. It would have put a four-star restaurant to shame. There were no less than three refrigerators, two large stoves, gleaming pots and pans hanging from ceiling racks, and in the middle of it, the cook and two younger women who were either her assistants or

271

children. She pushed the two of them in the direction of the pantry where she directed us.

"Follow them," she said to us in English. The so-called pantry was bigger than my whole apartment back in Texas. Industrial-sized dry goods filled the space. When you fed this many people, you had to buy in quantity.

I tripped over a fifty-pound sack of flour spilling across the floor and lost my grip on Marie's hand. She stopped and pulled me up. White flour covered my black clothes. If the attackers of the estate were at the end of the tunnel, I would become a large white target. A bit of hysterical laughter bubbled up in me. I bit down on it before I lost it completely.

I still had Garifullin's gun. It was bloody from where I'd hit him. When I'd fallen, it had remained in my hand. I still had a death grip on it. I wasn't sure I could even open my fist to drop it. It occurred to me that we might need it, and I was perfectly willing to kill someone if they got in the way of our escape.

If we got to the end of the tunnel and found ourselves face-to-face with the Ukrainian army, I would drop the gun and surrender. It would suck if our allies shot me because I was armed. If we found ourselves at the mercy of the Russians, I'd do my best to shoot our way out of it. If it were the Russians, it would be preferable for them to shoot us on sight.

One of the kitchen girls pulled on a rack of shelves, and a door opened. She grabbed a high-powered flashlight from the shelf and switched it on. The beam lit up a long, dark hallway hidden behind the door. The girl with the flashlight motioned for us to follow her. The second girl stepped in behind us. The kitchen staff seemed to want to help us, but for all I knew, they could be leading us right into a trap. I didn't trust anyone in this godforsaken household, but we followed the two young women. I was willing to do whatever it took to gain our freedom, especially when we were so close. There was only going to be one of two options from here on out. Our deaths or freedom.

At the end of the tunnel, the girl switched off the flashlight. Marie said something to her in Ukrainian. It sounded like gratitude for their help.

"You go out here," the girl said in English. "Stay behind the garage and go through the hedge. It will lead you to the road."

We thanked her again and ducked through the opening. If chaos reigned inside the house, the outside was worse. The Wolf Pack had barricaded themselves inside, firing at their attackers through broken windows. The attacking force threw everything they had at the dwindling Pack. Almost all the outbuildings were on fire. Smoke and noise were everywhere. I desperately wanted to pull out my camera and start shooting, but I restrained myself in the interest of survival. If Marie wasn't going to stop and administer aid to the wounded, I sure as hell could sacrifice a few pictures.

I grabbed Marie's hand again and pulled her at a run toward the garage. The incoming troops, if they were there to rescue Marie and me, were otherwise occupied. If we had any chance of finding out who was in charge, we would have to get past the front line. We had been so focused on getting to this spot, that neither of us had considered our next step. We could hike to the nearest road and hitch back to Kyiv. Or if we were lucky, some thoughtless driver had left the keys in one of the vehicles haphazardly parked around the garage.

We stopped when a large black Mercedes screeched to a halt inches from where we stood. A very angry Kostov stepped out of the driver's side. He barked some orders at two soldiers who tumbled out of the back seat with Sonja in tow.

I turned to Marie. "No matter what happens, if we get separated, I will find you," I said. "I promise."

Behind us, the entrance to the tunnel opened again, and Garifullin stumbled out. He held one of the kitchen servant girls in front of him as a shield. My hatred for him kicked up to a whole new level.

"Kostov," he demanded. "Shoot them. Shoot them both right now."

Kostov aimed his gun at a point between Marie and me. His breathing was ragged, and his eyes were just plain crazy. It took all my willpower not to drop to my knees and beg him to spare us. An intense rage over all the terror he'd inflicted on me in the past few weeks came boiling up in me. This man knew no mercy, but I'd die before I begged him for our lives. His gaze flicked between us and Garifullin. Without hesitating, he aimed his gun and fired. I flinched and waited for my body to tell me to lie down and die already. Instead, Garifullin crumpled to the ground behind me.

"Markar," Sonja screamed and ran to where her husband lay. Kostov had shot him right between the eyes. Even I knew he was dead. In the few seconds that the three of us stood stunned, I raised Garifullin's gun and pointed it at Kostov.

"Let Marie go, Kostov," I said. Surprisingly enough, my voice was level. "You can shoot me, but let her go."

He turned his attention back to me. His gaze briefly flickered to the gun in my hand, then he ignored it. The gun in his hand twitched a little bit to his right, back in my direction. His chest heaved as if the words he was trying to say were having to fight their way out.

"I have suffered that gluttonous fool and his vapid wife for months," he said. The words came through clenched teeth, but I could understand him, even with all the noise. "I have catered to their whims and kept my tongue. I have allowed myself to become a patsy for them for the sake of arming my troops and keeping them fed and clothed." He took several steps in my direction, closing the gap between us. "When he ordered me to take you and the doctor, I assumed we would kill you both. Lidiya, the whore you went through all this trouble for, is dead. All that was left was to find the boy and kill you."

My hand was shaking, and I wasn't too sure of how good my aim would be. But Kostov wasn't finished. I felt Marie let go of my hand and step away. I didn't know what she was doing, but I was positive she wouldn't desert me here. My attention couldn't be divided now, so I focused on Kostov.

"But would he let me kill you? No!" Kostov screamed. "He wanted to keep you around and make you write fluffy stories about him and his wife. All they wanted was to be members of Russian high society as if Mother Russia would have them. They made me their lapdog. Me! A decorated warrior, fetching croissants and tea. We needed his weapons, but we have them now, and I can finally kill you."

For a few seconds, everything around us faded away, and time stopped. I was going to do it, I thought. I was going to kill another human being. The gun in my hand went off as if my thoughts had pulled the trigger. I knew my brain had not given the order.

Kostov fired at the same instant. He went down first as a ball of fire tore through me. Without even realizing I had fallen, I found myself lying on the ground. Weirdly, I thought, damn, Pamela's never going to let me stay here if I keep getting shot. I could hear Marie screaming in the distance. I tried to struggle to my feet, but my legs didn't seem to be connected. Someone turned the volume down on the noise again, and the only thing I heard was Marie.

"Let me go. I'm a doctor. I can help her," Marie screamed. Someone was calling me by my name: "Nicole! Nicole!"

That couldn't be Marie. She always called me Press. The shouts faded, and I thought I saw someone dragging her away. I must have been asleep and dreaming. I certainly felt sleepy. Why was I all wet? A soldier bent over me. He said something, but I didn't understand him. If I was dreaming, wouldn't I have been able to understand the people speaking to me?

Two other soldiers picked me up, one at my feet and the other under my arms and laid me on a stretcher. They carried me past a body that looked like Kostov. From this angle, it was hard to tell. The headlights from the Mercedes illuminated his body. He lay on his back, slightly tilting his head. When the medics moved me past him, I thought he was still glaring at me. I shuddered and looked away. One of the soldiers pried Garifullin's gun from my hand.

They loaded me into an ambulance. I didn't see Marie. I tried to ask, but my mouth wouldn't move. A young medic climbed into the back of the ambulance with me. He assured me I would be okay while another one stuck me with a needle, trying to start an IV. The one who said I'd be okay stuck another needle in my arm, and a couple of seconds later, everything went dark.

CHAPTER EIGHTEEN

It was a long, slow crawl out of unconsciousness. My body felt heavy. When I tried to move, restraints held me down. I remembered lots of noise, fire, and excruciating pain. It was quiet wherever I was now, except for the hiss of something that sounded like air blowing through a tube and the occasional beeping. The excruciating pain was still there, and I felt hot all over like everything around me was on fire. Then, I remembered. The bastard had done it. Kostov had shot me.

I forced my eyes open and looked around. I was in a hospital room, that much was clear. Tatiana slept in the chair on the other side of the room, her body curled up into a fetal position. She was alive! I was so happy and relieved to see her that tears filled my eyes. I tried calling her name, but my throat and lips were too dry, and it came out as a hoarse whisper. She heard my croak and jumped up, instantly awake. She grabbed a cup of water off the tray next to the bed and held it up where I could drink. Water had never tasted so good as that one drink. When I finished drinking, I cleared my throat and tried again.

"You're alive," I said. I hoped every bit of the relief I felt was apparent. Tatiana nodded, but the happy grin I expected wasn't there. "Pasha?"

I'd heard the expression "tears sprang to her eyes," but the instant tears flooding Tatiana's eyes, didn't do justice to the expression. She tried to speak but couldn't. She shook her head. I dropped my head back on the pillow. A nurse rushed in to turn off the alarms on the machines. Tatiana and I stayed quiet until the nurse said the doctor would be in momentarily and left us alone again.

"I am so sorry," I said, choking back tears. It was my fault that such a kind, gentle woman had died. "The grenade that soldier tossed in the doorway. I saw it explode."

"Yes, Mama threw herself on it—" Tatiana's voice broke. "Three others died, and several were wounded, but my Mama, she saved everyone else in that room. They were able to put out the fires, and..." She stopped again, took a moment, then collected herself.

I struggled to sit up and wrap my arms around my brave little fixer. Tatiana's tears flowed freely this time. Because she'd saved everyone else, Pasha's death meant something, Tatiana said through her sobs. It struck me as unfair when women like her died, and women like Sonja Garifullin lived.

"Marie?" I finally asked. What if Kostov had shot her? Was she dead, wounded? If she was okay, why wasn't she here, sitting by my bed? Not that I wasn't grateful to Tatiana for being there, but I longed to see Marie. Panic rose in my throat. A feeling of fear and despair tore through me. It was far worse than any physical pain, and if Marie was dead, I didn't want to live either.

"The Russians took her," Tatiana said while scuffing her sneaker against the tile floor, making a mousy little squeak. "It took Papa days to find out what had happened to her. They are holding her in a Russian prison."

My heart sank. I remembered the stories from a few years ago of an American basketball player being held for months in a Russian prison. After the player's release, she'd spoken of the horrors she'd faced there. She spoke of unsanitary conditions, beatings, and little or no food. This was before the war. If the Russians were holding Marie as a prisoner of war, how much worse would it be for her?

"Papa and the French government are negotiating for her release," Tatiana said. Her words trailed off, and then she wailed. "No one will tell me anything. Every time I talk to Papa on the phone, he tells me they are working on it."

"Who was it that attacked us at Garifullin's?" I asked.

"It was the Ukrainian Army," Tatiana said. "But the Russians were not far behind. In the confusion, they thought Dr. Dubois was one of Garifullin's escorts. The Russians swooped in and grabbed everyone who wasn't wearing a Ukrainian uniform and took them away." She looked down at the floor again. "At least, that is what Papa told me.

It struck me as mildly amusing that Russian soldiers might think Marie was on the same level as the escorts. She will get a kick out of that when I tell her, I thought. If I ever got the chance to tell her. I refused to believe our story could end so abruptly and finally.

Tatiana reached down and pulled a box from a bag at her feet. In the bag was a new phone. After Kostov and his men had taken Marie and me away from the distribution center, Tatiana had contacted Pamela to let her know what happened. When my editor received news of my escape from my kidnappers, Pamela had instructed Tatiana to call every day with an update. When the fixer told her I had been rescued, I was ordered to call my editor as soon as I regained consciousness.

Tatiana had the phone charged and the numbers programmed for me. Instead of following my editor's order, I punched in Marie's number. It immediately told me it was not a working number in French, Ukrainian, and English. I dropped the phone on the bed. It had been a long shot, but I had to try. I would call Pamela later.

"Are we in Kyiv?" I asked.

Tatiana shook her head. "We're in Warsaw. Your injuries were severe."

"How long have we been here?"

"Five days," she said. "They took you to a field hospital in Kyiv, stabilized you, then sent you here."

The doctor's entrance interrupted any further conversation. This doctor was a young male of Asian descent. He talked about recovery time and possible future surgeries. The bullet was armor-piercing, but fortunately, it hadn't broken into a multitude of fragments once it entered the left side of my chest. It had barely missed my heart. A fragmented shot would have killed me, the doctor said. As it was, there were enough pieces to cause significant damage. One of my lungs had been nicked, and they hadn't been able to remove all the shrapnel.

I could do my physical therapy here in Poland, the doctor told me. Or they could send me back to the United States in a few days. Most likely, I would need support, a cane or walker, for an undetermined amount of time. I asked about going to France. He considered it and told me that might be another option. After he consulted with French authorities, he would let me know.

He asked about my pain levels. I wanted to tell him my physical pain was nothing compared to my emotional pain. I threw out a number to gauge my degree of hurt. It was the physical equivalent of fingernails on a chalkboard. The pain seemed to be moving in a slow burn down my whole left side. The doctor promised to give me something. He patted me on the leg and left the room.

Tatiana went to see if she could find me something to eat. I wasn't hungry, but I realized she needed something to do. I put on what I hoped was a brave smile and told her that would be great.

Pamela answered on the first ring, even though it was after midnight in Texas. In the first five minutes of our call, she chewed me out for getting kidnapped and shot again. The following five minutes were her telling me I had quite a few articles due and asking when she could expect them. The last five minutes were spent by me consoling my formerly stoic editor and reassuring her I would live.

"Jesus, Sheppard," she said after unleashing her feelings on me. I realized she wasn't angry as much as she had been terrified that I was going to die and relieved that I hadn't. "If you ever put me through that again, I will kick your ass back to Texas."

"Sorry, chief," I said. "But don't you dare tell Marge I was outside without my bulletproof vest and helmet. I'll start putting some words in right away."

"Better enjoy the rest while you can because you're going to owe me a fucking book by the time you get healed up and ready to work again," she said, only halfway kidding.

Tatiana had retrieved my things from her house and from the soldiers who had overrun Garifullin's estate. Like the faithful companions they were, my messenger bag and camera were still there. I grabbed the bag and dug through it, searching for the flash drive where I'd saved everything from Kostov's computer. I panicked when I couldn't find it. I forced myself to calm down and go through the bag again. I found it stuck under a loose flap in a hole from the first time I was shot.

"You are not going to believe some of the stuff I've got," I told Pamela.

She told me to get started then. Work could be a balm for me, she said. After a brief silence, she said she was glad I was going to live. Before we signed off, I told her about Marie and asked, begged her to use whatever connections she had to help get the doctor released.

"First, you want me to adopt a kid, and now you want me to play Cupid." She groaned. "Don't tell me you went and fell in love over there."

"I'm afraid I did," I said.

Pamela sighed. "That's how I know you are never going to be old, bitter, and cynical, Sheppard. I send you to a war zone, and you fall in love. Okay, give me her name and everything else you know about her, and I'll see if I can track her down."

I told her everything I could think of about Marie. I described her beauty and compassion. Tatiana had reentered the room while I was waxing poetic about my love. Tatiana put the tray of food she was carrying down and took the phone away from me. Pamela needed facts, not lovesick poetry. Tatiana gave Pamela the practical information she needed and then returned the phone to me. Pamela told me to get better fast and hung up.

I glanced over at Tatiana. "How did you get here?" I asked.

"The manager at the hotel contacted me when they brought you in to be treated by the doctors there," she said. "When they decided to move you here, I asked Papa if I could come with you."

Her father had encouraged her to come. Dimitri now spent most of his time in the city at his office. Neither of them could bear the house without Pasha. She was what had made it home.

I reached over and patted Tatiana's hand. "I'm glad you're here," I said. I promptly fell asleep as soon as the nurse came in and injected painkillers into my IV.

For the next few days, I was in and out of consciousness. It was better than being completely out of it or completely awake. When my heart felt like it would break from Marie's absence, I welcomed the sleep. The pain from the wound constantly asserted its presence under a dull blanket of painkillers. Thankfully, because of that, I didn't dream much. During my more lucid moments, I tried to find out what I could about Marie. The lack of information was infuriating. I pulled out every bit of my experience as a journalist. I excelled at finding people and finding answers. Not this time, though.

Doctors Without Borders patiently explained to me multiple times that they did not release any information on their volunteers. They could neither confirm nor deny the actual existence of Marie Dubois. They also could not confirm or deny that Doctor Dubois was being held in a Russian prison. They thanked me for my interest and asked me if I would like to make a donation.

The French government told me they would take my number, and if any information came through, someone would call me. It was the French equivalent of, "Don't call us, we'll call you."

The US State Department was polite at first and directed me to their online forms to fill out as a United States citizen seeking assistance with a Russian prisoner. When they found out Marie was not an American, the woman told me in no uncertain terms that they had their hands full trying to get Americans out of Russian prisons and did not have the time or the resources to worry about the French. Unless I was Marie's next of kin, they couldn't help me. I told Tatiana I was beginning to think Marie was a figment of my imagination.

"You've got a pretty good imagination, then, boss. I thought she existed, too," she said, laughing.

After several attempts and a lot of Google Translate, I was able to get the phone number of Marie's parents' clinic in Saint-Malo. It took several more painstaking minutes to make the receptionist understand that I needed to speak to Dr. Dubois. Marie never told me her parents' first names, but she did tell me they were both doctors at this clinic. Finally, a woman's voice came on the phone. If my rudimentary French was anything to go off of, I think she was asking if she could help me.

"Please, madam," I said, cursing my strong Texas accent and dragging my memory for the right words and phrases. I explained I didn't speak French very well and asked her if she spoke English.

"Yes," she answered. "I am Dr. Dubois. How may I help you?"

I almost fainted in relief. I was speaking to Marie's mother. I only hoped that Marie was right in telling me that her parents fully accepted her sexual orientation. If they didn't, this was going to be a very awkward conversation.

"My name is Nicole Sheppard," I began.

Dr. Dubois interrupted quickly. "Nicole!" In her excitement, she lapsed back into French for a minute. Then, she resumed her English. "Yes, Marie has told us all about you. Have you heard from Marie? Have you had any news?" If she was desperately asking me these questions, then she hadn't received any valuable information either.

My heart broke all over again, knowing that I was going to have to break this woman's heart.

"No," I said, barely keeping the tears at bay. "I was hoping that you had heard something. Or at least made some progress toward getting her released."

The tears in Marie's mother's voice were as obvious as mine. "No, *cherie,* I'm sorry to tell you. It has been so frustrating. The French government keeps telling me to be patient. Obviously, they do not have children."

We talked for a bit longer. Marie's mother told me to call her Annette. She asked how I was doing. The French government had told her that I had been shot while Marie and I were trying to escape and that I was hospitalized in Poland. Annette told me she had been trying to get my number. She was very glad I had called. We exchanged numbers. I also gave her Tatiana's number and Pamela's office number in case she received news and couldn't reach me.

"Marie is my heart and soul," Annette said. "If she loves you, then I love you too."

This time, I couldn't stop the tears. For most of my adult life, I did not have a mother. So having someone extend motherly love toward me was a wonderful gift. That was one reason Pasha's death hit me so hard. I thanked Annette, hoping she could tell how much her words meant to me. I hung up, both elated that I was accepted by the mother of the woman I loved, and dejected because she did not have any more news about Marie than I did.

It was going to take every bit of strength and resolve I had to bring myself back physically from getting shot a second time when the first wound had barely healed. Adding the difficulty of finding Marie was going to take all my mental and emotional strength. For the briefest of seconds, I just wanted to crawl under the blankets and cry.

Tatiana stuck by me through the long days, even though her grief weighed heavily on both of us. Coupled with the loss of Pasha and Marie, and the physical pain, we spent a lot of time holding each other while one or both of us cried.

We talked a lot about what Tatiana wanted to do going forward. It was tough losing a mother, especially one as well-loved as Pasha. Tatiana put up a good façade but confided in me that she wanted to study abroad because she couldn't stand being in that house knowing her mother wasn't there. That was something I believed I could help her with, and I bullied Pamela into starting the process of getting a student visa for my faithful fixer.

Between desperate attempts to locate Marie, I spent several hours a day in physical therapy. A fragment of the bullet had caused some minor damage to my spinal cord, forcing me to learn how to walk again. My physical therapist spoke very little English, and I knew no Polish. I leaned heavily on Google Translate during this time. I did learn a lot of Polish curses.

I called Pamela daily, reporting on my progress and turning in stories. Writing kept me sane, and I had plenty of notes and photos stashed away on my computer and the flash drive. My editor told me the stories were having a profound effect on our readers. She had to hire another receptionist to answer the increased number of calls and letters. Every day at the close of our conversation, I asked if there was any news about Marie. Every day, Pamela said no.

Every bit of pain, anger, and hatred went into the stories I wrote. I wrote about the Garifullins and their mini-empire of sex, drugs, and guns. I wrote about Sonja's indifference to the war and the blind eye she turned to her husband's business dealings. Marie Antonette had nothing on Sonja Garifullin.

I wrote about Lidiya's murder. I wrote about the brutality of Kostov and his men. Pamela told me that when our readers read about Kostov telling me rape was a tool, the Titan switchboard lit up like a fireworks display with the public outcry. I held nothing back. If I did, then my time in Ukraine was worthless.

Tatiana and I frequently spoke of our plans to return to Kyiv. It would be sometime in the distant future. Even after the war was over and the Russians were pushed back to Moscow with their tails between their legs, the stories would still be there. After we found Marie and we'd both recuperated. I didn't kid myself about what kind of shape she might be in after being in a Russian prison. What would Marie want, I wondered. Would she want to go back? Or would the trauma push her to return to France and spend the rest of her days working in her parents' clinic? Whatever she wanted, I was on board for.

Not knowing was driving me crazy. It was so frustrating not being able to do anything but make endless phone calls that led to half-hearted reassurances from overworked bureaucrats. I still made the calls daily, despite meeting an endless wall of, "Sorry, there is nothing we can do." I wrote passionate letters to the French government, the United Nations, the Russian government, and my useless state senators. I wrote to Doctors Without Borders and even contacted a few private investigators to see if there was anyone on the whole damn planet who could help me find the love of my life.

Pamela gave me evasive answers when I expressed my desire to either return to Kyiv or go straight to Russia to look for Marie. Pamela told me to keep working on the stories about my kidnapping and how Russia was using the mercenaries. For the time being, she purchased stories about the ongoing war from a freelancer in Kyiv.

She did tell me the stories they purchased were subpar to mine. They didn't have the heart and soul my stories conveyed. At least that was something. She insisted I come home when I was released from the Polish hospital. She needed to lay eyes on me to make sure I wasn't going to die. Then, and only then, would we talk about the future.

When I asked about Akim, Pamela told me that since both of his parents were now dead, an American couple who had some pull with the US State Department was working on adopting him. That was also good news. Pamela had located the infant after making a few phone calls. Bitterly, I thought if Garifullin or Kostov had known how easy it was to find him, probably none of this would have happened. If the American couple was able to adopt Akim, at least one happy ending would come from all of this.

Pamela also agreed to sponsor Tatiana. After many discussions about her future, Tatiana applied to attend the University of Texas. The university had an excellent engineering program. She would stay with me, and Pamela offered her a part-time job as a gopher in the newsroom. Tatiana overcame the last hurdle when her father agreed to let her come to the United States.

There seemed to be nothing left for me to do except to go home.

EPILOGUE

Pamela, Tatiana, and I were on our way to New York for the Pulitzer ceremonies at Columbia University. I wasn't as thrilled about getting the prize as I'd always dreamed I would be. Having spent most of the last few months trying to get Marie released from a Russian prison had occupied more of my thoughts and emotions than anything else.

Pamela didn't know it, but tucked away in my battered, bullet-ridden messenger bag was my resignation. I would camp out on the United Nations doorstep until I got some answers. If that didn't work, I'd fly to France, meet up with Marie's parents, and the three of us would do whatever it took to get her released. Even if it meant we had to go to Russia ourselves.

Before that happened, I would go to the Pulitzer ceremony, and I would graciously accept the award and make the appropriate speech. I owed Pamela that much.

During our visit, we were scheduled to meet Akim and his courier at JFK. It would be my last story for Titan Global News. I'd looked forward to seeing the little guy but couldn't help wishing Marie had been there to share it with me. They'd told us his flight was delayed when we'd arrived at the airport. It was another disappointment. We'd gone back to the hotel to prepare for the award ceremony.

When the time for the ceremony came, I was nervous. Pamela had graciously allowed me to dress in a suit and hadn't forced me to don a dress. She probably knew I would put up a fight and even refuse to attend if she did. Everyone kept telling me I looked great, but my mind kept returning to the way Marie had looked at me the night we'd dressed up at Garifullin's mansion to attend Sonja's dinner party. I'd have returned my Pulitzer to see that look one more time.

When they called my name, I walked up to the podium, cleared my throat, and began my speech. I thanked the prize committee. I thanked Pamela and the staff at Titan Global News. I thanked Tatiana and her family because I couldn't have done it without them. Pamela was live-streaming the ceremony, and Tatiana had promised me the whole family would watch. Marie's parents had tuned in as well.

When I got to the part of the speech where I thanked Marie, I couldn't speak past the lump in my throat. The silence dragged on while I fought to control myself. During the pause, I noticed a stir at the back of the auditorium. Pamela stood up, holding the door open for someone. I expected to see some stranger holding Akim. But it wasn't a stranger. For a second, I thought I must have been hallucinating.

While Pamela held the door open, Marie walked in carrying a small boy who could only be Akim. My love had lost weight, and her hair was a lot shorter, but she was still beautiful. I told myself it had to be a vision brought on by my grief. When she graced me with that smile, my heart knew it was her and jumped in my chest.

Forgetting the rest of my speech, I leaped off the stage and ran down the aisle to meet her halfway. I grabbed her and Akim in the tightest hug I could. My heart was doing triple time as I kissed her. When we broke apart, I realized the entire room was on its feet, clapping, stomping their feet, and cheering.

"Good job, Press," she said, and kissed me again.

ABOUT THE AUTHOR

Stacy Reynolds is a Renaissance woman. She's been an award-winning journalist, a DJ, a stand-up comedian, a government drone, and a writer of both fiction and non-fiction.

She is extremely happy to be a member of the Affinity Rainbow Publishers team of authors with her first romance novel, *Without Borders*. She hopes to provide many more to come.

An avid reader, Stacy leans toward science fiction as her preferred genre. She also loves a good mystery.

Stacy's hobby is photography. She also enjoys spending time with her four grandchildren, bird watching, trading sarcastic barbs, going to Joan Jett concerts, discussing art, and photography.

Currently, Stacy lives in San Marcos, Texas, with her son, daughter-in-law, grandson, their two cats, and a dog.

You can find Stacy on Facebook https://Facebook.com/stacy.reynolds2

Instagram and X @daather

OTHER AFFINITY BOOKS

The Invisible Woman by Annette Mori

In a world where logic meets the extraordinary, Tamara, a brilliant forensic scientist, discovers a mysterious purple plant that blesses her with superhuman abilities, including invisibility. Teaming up with her best friend, Annalise, a passionate FBI agent haunted by scars from her past, the two friends embark on a quest to bring down a brutal serial killer known only as The Hunter. As the danger intensifies, their bond deepens, and secrets are revealed. Will Tamara and Annalise finally admit to their feelings despite being polar opposites? Join these extraordinary women in this gripping tale of love, friendship, and the fight for justice, where heroes are born from pain.

Never Too Late by Glenda Poulter

After the death of her long-time partner, and a scandal at the school where she taught music and art, Janice Halston emerged as a shadow of herself. Feeling shaken, cautious and artistically blocked.

Tam Murphy lost her wife and son within a short time of each other. She tries to fill her emptiness with her daughter Mae, and granddaughter, Ocee.

Janice and Tam are brought together by the precocious Ocee. As their friendship deepens, so do their feelings for each other. Their deepening feelings send both women spiraling…in different directions. One toward what could be, the other away from fear of another loss. Will their spirals lead them back to each other, or further apart?

Nothing But Net by Ali Spooner

Hunter James, a rising star in college basketball, has her career and life sidelined after experiencing a family tragedy.

An opportunity for a fresh start opens the door to return to what she loves most: playing basketball. Hunter rushes through that door to make the most of her second chance.

Back in the basketball arena, doing what she loves, will she open herself and her heart to another chance to forgive herself and fall in love?

The Kitten Trap by Annette Mori

Inspired by the classic movie, *The Parent Trap*, two adorable black kittens, Midnight and Onyx, play matchmakers for their human mothers, Mac and Carmen. Struggling with the complexities of farm life, Mac can barely believe her beautiful girlfriend, Carmen, has agreed to move to the drafty old farmhouse to live with her and her beloved Pops. When Carmen is forced to leave the farm to care for her ailing mother, Midnight and Onyx as well as Mac and Carmen must struggle with the difficult separation. Just when it appears Carmen and Onyx may come back home to the farm, cruel fate raises a further challenge, one that will need the help of two mischievous kittens to overcome.

To Autumn by Katie M Hall

Sixteen-year-old Robyn Gale, along with her younger sister Anne, is sent away for the summer holidays of 1997 to stay with her grandmother at a caravan park in Devon. Robyn's had a tough few months: trying to cope with the fallout of their mother's attempted suicide, messing up her GCSEs, and finding herself attracted to girls. Perhaps getting away from her real life is just what she needs…she can focus on finding a boyfriend, watching *Neighbours,* and swimming. A solid plan, until she meets charismatic Australian lifeguard, Autumn, and her life is turned even more down under.

Fairytail Farm by Ali Spooner

Dr. Hill McCall and her wife Alice dreamed of developing a sanctuary for unwanted cats and dogs to live out their lives as a retirement project. Hill has secretly worked on the project for months when a wealthy benefactor surprises her with a large donation, allowing Hill to be more aggressive with the project's opening. A group home operator approaches Hill about summer volunteer positions for four girls as Fairytail Farm becomes more than just a sanctuary for the animals. It creates an environment of love and kindness for the animals and all that support the project. Several love stories develop from first love to mature couples who have found their forever person. Fairytail Farm is more than a dream come true. It is a home for happily ever afters.

The Love Demand by Annette Mori

In the dazzling realm of reality television, where love and drama entwine in a complicated dance as old as time, a groundbreaking series emerges that transcends the ordinary. *The Love Demand* is not your typical reality show. Lacey Fellows isn't sure she wants to subject herself to further humiliation, however, on the off chance her girlfriend may agree to accept a second marriage proposal, Lacey reluctantly consents to participating in the new reality show. What she doesn't count on is meeting a kindred spirit—one she can't seem to shake from her thoughts. Jaimie would do almost anything for her girlfriend, including following her to the ends of the earth and participating in a conniving television show that puts her in front of a camera, which happens to be her least favorite place. Her girlfriend, Sabina, hasn't met a camera she doesn't like. They couldn't be more opposite, but Jaimie still hopes Sabina will want marriage, kids, and the whole shebang. The last thing she expects is to fall in love with someone else. Let the games begin.

Sullivan's Trace by Ali Spooner

Micah "Sully" Sullivan has settled into a solitary life at the family horse ranch after her father's death. When her long-term vet, Doc Barton, plans to retire, his granddaughter, Bryn, arrives to take over his practice. An attack on one of Sully's prized horses throws Sully and Bryn into a whirlwind as they fight to save the young animal. Just as Sully is becoming comfortable with her growing attraction to Bryn, tragedy occurs, and her brother and his wife are killed in an accident. Sully's solitary life drastically changes when a family of three is born.

Love Sins by Annette Mori

Jessica Green's life is predictable and boring. As the chief engineer for Solar Flair, her career is right on track. Her love life, not so much. The last thing she expects is a call from her estranged father's attorney. Too curious to ignore the message, she can't resist meeting with him and discovering more about specific instructions related to his estate, as well as the letter her father left for her. Rattled by what she finds at her father's home, she promptly dials 911.

Special Agent Amanda Forrester is perplexed by a call to join a homicide investigation until she arrives at the scene and learns the victim is not only a serial killer but an elite assassin the authorities have been after for years. To Amanda's increasing irritation, the daughter recognizes a picture of the last target and insinuates herself into the investigation. As the case takes a surprising turn, Amanda finds she has landed smack dab in the middle of a complicated and dangerous situation. The facts lead her to a puzzle weaving together the recent suicide of a wealthy businessman with the activities of several prominent politicians. Amanda must join forces with a mysterious organization and the persistent woman she finds increasingly hard to resist. Her instinct to protect the alluring and vulnerable Jessica Green kicks into high gear, taking the reader on a roller-coaster journey for the last book in *The Next Generation* series.

A Wild Moon Rises by Jen Silver

Successful author, Malory G Holmes, has had a rough year. Wounded by an emotional breakup and writer's block she returns home after eight months travelling to discover the startling results of a DNA test. Apparently, through her mother's side, she is related to a baronet with an estate in Briarbay, Northumberland. She decides to visit the place to find out more about this unknown side of her family.

Selene Wylde is content with life, running a bookshop in the small hamlet of Briarbay. She also looks after her father, Reginald, who is grieving over the recent death of his husband, Sir Alan Guyatt. Reginald is worrying about his claim to stay at Briarbay Hall as the Will of Sir Alan has not yet been found.

With the arrival in her shop of a very attractive, well-known writer, Selene's world begins to tilt alarmingly. Malory and Selene become entangled in a web of secrets and deceptions with the added complication of a rapidly growing attraction.

The Wolf and The Unicorn by Ali Spooner (Erotica)

Ready to explore a steamy, passionate, and tantalizing erotica romance....

Keagan and Celeste have built a solid relationship on trust and independence. A successful surgeon, Keagan understands Celeste's supercharged libido and her desire to experience a variety of sexual encounters. Everything changes when Sky, a new doctor, arrives at the hospital, and Celeste is immediately drawn to the younger woman. Keagan is surprised when she is also attracted to Sky, who shares common interests with Celeste and her. When more than a physical attraction develops, the three women discover a loving relationship beyond the bedroom.

The Blank White Page by Ali Spooner
Tatum Chastain, Corporate Officer of Chastain International, her family's real estate empire, accepts the challenge her father, Charles, has set forth. Charles has tasked Tatum and her brother, Charlie, to survive in the wilderness for six months to prove their skills in taking over the family business once he retires. Charles fails to realize that Tatum would fall in love with the southeastern Alaska cabin he has chosen for her to test her resilience and creativity. Tatum prepares for life in the bush, and shortly after she arrives, Poe, a beautiful raven, becomes her companion and guardian. When River Foster, a designated hunter for her village, crosses Tatum's path, she finds a different kind of love awaits her.

Love Hacks by Annette Mori
Joy Stiles is adrift. Having finally finished her graduate degree at the National Defense University, the only thing keeping her interest is an ongoing feud with a fellow hacker to gain access to sensitive information. Against all odds, the person snuck their way into her tech and kept leaving taunting messages. It's driving Joy crazy. She doesn't have time for this. Operation Elephant Bites isn't working as The Organization thought it would when they started down that path two years ago. Now they have a new worry. Someone is desperately trying to find out more about The Organization, believing they are behind the attacks on the mines. Whoever that person is has not only ties to the Chinese and Russian governments but also members of the US Government. Top

secret files at the NSA call their unknown group The Crusaders. Joy's efforts to uncover the identity of the enemy lead The Organization to a lot more than evil plans, and it's up to The Next Generation, with support from senior members of The Organization, to thwart the inevitable trajectory, perhaps with the assistance of Joy's irritating foe.

Strength Within by Mia Barnes

Samantha Wilson is an award-winning freelance writer with a passion for being the voice of others. Despite vowing never to go back, she returns to Milwaukee, Wisconsin, for an assignment. Her return awakens memories that force her to confront her sad and lonely childhood, including the violent attack she'd rather forget. Moving away and making a quiet, successful solo life for herself, leaving the life she knew behind cannot keep Sammie from facing her past.

Fortunately, her best friend, Zoë, flies in from New Mexico to be by her side while she confronts the demons of her past. Sammie has a knack for helping others find their happy endings. Will she finally let Zoe help her become whole again and maybe discover her happy ending in the process?

Affinity
Rainbow Publications

eBooks, Print, Free eBooks

Visit our website for more publications available online.

https://affinityebooks.com/

Published by Affinity Rainbow Publications
A Division of Affinity eBook Press NZ LTD
Canterbury, New Zealand

Registered Company 2517228